THE ROAD TO NOWHERE

THE ROAD TO NOWHERE

Rodolfo Martínez

NewCon Press
England

First edition, published in the UK May 2018
by NewCon Press

NCP 159 (hardback)
NCP 160 (softback)

10 9 8 7 6 5 4 3 2 1

Cover art by Ben Baldwin
Cover layout by Ian Whates

Edited by Ian Whates
Interior layout by Storm Constantine

CONTENTS

INTRODUCTION

Rodolfo Martínez

I am, above anything else, a novelist. I have written quite a few short stories, though, and I continue to write them. It is true that I don't write as many as I used to, but sometimes, here and there, I find the time and the motivation to do so. The truth is, I wouldn't ever like to stop writing short stories.

But I am mainly a novelist (well, I am mainly a story-teller, but this is another story for another occasion). When I begin to work on a new tale (and I always think in terms of tales, of sequences and scenes and things that happen to someone rather than in terms of ideas or concepts), it is not long before the story begins to grow, to branch out, to become more complex and, finally, to transform into a novel. Or maybe, if I am lucky, just a novella, but rarely a short story any more.

From my distant origins (I won't say when that was, let's just say it was in another century) my mind was filled with novels. Well, it was filled with other things also, such as sex, the future, sex, the past, sex, a lot of questions about what I was going to do with my life and, of course, sex.

When I wrote something in those early years it was invariably a novel.

Once on paper, it didn't seem *quite* a novel. Since I was only twelve of thirteen at the time, what I produced was nothing more than thirty or forty pages handwritten in an A5 notebook. But these thirty or forty pages had the structure, the ambition and the essence of a novel. They were, we could say, frameworks, dehydrated novels to which I hadn't yet added the necessary water (mainly because I didn't know how). But they were novels. Or at least they were intended to be.

It took me a long while to think of writing short stories. And that's funny because most of what I read then (mainly science fiction) were short stories.

I think I learned quickly how to build a novel. How to frame it, how to adjust the story to such a structure, how to give it the pace it deserved... those kind of things. I did so instinctively, without really thinking too much about it, just taking a lot of things for granted and, fortunately, without making too many mistakes along the way.

But when I tried to write my first short story I found I didn't know how. I hadn't the slightest idea and, if that wasn't handicap enough, it proved a difficult and slow process. Compared to the frantic pace I employed when writing a novel, the effort and time it took to write a few pages was frustrating.

I guess it took me so long (I'm a slow learner sometimes) because I had moved on and all those things I had learned writing novels didn't necessarily apply to a short story. Not without adaptation, at least.

It was a long and painful process and, as I always do, I was learning on the job. I jumped into the water and began to splash, confident that sooner or later I would manage to stay afloat and go where I wanted, or close enough.

During the '80s and the '90s I wrote short stories at a frantic pace. I didn't abandon novels (tales were still filling my mind and branching out) but during those years I focused on short stories.

With every new story I learned something which I used in the next, and I like to think that, beyond occasional slips and some plummeting, I was heading in the right direction, that each new story was a little better than the previous one.

When I published my first novel, *Cat's Whirld*, in 1995, my focus switched back to novels. I was writing fewer and fewer short stories. I went from producing half a dozen a year to just one or two. That remains the case. In fact, there have been years when I haven't written a single short story.

Well, I told myself, these things happen. I *think* as a novelist and I guess short stories are not my natural territory. So I had better focus on my true calling and forget about short stories.

The problem was, I didn't want to.

Short stories are essential. Some of the brightest pages of literature are found in short stories. In fact, it is in short stories where science fiction (that genre that, though it may no longer be my main focus, remains the apple of my eye) has enjoyed some of its greatest moments.

And on a strictly personal level, I like to write them. I like to because they are hard, because they are a challenge and because they allow me to test ideas I can use later in a novel.

But still the process is hard for me. Finding an idea that is perfectly suited to a short story becomes more difficult as time goes by. Besides, a short story has to be flawless. A novel can have ups and downs, it can afford the luxury of not being perfect at every turn and still emerge as a good novel. A short story can't. It succeeds or it fails in a few pages and each one of them has to be up to the standard of the others.

I have never written a short story that satisfied me a hundred per cent (nor a novel, come to that) but there are a bunch that make me proud enough to let them be read by other people in the belief they may find in them something of worth.

In the pages that follow, I have collected some of these short stories, those that are mainly science fiction. I hope you enjoy them and, who knows, perhaps on another occasion I can introduce some of my fantasy short stories to you as well.

So turn the page and enter a bunch of universes that don't exist but, if I have done my work well enough, should seem real to you.

Best wishes.

Rodolfo Martínez
Gijón, Spain,
September 2017

A TALE OF NO CITY

"What are you doing?"

As usual, Sarai appears out of nowhere and throws her question to the air as if she did not want an answer.

"A new building."

My words arouse her curiosity.

"What kind of building?"

"A church."

She frowns. Last week she heard about religion and insisted on learning everything about it, as she always does. She did not like it.

"We don't need a church."

"Don't use it as such," I say. "Use it as a playground or a museum, or… Well, as anything you like."

She does not seem convinced at all.

"Let me show you," I insist.

I display the blueprints and show her some old photographs I scanned a few days ago. Reluctantly, a spark of interest appears in her eyes. She tries hard not to be impressed, but she knows she isn't fooling me.

"All right," she concedes. "It seems nice. Where are you going to put it?"

I upload the city map and show her.

"There," I say. "At this spot, between Marina and Provença Streets."

"There's nothing there."

"But there was. And there will be."

She frowns again. Then, without a word, she disappears. I smile and go back to work.

Morning passes quickly. It is midday before I notice. I go to the refrigerator, take a can of food and a bottle of water and go to the roof. It is a pretty autumn day and no cloud stains a sky as blue as a dream. Behind me, what once was the National Park of Serra del Collserola is now an entangled jungle full of disturbing noises. In front of me the slope descends into the city in ruins until it dies in the sea. Sun reverberates in the quiet Mediterranean waters and everything around me seems to be asleep.

I open the can and eat without tasting the food. When I finish I drink the fresh water in the bottle at a gulp. I put can and bottle in a bag and, as every afternoon, I check the solar panels. All of them seem to be fine and I end my inspection with a shrug.

I go back into the building. I sit again and continue working until the dusk transforms everything around me into ghosts.

I get up, take a good look around and decide to go for Sarai as I do every night.

The city is a delicate gem, a flower always in the brink of blooming. In the beginning, long before I let my siblings get out and wander its streets, it was just an empty landscape, contoured by the sea to one side and the distant mountains to the other. I know the original has no such mountains, but I added them because they provide a good point of reference and come in handy to delineate the borders.

I began to construct the first buildings five years ago and two years later I released my siblings into the streets. There are still too many empty spaces but I do my best to keep them out of sight. I usually succeed and my siblings are not aware of all that is missing in the landscape. For them, the city is complete, and it has always been that way.

Not for all of them, of course.

Sarai is different. She is fully aware of the empty spaces. And she recognises the new buildings as such when I add them. As witness her words this morning. Nobody has ever noticed that there is nothing between Marina and Provença Streets, that the place where once the Sagrada Familia stood is just an empty spot full of darkness and noise.

Not for long, I tell myself.

"You're late," says Sarai, appearing suddenly by my side.

"You're early," I answer.

She smiles, though my words are exactly the same as last night's and the ones from the night before. As usual, she looks like a teenage girl with tousled ginger hair and mischievous green eyes. She is tall, a little taller than me, and looks skinny at first sight, but that impression vanishes quickly. She has strong cheekbones and a stubborn jaw that always trembles when she is about to acknowledge she is wrong.

We walk by the darkened streets without saying a word. This part of the city is almost empty and the moon seems to be playing hide-and-seek with the tall buildings. We descend to Via Augusta and turn right to Montaner Street until we arrive to Diagonal Avenue. We see groups of people here and there. Some of them are sitting in a circle, discussing passionately something we cannot hear, and some are walking lazily and pausing every few steps. I see Provença Street to my left, but I pretend to go straight as if ignorant of where Sarai is taking us. Impatient, she takes my arm and leads me to Provença. I smile and notice she is making a great effort not to do the same.

We arrive at last. There are not many people around us and those that are cannot see the empty space we are looking at. A cluster of clouds hides the moon and suddenly the entire world transforms into a cold empty space. The moment passes as quickly as it came and I wonder if I imagined it. A glitch in the system, maybe. I will have to check later.

"Did you know the original Sagrada Familia was never finished?" asks Sarai, who does not seem to have noticed anything untoward.

I nod. She has been reading the database. Not that I would have expected otherwise.

"And did you know that it was financed by private investment?"

I nod again. Sarai's questions are not a surprise. I was expecting something of the sort since this morning. I am sure she has been researching most of the day, with every piece of discovered information increasing her curiosity.

"But I don't want it to be a church," she says. Her voice is now firm, sharp, and she is ready for a long battle.

"Then it won't be a church."

She stumbles, as if she had pushed too hard against a wall that wasn't there.

"All right," she says, frowning. I guess she is waiting for the catch. There is no catch, but she doesn't know that.

"Great," I say. "Can we go on with our walk?"

Not entirely convinced she has won before the battle even started, she nods. I savour the moment; surprising Sarai is not something that happens every day. She takes a couple of steps, stops suddenly and turns to me.

"It was as if the building belonged to everybody," she says. "To all that had participated in its financing, at least. Wouldn't be great if we could do something like that with this one?"

"Of course," I say. "We can make a public call and people can donate…"

"No, not just this. Not money. Something more personal."

"Like what?"

"Their work. Let them erect the building, dig the foundations, raise the walls, decorate the… Let them make it with their own hands."

Now it is my turn to be taken by surprise. Where does she get these crazy ideas from? I consider it for a moment. I like it, but…

Sarai is staring at me. She looks nervous, almost anxious, as if her future depended on my response.

I consider her proposal at length. The idea is appealing, but at the same time it implies changing everything around us. Until now, my siblings have been living a perpetual now, without memories of the past or desires for a future. What Sarai is proposing would change everything. She is talking about a process that will last months, maybe years. The citizens will see the Sagrada Familia growing up before their eyes and they will have a landmark to show the passage of time. They will be conscious of the past. They will imagine the future. They will change, they grow older, they…

Nothing will be the same.

But, is this not exactly what the Parents intended when they put me in charge? Sooner or later, my siblings will have to leave their perpetual present and begin to live a real life.

Has the moment arrived?

The answer is waiting for me in Sarai's eager green eyes.

I knew this moment would come, but I expected it to arrive later. When I'm older, maybe wiser.

But what Sarai proposed makes sense. It is the next logical step. The only step I can take, in fact. I have known it for some time, but I have been postponing it again and again.

It was one of the very first things the Parents told me when they began to train me.

"For them to have a real life, they must have a past and a future. They must grow up, get older. And they must die."

I remember vividly their long solemn faces, the five of them.

"Someday they will be ready. You must decide when."

Is now the time? One part of me wants to insist not: they are not ready; it is too soon. But even that part of me knows deep down that I am lying and they have been ready for some time now.

From the roof, I gaze at the lazy clouds. Below me brushes, weeds and trees are the new masters of what once was a city, a jungle that spreads its arms around the frame of a dead body. I finish my lunch and make a decision.

Good-bye, Sarai, I think as I walk down. Good-bye my stubborn child, my sweet, innocent, wicked girl. In the blink of an eye you will be a full grown woman, and your head will be filled with hundreds of things more interesting than spending time with me.

The rest of the day passes with me revising calculations and implementing new algorithms. I check them rigorously and when I am sure everything is right I stop the running of the city and wait while the system saves a backup of its actual status.

All lights are green. Everything is ready. I upload the new algorithms and integrate them into the system. I wait a few eternal seconds with my finger hanging over the EXECUTE key and I finally strike it with a desperate rage that vanishes in quiet resignation.

The city is running again. Its citizens are waking up without knowing they have been asleep. Their clock starts ticking. They begin to live.

The first time I plugged myself to the digital world and played with my digital siblings I was only a child. It was amazing. I was not alone; there were other children like me and I could play with them. Everything seemed more real than the flesh and bone world, more vivid, more intense. My siblings were little more than babies and they were full of curiosity and eager to know new things. My arrival was like a birthday present for them. Of course they had met the Parents, but the gap between them was too big. I could interact with them far more effectively than an adult.

Once I returned to the flesh and bone world I asked Aurora why I could not remain there forever. She shook her head and said:

"You could. But then you couldn't help us develop your siblings."

I must confess the subject did not seem very important to me then. I was nothing more than an ignorant child, without a real sense of what was important and what was not.

"Besides, if you are going to be a permanent resident of the digital world you cannot remember who you are."

I did not understand.

"The system has safeguards to prevent certain things. Among them, it prevents a person of this world taking his preconceptions with him. If you are going to be a permanent resident, the memory of your digital self will be erased, only your personality patterns would remain."

"I don't want to forget what I know."

"You would also forget who you are."

The public call to build the Sagrada Familia has been a tremendous success. There are just four hundred citizens and sometimes I have the feeling that every single one of them is at the site digging and working on the foundations.

Sarai is among them, of course. She stills walks with me at evenings and nights, but we walk now by streets full of people, anxious to celebrate their lives. And the construction of the new building is her main topic of conversation.

I did not expect anything else, but it hurts just the same.

I realise Sarai notices and tries to restrain her enthusiasm, but with limited success. She is happy, excited as I have never seen her. And why not? For the first time in her life she is truly alive.

Weeks pass and our relationship returns to normal… almost. Something is lost, but what it remains is enough, at least for now.

The foundations are advancing at a good pace and having something to construct together has given the citizens a sense of community they did not have before. I should be satisfied, exultant. The project has entered a new phase and I sense that in no time the citizens will be ready to fly by themselves.

But I am far from content. I do not mind they no longer need me, but I cannot bear the idea that someday Sarai will be able to manage all by herself and I will become just an appendix; nice but not essential and maybe even annoying sometimes.

Some nights I have the feeling she is reading my thoughts. There are moments she seems about to say something. But she always changes her mind and the words that hover on her lips vanish in the thin cool night air without a trace.

These are busy days, not only for the citizens but for me. I spend my mornings in the flesh and bone world fighting again unexpected bifurcations in the code and tracing all the programing modules, searching for bugs. Everything seems to be fine but, as one of the Parents used to say (was it Carles or maybe Roberto? I cannot remember), "Everything seems to be fine even a nanosecond before the collapse."

So I do not relax but work hard, harder than I have worked before. There are hundreds of thousands of code lines, some of them in almost unintelligible obsolete computer languages, and the integration of the entire system seems sometimes a Christmas tree designed by a drunk engineer.

After all, many of the pieces that are now part of the system were originally designed for other tasks. It is a miracle the Parents were able to assemble all this and make it work. I am a midget walking on the shoulder of giants, I am very conscious of that.

Another week passes by and I relax and try to enjoy this new phase of the project. Things seem to be fine. The foundations will soon be finished and Sarai and I are satisfied with the way things are developing… though that satisfaction is not entirely genuine. At least as far as I am concerned.

But we have found common ground when we walk and talk and look at each other. We can fool ourselves into thinking there is no one else around and nothing has changed. An illusion, we both know, but it's enough for the time being.

I remember last time Aurora and I talked. She was in her bed, which was about to become her shroud. Her head and one of her arms were plugged into the autodoc, whose lights were blinking frantically, passing quickly from green to red. She was the last of the Parents alive and she was infinitely old, the oldest person in the world she seemed to me. And maybe she was, who knows? The autodoc had been trying to keep her alive for the past week, but there was nothing more it could do.

She looked at me.

"You're on your own now."

I nodded. I could not talk. What could I have told her? Words were meaningless.

"I must go, my beautiful boy. It's time to rest."

I noticed the tears in my eyes but did nothing to wipe them away.

"Good-bye, my sweet prince," she said. Her green eyes looked at me one last time. She smiled. "Until our next meeting."

Those were her last words. One moment her eyes looked at me with something I like to think of as 'love', the next they were just two empty glass marbles.

From that moment on I was alone in the flesh and blood world. Forever, or so I thought.

"Hi! 'Body home?"

It is a young voice, one that sounds almost amused. For an instant I am convinced I have imagined it, until a silhouette appears in the threshold, framed by the outer light. I blink and shake my head.

I am awake and I am not hallucinating. It is another human being. A flesh and blood human being.

No, that is not possible. What are the odds? The war and the post-war fertility disease finished everyone... That was what the Parents used to tell me again and again, though Aurora admitted one day this was an assumption. They thought mass extinction was the most probable consequence, but had no way of being certain.

I stand up.

"Hi," I manage to say. "Welcome, benvingut."

My voice sounds harsh. It has been a while since I used it in the physical world. It seems an old man's voice. A drunk old man's voice, I tell to myself while I hold back a giggle.

"Wow! Ar'u real?"

I increase the light intensity and let him examine me thoroughly.

"Come in," I say. "You are welcome."

He still hesitates. Suddenly he bows and says,

"May'ur days'll be fill'd with joy and 'ur nights with excitement."

He seems to expect some kind of answer from me.

"Thank you," I say. "I desire the same for you. I don't know the proper words. I'm sorry."

He smiles while he slips inside and takes an amazed look around. Now that he is no longer backlit I can see that he is indeed a young man. Almost ten years younger than me, I would say. He seems to be about seventeen at most. He has nice and frank features, and is almost barefaced. A short blonde fuzz crosses his jaw and upper lip and his hair spreads upon his shoulders like a golden cascade.

"Fabri," he says pointing to his chest.

"Abraham," I reply, guessing he is telling me his name.

"Come from Novuporti. 'S south two days walk from here."

"I… I don't come from anywhere. I'm home," I say, and I notice my words surprise him.

"U… U'r born here, in Barslona?"

I do not correct his pronunciation. Why should I?

"Yes."

"U… no, 's impossible. U'r not old enough. U can't've known ancient world."

I smile and shake my head.

"I didn't. My Parents did, though."

He seems fascinated, not only by my words but by everything that surrounds him. He is like a child in a candy store. Well, he is in fact a child, no older than Sarai.

"Adulthood voyage's been more interesting than anticipated," he says, enthusiastic. "My folks won't believe when tell'em."

"Didn't you expect to find anyone here?"

"Of course didn't! This Barslona, ruins of ancient world. Nothing should live here. Should be no more than ghosts and spectres…" Suddenly he bites his thumb and spits on his palm. "U'r no ghost… ar'u?"

I laugh.

"I'm a man, just like you," I say.

He walks towards me, not entirely convinced. He stretches one arm and touches my face. I let him do it and try to be as still as possible. He ends his inspection and nods, satisfied at last.

"Ye', u'r man. Ghosts don't sweat or breathe. Guess."

I smile, trying to be as soothing as I can. He smiles back. Suddenly I see a weird glow in his eyes.

"Do'u wanna've sex?" he asks, stammering.

"Just like that? Is that a custom among you when you meet a stranger?"

"Sometimes. When wanna be sure 's no ghost."

"I see. Why not? Follow me."

"This compound was created as part of the war efforts," Aurora told me once. We were alone. I suspect she would not have told me anything if the other Parents had been there. They did not like to talk about old times but there was nothing Aurora did not want to talk about. "We created drones and robots faster and more versatile than those existing ones. We learnt to play DNA as a virtuoso musician plays her instrument. We developed AI algorithms more complex than anyone could have imagined."

She stopped and looked me right in the eye, as if she wanted to be sure I understood everything she was telling me. I sat straight and did not blink.

"And that's why we couldn't leave. When everyone ran, when the world fell apart and there was nothing to live for, we didn't give up. We couldn't. What we had achieved…"

She pointed to the line of servers, to their blinking lights. Her green eyes welled.

"They're alive. They think. They're people. Not just information, not just a bunch of ones and zeroes in a flow of data. Nobody intended to create them, but they exist. They are our children. No, not mine or the other Parents'. They are the children of humankind. They will inherit the world and, hopefully, they won't make the same mistakes we did."

I do not know how old she was. All five of them seemed terribly old to me when I was a child. But she had to be very old. Ninety? A hundred? Maybe more. She and the others had been working by their own so many years, trying to develop those digital children they had accidentally created. And in their last years they created a flesh and blood one. Me.

So old. Will I someday be as old as she was? Will I endure long enough?

He is sleeping now. I watch him and wonder what is he dreaming of. He is so young, just a boy, and in same strange way he reminds me of Sarai.

He turns round and faces me. There is a smile in his lips and his breathing is calm, regular. What kind of person is capable of sleeping like that in the presence of a stranger? What kind of community breeds people like that, so confident, so trustful?

After the sex we have been talking. He was curious about me and the place, of course. He said he was not expecting to find anyone in the old city. Only ruins and maybe ghosts. I told him a few things, nothing really important, and while I was talking I saw he could not stop looking at the blinking lights of the servers. What are they? he asked. Machines, I answered. What kind of machines? he wanted to know. Machines that handle information, I said.

His curiosity seemed boundless. But he was polite enough to curb it when I asked about him and his people.

They number just over a hundred and fifty, though a traveller who came from the south five years ago told them there was a community of about five hundred people at the banks of Guadalquivir. That visit was the most thrilling moment Fabri and his people can remember. They are an agricultural community and have lost most of the technological knowledge of the ancient world. Fabri recalls they had electric light when he was a child, but not anymore.

I did not dare ask if there are many youngsters like him among his people or if he was an exception. He would have found the question too weird and I did not want him to suspect anything strange. I told myself that a community so small was not genetically viable and tried to convince myself that, even if they could conceive and deliver as before the war, I should not be worried.

But I am. Of course I am.

I watch him again and consider the idea of trying to convince him to stay here and help me with the project. I could teach him and it would be gratifying to have a companion after all those years, someone who shared my goals, someone to talk to, to touch, to caress…

But I do not dare try. I cannot afford to take the risk.

He is innocent. He does not mean any harm. He is just an ignorant and enthusiastic child, eager to learn and to discover new places, not very different from my siblings. And when he returns to his community he will tell the others what he has found in the ancient city of Barslona and…

I cannot allow it.

The Parents were very specific regarding that. The viability of the project stands on secrecy. Humans must not know they are a dying species, much less that they have a replacement.

"If someone has survived they mustn't know what's happening here," Aurora told me time and again. "Not for the next thousand years at least, assuming they survive."

I can see her before me as if she really were here. Her skin is like an old map road and her hands tremble, but her green eyes still keep the fire of youth.

She was right. No one must know.

And I know what I have to do.

Slowly, quietly, I put my knees on his shoulders, I bend down and pass my hands around his neck. Little by little, I begin to tighten. I try not to look at him but I cannot help it and my eyes stay fixed on his face.

He wakes suddenly and looks at me, incapable of understanding what is happening. He struggles, but I am strong. He opens his mouth; I am not sure if he is trying to breathe or if he wants to say something. It does not matter. The air will never reach his lungs and I do not want to hear anything he may wish to say.

There is a crunch. His eyes turn to cold glass. All struggle ceases. I relax, loosening my grip. His mouth is half open and there is a look of astonishment in his dead eyes. He has died without understanding why and he will never have the chance to do so. If there is an afterlife, as Carles thought (an idea Aurora heatedly refuted), he will spend it haunted by the knowledge that he will never understand why he died.

I wish I could have explained it to him, I wish...

I stand up and wipe the tears from my eyes. It is late in the night and I should sleep, but I must dispose of the body. It will be a hard and nasty work and the sooner I get to it the better.

Next day I walk around the compound and make a thorough inspection. The compound should have been effectively hidden, but Fabri had managed to find it. Even if it was only by chance I cannot take the risk of anyone else stumbling upon it. So I look for weak spots and try to find a way to strengthen them.

If someone walks by again someday he should not see anything of interest, just weed and brushes and the ruins of an old building. He should go on his way without taking a second look. I cannot afford another Fabri...

Why did he have to tell me his name?

I push aside the thought as firmly as I can. I have no time for this. I am going to be busy for the next few years, working not only on the developing of the digital world but on its protection from the physical world. Between them these tasks will consume all my waking time. I will have no time for anything else.

Why did he have to tell me his name?

"I've missed you"

I am about to say sorry, but I know that is useless with Sarai.

"I had things to do."

"Very important things, it seems."

"They were."

She hesitates for a moment and then she shrugs.

"What do you think?" she asks, pointing at the people working on the building. Foundations are finished and the walls are beginning to take shape. It is remarkable what they have achieved in the months I have not been here.

"It seems fine," I say.

"Better than fine. It has given us a common purpose."

I nod. "I know."

Yes, how could it be otherwise, I suspect she is thinking. As far as she is concerned I know everything. Sometimes I wonder if that is the only reason she began to talk to me, because I seemed to know everything.

When I began to plug myself into the digital world after the death of the Parents, I did so only because I wanted to see for myself how things were going... Or at least that was what I told myself. I tried to keep my interactions with the citizens at a minimum. And I managed to do so until she appeared.

"You're new," she told me the moment she saw me.

That aroused my interest. How could she know that? It should not have been possible for her to remember previous iterations of her world.

It did not take me long to discover that Sarai was unique in many ways. At first she only asked me questions, one after another. Surprised by the fact that I seemed to have an answer for everything, she redoubled her efforts and her questions became more complex and elaborate.

One day she asked me where I went when I was not there. That shocked me in ways I cannot describe. She should not have been aware of my absences.

I know I should have checked her records, examined her behaviour parameters and tested her access levels. I did not, afraid of what I might find.

By then, Sarai was the most important part of my world. I just could not risk discovering that her behaviour and her personality were the consequences of a system bug. Though there were far worse alternatives...

"What was the ancient world like?" I asked Aurora one day.

She smiled, a sad and homesick smile, and then stared at me with those green eyes. They were the eyes of a young woman, maybe a child. The only aspect of her that did not age.

"It was the best of times, it was the worst of times,", she said, as if she was reciting a verse. "It was the age of wisdom, it was the age of foolishness, it was the epoch of belief, it was the epoch of incredulity, it was the season of Light, it was the season of Darkness, it was the spring of hope, it was the winter of despair."

"I don't understand," I said, perplexed.

She shrugged and then did something no one had ever done to me before. She bowed and gave me a kiss.

"It was a time like any other," she said. "Just like any other."

The construction of the Sagrada Familia is progressing well. Very well, in fact. The original building took more than a hundred years and it was never finished. This one could be completed in a few months, a year and a half at most.

Everyone is working on the project and, in doing so, they are discovering new abilities. As work progresses they are beginning to differentiate one from another. Some of them discover they are good at maths, others develop unsuspected manual skills, still others… They are becoming more and more individual, each with a distinct personality and different abilities. And at the same time their bonds as a community are strengthened by the task.

Sarai was right. That kind of involvement was just what they needed to take the next step in their development. How could she know? And how could I not?

She looks at me and smiles, as if she is reading my mind. Sometimes I think she is. And, well, it is not impossible. Just now my thoughts are nothing more than data bits in the server cloud. Anyone can read them if she or he has the right access level. Has Sarai?

"You're paranoid," she tells me. Is she just joking or it is her way of telling me I am right?

"That doesn't mean nobody is after me," I answer.

She laughs. And her laugh is so genuine, so naïve that it puts an end to my suspicions… almost.

There is so much work to do.

The Parents were old people when I was born. And I was the only success in a long list of failed attempts. They had been working all their lives, trying to preserve the precious discovery they had made at the end of the war, just a few months before the fertility disease spread around the world.

"Humankind is doomed," they told me the minute I was able to understand them. "But there is another possibility, another form of life, another…"

Roberto, impatient as usual, pushed Carles aside and said:

"They are our children. Your siblings, in some ways. You must protect them and help them to develop."

There was so much I did not understand. But Aurora, more patient than the others, explained things to me until I understood.

She was my favourite Parent. Carles, Roberto, Farya and Chihook were fine, but Aurora… She never got impatient with me, she never thought I was not up to the task, she never refused to answer a question. She always paid attention to what I said and I could tell she was not merely being polite; she was really interested in what I had to say.

"We were lucky," she once told me. "This facility was secretly built in the last years of the war. Only a few knew of its existence and location, and it was designed to be self-sufficient. Sheer luck. Our discovery could have taken place in a less protected site… or nowhere."

She taught me to work hard, to never give up. But there is so much to do. And there are dangers I have not considered, as Fabri's visit has shown me.

I wish Aurora were here now. I could ask her. Because Sarai is wrong. I do not know everything; I do not have all the answers. Aurora and the others did. They were the creators of this world, I am just a gardener, a caretaker. Aurora would have known what to do.

But you do know what to do, her voice says inside my head. You must protect your digital siblings. They are the future.

What I do not know is if I will have enough time to do everything I must. And not only time. After all, I am only one person and there are so many tasks involved.

I can control the digital world, its programming and its developing. But what about the other machinery, the solar panels, the construction robots, the… So long as nothing serious happens I can take care of maintenance, and the machines were designed to repair themselves as well as other machines, but there are some things they cannot do, things that require a human hand. I am not sure mine are capable enough.

No matter how many years I live, sooner or later I will die. By then, my siblings have to be able to control not only their digital world but the machines of the physical world also. If a solar panel fails, they have to be capable of sending and controlling a drone to make reparations.

Yes, I worry too much. Before the arrival of Fabri I rarely thought about the future. As my siblings, I lived in a perpetual now and that was enough for me.

Things have changed. He has changed everything. Am I doing what I must? Is the world out there really a dying place without hope? Are Fabri's and the other communities that exist doomed to a long decay that can only end in extinction?

I have no answers. I have only memories of an innocent laughter and a pair of trustful eyes, of someone I killed before I really knew him.

But I cannot afford to hesitate now. Right or wrong this is my life, the one I know. I am the caretaker of the future, I tell myself, I must not give up.

But what future? I wonder. Not my future, but theirs. Fabri was lucky, I killed him in the prime of his life, he will not have to endure the indignities of old age. He will never grow old, his body will not betray him, he will not...

Enough. Enough. This is my life. Nothing else matters.

Time goes by. Weeks turn into months and months into years. The drones under my command have almost completed their tasks. When they finish it will be all but impossible for anyone to find this place... At least that is my intention. I have done my best. I hope it will be enough.

In the digital world the city develops fast and my digital siblings with it. They have taken matters into their own hands and now decide by themselves what to construct and where. The city is taking shape; the empty places are empty no more and new buildings are being erected.

The new city is very much like the original but it is not an exact copy. There are new places and streets and buildings, and even those that are like the old ones are slightly different. My siblings go on evolving and they are beginning to get creative. The Ramblas are a good example: they have transformed them into a series of pools, each them home to a different kind of fish.

The population grows as they learn to interact and create new life.

The Parents would be proud, I hope.

Though everything seems to be fine there is something that disturbs me. Something that it is not as it should be. And even though I rather like the anomaly it worries me in ways I cannot describe.

The compound is hidden and safe. The digital world has grown complex enough to almost develop by itself. My siblings grow up steadily.

All of them but one.

"You're not getting older."

"You are."

Sarai is right. My digital self reflects with painful fidelity the ten years that have passed. But she is the same teenage girl I met so many years ago. She has not changed a bit.

"This is how things are," I say. "All living things grow up, get older and, some day, die."

"Am I not alive, then?"

A good question. Is she alive? What is she?

"Not entirely," I answer, measuring every word. "Life is change. You must change if you want to be entirely alive."

She hesitates a moment. She shrugs.

"I'll change," she says.

"But not today."

"No, not today."

Her words fill me with joy… but they also scare me.

When I get back to the physical world I do what I have been avoiding all these years. I enter the system and look for Sarai parameters.

I fail.

Time and again the system stops me and tells me with its annoyingly polite voice that I do not have the required security level.

I try to keep calm and not to wonder how it is possible for the only system administrator to not have a high enough security level. I will consider that question later, once I have solved the mystery of Sarai.

But despite every effort I fail. For two days I try and my frustration grows and grows after each failure.

I decide to go back to basics, to the beginning, to the original system specifications as the Parents wrote them.

I find what I am looking for after several hours of reading machine code. The system itself has the highest security level and can override any request by the administrator if it considers that request endangers the project. A programmer remark informs me that it was Aurora who implemented that code.

It makes sense. Not that I am capable of seeing that at first. But after a few hours working in the solar panel maintenance I can get back to the server room and face the problem with a cool head. Yes, it makes sense; the system has to be capable of defending itself against anything that threatens the parameters of the project. It does not matter if the thread is internal or external. In fact, internal threats may be even more dangerous than the external ones.

But that leaves an unanswered question. Why would my trying to see Sarai's parameters put the project at risk?

I spend the next two days designing a spy module. When it is ready for release I hesitate. Should I do it? What if the system is right and I am putting at risk everything the Parents and I have done? Is it so important for me to know what Sarai is that I am willing to endanger my life's work to find out?

Seconds turn into minutes and minutes are about to turn into an hour when I finally give the order.

Ten endless minutes later my spy module returns with the information it has managed to get.

Almost nothing. The system is shielded well enough to protect itself from my feeble attempts to trespass. The only thing the module can give me is the creation date of Sarai's parameters and when she was activated.

Nothing. A trifle. What good is knowing the exact moment the Parents created and activated her?

But it is the only thing I have, so I open the file.

It cannot be. It makes no sense.

Sarai was created and defined several years after my other siblings. Many years later, in fact. Why? What happened? Did the Parents develop some new algorithm and implement it in Sarai? If so, why did they not tell me? I was alive and working when Sarai was defined and activated.

I was...

I make a quick mental calculation. The year, the month, the day. Yes, of course I was alive, but none of the Parents were... except Aurora. But not for long. She must have died a few days after...

Or was it the same day?

I upload Aurora's vital data. I look for the date and time of her death. When I find them I do not need to compare them with the date and time my module has retrieved.

Sarai was born less than a picosecond after Aurora's death.

The system has safeguards to prevent certain things, I recall. Among them, it prevents a person of this world taking his preconceptions with him. If you are going to be a permanent resident, the memory of your digital self will be erased, only your personality patterns would remain.

But that is not the only thing that remains, I tell myself. Maybe Sarai has not my mother's memories but does have her access level to the system. That is why she was aware of time passing, and knew that I did not belong to the system. She is a preferential user, so she can do things my other siblings cannot.

Such as refusing to grow up and being a teenager as long as she wants, for instance.

An accident or did it happen deliberately? Had Aurora tricked the system in some way to allow her digital self to become a super user?

A new memory comes out of the blue and strikes me suddenly. I see Aurora again, at the time of her death. I remember her last words to me:

"Until our next meeting."

She told me. She told me what was about to happen with her last words. I have been so stupid. A perfect and complete moron. All these years I had the truth in front of me and I did not see it.

Maybe I did not want to.

Time goes by. It is hard for me to distinguish one year from another. When I look back it seems only yesterday when the Parents died, when Fabri arrived, when my siblings began to build the city by themselves. A sigh. A blink.

But it has been twenty years since the Sagrada Familia was finished, since the first fireworks were launched to celebrate the completion of the building, since...

I am not a young man anymore and I have not been for several years. I am not as old as the Parents, but old enough to be younger than my body. My eyes reflect the passage of time, also. It has been a while since they seemed innocent and eager. And maybe those eyes I remember were not even mine, but Fabri's...

I am in good health. If I am careful, I have several years before me. What kind of years? I wonder. Living in a dead world and taking care of a newborn is not for me. My siblings will go on evolving, developing, building and changing their environment, creating their own universe as they explore it and imagine it. I... I will simply grow old and one day I will die. I will be as dead as the rest of the world.

As dead as Fabri.

Funny. As years go by I think more and more of Fabri and I wonder how things might have turned out had I made a different choice. Would I have been able to convince him to help me? Had I given him the opportunity, would he have seized it?

It does not matter. Not really. Thoughts and remorse cannot change the past. But these thoughts persist. Old man stuff, I guess.

In those twenty years my visits to the digital world have become less and less frequent. My siblings evolved quickly and in no time they were managing the world by themselves. A world whose shape has begun to change in ways I could not have imagined. After twenty years, the city has become something very different from the original.

Well, the original was a ghost invaded by the jungle when Fabri arrived and today it is nothing but a distant memory.

Some things remain: The Sagrada Familia and a couple of other places that still hold meaning for the citizens. They are building their own city... If what they are building is in fact a city. Sometimes I have my doubts.

And why not? The Parents wanted them to be free of the mistakes of the ancient world. Yes, let them make their own mistakes. They are entitled to, after all.

During these years, Sarai and I have seen each other from time to time. She still looks like a teenager and behaves as one, but her eyes belong to an older person. Funny, because it was just the other way around with Aurora.

My work here is done and my presence is now more and obstacle than a help. Time to go; time for them to live their lives without outside interference, not even mine.

It is time for Sarai and I to say good-bye.

"You are leaving," she says the moment she sees me.

"I am. And it's time for you grow up. Thank you for having been the same for me all those years. There is no need for that anymore."

She does something I do not remember seeing her do before: she begins to weep. Quietly, solemnly, tears slip through her check.

"Shhh. It's all right," I say. "You need to live your lives on your own. No more supervision. I will protect you until my last day, but I don't belong here. Not anymore. This is your world now."

She is about to say something. I am almost sure she is about to say this can be my world too, but she suddenly keeps quiet. All my plans fall down like a house of cards and I cannot say a word. So I keep watching her.

And do as you did, mother? I would have replied to the proposition she has not made.

I know she would not have been surprised by my words. I am positive that, in some way or another, she has learnt about herself… Well, I am not sure that 'herself' is the right word. The person whose thought and behaviour patterns were used to create her, then.

Maybe she would ask me how long I've known. What could I tell her? That I knew for a long time? That, in some ways, I always have known but I did not want to find out? All the clues were right there in front of me.

But it does not matter. Maybe she has inherited the personality patterns of Aurora, but she is not her. She is Sarai. And I have loved them both.

I take a long look around. One last look, at least with these weary old eyes. There are so many new things, so many changes, so many people. I guess I did my work well, after all, though sometimes I regret that the new city is not more like the original.

But why should it be? This is their world, not a ghost copy of what once was. Something entirely new. And they see it with their own eyes; fresh eyes that do not carry the weight of a past that is nothing more than a ghost. I cannot look with eyes such as theirs and, if one day I do, I will not be myself anymore.

"Good-bye, my love," I say. And it is indeed a farewell. The next time I see her, many years from now, I will be another.

After a while I smile. "Until we meet again."

In July, 2016, in Avilés (Spain), Ian Whates asked me for a short story of about 5,000 words to be included in an anthology he was going to publish at the 2016 EuroCon in Barcelona. Apart for its length, the only condition was that Barcelona should appear in the story in some way. I said yes almost without thinking: I liked the idea and Ian is such a nice guy it's hard to say "no". But the truth is I hadn't the slightest idea of what I was going to write.

Eventually, something came to mind and I got to work. Instead of writing in Spanish and translating it afterwards, I decided to write in English from the start, something I had never done before, at least in fiction. It was a fascinating process; sometimes hard but always enjoyable. In fact, I enjoyed it so much I'm sure it won't be the last time.

In the end, the story was longer than expected and I finished with more than 8,000 words. I sent it to Ian nevertheless. Fortunately, he liked the piece despite its length. It appeared in November, 2016 in Barcelona Tales *and is reprinted here for the first time.*

The funny thing is that, if someday I want to publish it in Spanish, my native language, I will have to translate it.

LOADED DICE

I check the sound system one last time. The hidden mic works fine and in my ear the headphone picks out in high definition all those sounds we make and never notice: a hawking, a lip smacking, a mutter just at the edge of audibility. From my position I can see the Wildling perfectly. He's sitting by a corner, waiting for his drink to reach the right temperature, and gazing lazily at the window. The Agent comes in and stands next to the Wildling, but he isn't aware of his presence, so the Agent clears his throat. The Wildling turns to him and looks up.

"I see," he says. There's no surprise at all in his face, just weariness. "So it's you, again. Take a seat."

There's a moment of hesitation before the Agent sits where the other man has pointed.

"There's no need for you to make the usual speech. Unless you feel you must, of course," says the Wildling as he checks the temperature of his drink, nods and brings the cup to his lips.

The Agent smiles. It's a harsh smile: he's not going to let the Wildling win the game.

"And how does that 'usual speech' go?" he asks.

"You're not gonna make it easy, eh? All right." He clears his throat. "Let me see: 'I am an authorised representative of the Panuniversal Transtemporal Agency. I am here because two years from now you are going to create a time machine. That event would change history as we know it. I have come to prevent you from creating that machine.' More or less. No doubt I've misplaced a few words and maybe I simplified your speech a bit. But I'm essentially right, am I not?"

For three seconds that seem endless, the Agent is incapable of moving.

"You're not the one I've come to see," he says at last.

The other nods.

"Excellent! You've hit the jackpot. You've been faster than most of your... colleagues. And I'm sure next time you'll be even faster."

"Next time?"

"Next time we meet. At least from your point of view. From mine, it will be the previous time."

The Agent nods and I think he is beginning to realise that he's facing the biggest challenge of his career. His opponent is not just skilled and farsighted; he has met with the Agent in the Agent's future, so knows his modus operandi and maybe his weak spots.

"All right," he says. "Let's be frank, then." He stretches his hands, palms up, in a gesture I know very well. "No tricks, no catches, no excuses. We both know what to expect."

The Wildling smiles and joy gleams in his eyes.

"As you wish. But you used that trick once and it failed."

"We've never met before, am I right?" says the Agent. "You're just bluffing. And you're good, I have to say. I almost believed you, which would have given you an advantage."

"It is an advantage, whether you believe or not," says the Wildling while he puts his empty cup in the table. "Right now you're not sure. You don't know if we have really met before or not. And if we did, you ignore what you told me then, what hidden weak spots you showed me in our second encounter. Or in the first one. Sorry, this is a bit confusing sometimes."

"I won't take your bait. As you say, I have no means of knowing if I'm going to meet you again. And if that *does* happen, I don't know what I'm going to tell you. So it's easy: I won't take into account that fact when I talk to you."

The Wildling shrugs, looks at the menu and requests something with a touch of his finger. A cigarette appears in his mouth. He inhales and there is a spark at the edge of the tiny white cylinder that becomes a little hot coal. He fills his lungs and exhales and the smoke vanishes a few centimetres from his mouth. From my vantage he seems a strange mythical creature, surrounded by an aura of smoke whose tentacles vanish as the further they go from him.

"As you wish," he says. "Now we can begin a dialectic battle that will take hours or I can explain why you will never be able to stop me. Then you leave, and we put an end to this."

"Explain everything you want. Surely you aren't expecting me to believe you?"

"I'm not. No yet, anyway."

The Agent doesn't answer.

"All right," says the Wildling. "Here you are, the PTA, with your shining brand state-of-the-art quantic time machines, all of you convinced that someone has put you in charge of everything everywhere and it is your duty to ensure the proper development of events. When an unauthorised person – I think you call that 'a Wildling', correct me if I'm wrong – is about to create his own version of a time machine, you prevent that from happening, one way or another. In our previous meeting you didn't go into details but you managed to make it clear that things can get very unpleasant for the poor Wildling if he doesn't agree to a deletion and reconstruction of his memory. You are always successful because it doesn't matter how long it takes, you have all the time in the world to accomplish your task. Am I right so far?"

"Pretty much."

"Let's take a look at my case, then. I am, it seems, a twenty-two year-old mad genius who has developed a set of revolutionary equations that describe the collapse of the wave function in a completely new way. These equations will allow me to build, in a couple of years, my own time machine. It will be a primitive device, of course, capable of moving longitudinally across time, but not transversely between universes. Your research reveals that, if I am allowed to build my machine, this reality will be severely affected and the echoes of that alteration could reach other regions of the panuniverse. So you have come to give me a choice. I can refuse to develop my machine and agree to forget everything about it or I can work for you, the PTA. An honour, it seems, because according to you this second choice is not common. Usually there are no alternatives to oblivion."

"You're right on all counts."

The voice of the Agent doesn't betray him, but no doubt he realises that the Wildling's knowledge confirms that a second meeting *will* happen. Or it has happened, depending on your point of view.

"You're wondering now what I'm doing here. Why my current self, the one of the right age, the one that belongs to this moment, is not sitting at this table taking his beverage, ignorant of what is to come, instead of this older version that has supplanted the appropriate me."

The Agent nods. I can't help smiling as I listen to the conversation while pretending to focus on my soda. The Wildling speaks fluently; he doesn't make a mess of pronouns or verb tenses. It seems clear he has plenty of experience with time travel.

"You say you have all the time in the world. As do I. The me who should have been here talking to you is twenty-two. The actual me is about thirty. I have spent six years – and I guess I'm going to spend a few more – finding the exact moment you reached my previous self and, one way or another, prevent him from being at that place at that time. For instance, I have managed to be me, instead of me, here and now. Do you follow me?"

"I do. But surely you appreciate that it's impossible for you to win. Sooner or later we'll find one of your previous selves in a moment you haven't reached."

The Wildling shakes his head and smiles again while he takes the burned-out cigarette and throws the butt into the recycler.

"You don't understand yet. I didn't expect otherwise. According to my calculations you are the original one, the first Agent the PTA sends to stop me. So all this is new to you, maybe even baffling. Let me explain; there isn't any moment from my past – my past before I built the time machine, I mean – when you can contact me because I don't remember being contacted by you."

Now it's the Agent who smiles, who almost struts while he explains the situation to the Wildling and reveals the mistake he has made. Time is fluid, he says, and if his actual incarnation doesn't remember having been contacted in the past it just means they haven't done so yet. But they will and then all his memories will change to accommodate the new reality.

The Wildling looks at him, astonished. And I see, beyond doubt, that he is faking.

"It can't be. If you had contacted me in a moment I don't remember, that would only have created a new universe, divergent from this one from that moment. But this universe would remain untouched."

"So it seems, right? It would be nice, really, if things worked that way. But I'm afraid they don't." I find the self-confidence I hear in his voice unbearable. "There are infinite realities, true, but what you do in one of them affects just that one, not the others. Sometimes a change can echo through adjacent realities, but it's infrequent."

"I see. And according to the theory you work with I should give up because you'll succeed in the end no matter how long it takes."

"Something like that. You're just one man. We are many and can cover many more moments in your timeline than you're able to."

The Wildling puckers, thoughtfully.

"But that's a fallacy, you know. I can cover as much of my past as you. Being only one implies I have to work harder and travel to more past moments than each one of you, but at the end of the day it makes no difference."

"All right," concedes the Agent. "Let's suppose you can do what you say. There are no guaranties you're not going to make a mistake. Maybe you have forgotten to cover one tiny moment and we take advantage of that. There's no way you can know."

There is an instant of hesitation, of uncertainty. I finish my soda and strike the combination for another one while I wonder if the moment to intervene has arrived. No, not yet, I decide. But soon.

"Well, maybe," says the Wildling. "But so what?"

"Do you remember our proposal? You're a skilled man, with a sharp mind and good reflexes. Join us. You would be an excellent field Agent."

"I see. Your offer flatters me. Maybe I would be tempted but for the tiny detail that I don't accept the PTA's authority to do what it does."

"That's... ludicrous."

"Is it? Who put you in charge? Who told you to interfere as you see fit? Who authorised you to decide which is the right timeline for any given reality?"

It's not the first time we've heard these questions, the Agent and I, but usually they are spoken with passion, with anger and frustration. The Wildling sounds indifferent; the only apparent emotion is one of mild contempt. That disconcerts the Agent, as it disconcerted me the first time.

"The truth is you're nothing more than a bunch of frightened bureaucrats obsessed with control," the Wildling adds.

"What would you have us do, then?"

"You? I guess you'll just keep on trying no matter how many times you fail."

"I didn't mean that. We could kill you."

"Here and now? You can, but it wouldn't change anything. What happens if in this moment of my life I have already covered every possible point of my past? I've mentioned my age before, but was I telling the truth? Maybe I have travelled to the right time – let's say a future when our biological and physiological issues are solved – and I've got an immortal body. And then I have spent several thousands of years getting myself out of your way. How can you know?"

He's right.

"Besides, and believe me when I say this, you've already failed."

"That is…"

"Ludicrous? Ah, you haven't realised yet. You will soon, I'm sure, because in our second meeting you will seem defeated and tired."

"Don't bluff."

"I'm not. Here, let me explain. The funny thing is that you told me why it's impossible for me not to win and why you've already lost."

"When? During that second meeting I'm not even sure is going to happen?"

"No. Right here, a few minutes ago. When you thought you were showing me my naïve mistakes. What changes in one reality affects only that one, right? It doesn't create a divergent timeline but reshapes that region of the panuniverse in such a way that everything the change has created will seem to have been there from the beginning. Now think of that pretty quantum theory you use in the PTA, remember the premise that the eye of the watcher affects the experiment. Then, allow me to explain to you how my 'primitive' time machine works and how it differs from yours. I think it'll be enough."

"All right. Go on."

"My equations, quantum equations as I'm sure you remember, describe and permit an artefact that collapses the wave function of an entire universe. My time machine."

"Your…" The Agent stops talking. He turns to the window and, though I cannot see his face, I know the implications of what the Wildling has said are permeating his mind, filling it with a weird and languid horror. "That's not possible."

"Why? Doesn't quantum mechanics predict its own failure in the face of a singularity? You can see my time machine just like that: a deterministic singularity in a probabilistic universe. In fact, if you allow me the verbal pirouette, we can see my machine as a naked deterministic singularity: the universe can look into it in a way it cannot look into a black hole." He smiles, as if a sudden idea has occurred to him. "To be more accurate, it is my singularity that looks into the universe and forces it to look back. From there, the consequences are clear, are they not?"

Now. Now is the time. If I do something, if I'm going to stop this and save the PTA from disaster it must be now. I stand and go to their table. Someone holds my arm. I turn around and see him.

"No," he says. "You can't."

Has he foreseen even this? Of course he has, if he's right about his machine. I try to break free, only to discover that my other arm is similarly held. I look from side to the other: both of them look at me with a half a smile on their lips, the same smile I can see in the Wildling at the table. Each of them holds a tiny metal tube pointed at me.

"Don't try anything. We don't want to hurt you. Let it end," they say. I'm not sure which one of them, maybe both.

For a moment I consider trying, in spite of everything. Would his shooting me change anything? I surrender. I do nothing while the conversation in the table crawls to its conclusion.

"Yes," says the Wildling. "My time machine is not a probabilistic artefact, but a deterministic one. And that determinism is not hidden behind the protective layer of an event horizon. The consequence is that any universe that contains it becomes a deterministic universe. And in that universe, this one, there cannot be reality changes; reality is fixed. In a way, the entire universe is a singularity and is naked: the other universes can look into this one. If I don't remember you in my past it's because you were never there. If I remember having travelled in time to take my younger version out of your way it's because that has already happened."

"No…"

"Yes. Funny. I wondered what it would be like when I told you this. What I would feel when I saw the face of the first one of you the moment he understood. It's rather disappointing. Anticipation ruins the moment; don't you agree?"

"No…" the Agent repeats, desperately trying not to believe but unable to refute the Wildling's words. A deterministic universe, he must be thinking, infecting everything around as a tumour, becoming the vortex of an infection that will destroy the PTA. Because what's the use of an Agency that controls the correct flow of time if time can only flow in one way?

"Leave," says the Wildling. "This doesn't make sense any more. We'll see each other again, but today I'm not in the mood."

The Agent obeys. He stands and walks out like a puppet with severed strings. I watch him leave the place, trying to pretend he has not been defeated, but it's an act that doesn't convince anyone, not even himself. I know he'll return to his cabin and will hesitate a long time before pushing the button that will take him back to the distant future where the PTA is based.

I notice in that moment that the two men who held me have disappeared. Now that it doesn't matter I can move at last. What do I do? Do I stay, do I leave? I go to the table. He sees me and at first he doesn't understand. Then he nods.

"Good disguise," he says. "How much have you heard?"

"Everything."

"Ah, of course everything. Haven't you tried to interfere? Haven't you tried to change the conversation, to make it different from the one you remember, to prove me wrong?"

"I have, but you have stopped me."

"Of course I have. Or I will. It couldn't have been otherwise. Are you convinced now?"

"I'm not."

But there is no real conviction in my words. I know next time we see each other (the first time for him, the second one for me) it will be even worse. I will face him just because I think it's my duty to do so, but knowing in advance that I'm destined to fail, that in this deterministic universe his machine has created there is no way to change things, that if he doesn't remember being beaten by me, I cannot win in his past, though his past be my future.

The Wildling looks at me and nods. We both are doomed to repeat the same predetermined dance, again and again. Nothing can change that.

"Let me tell you something," he says. "Maybe God plays dice everywhere. But here he uses loaded dice."

A few of my short stories come from dreams. This wasn't entirely the case here, but almost. One night, when sleep was proving elusive, I began to play with a couple of ideas. I always wanted to write something about time travel, but I had never found an idea compelling enough. That night, though, something happened and the entire story came to mind almost in a flash.

To hell with sleep. I got up, turned the computer on and began to write. A couple of hours later I had written the first draught of "Loaded Dice". It seemed a good moment to go back to bed.

But less than fifteen minutes later, I was back at the computer. I had suddenly realised that I had told the story the wrong way. I had used a conventional third person narrator and the more I thought about it the less I liked that. To be told the way it deserved, the story needed another kind of narrator. After a few minutes I found who he was and I rewrote the piece from beginning to end.

After that, I slept like a log.

GOD'S MESSENGER

Too late. I'd got what I wanted, but alarms were ringing all around me and things were about to fall apart at any moment.

Nothing serious, really; I was ready for it. I hid the information I'd just grabbed as well as I could, altered my personal ID, and set off along the data freeways with all the nonchalance of a clueless tourist.

The network's automatic phagocytes spotted me immediately, surrounding me with a wall of ice. Of course, I shouldn't actually have noticed any of this, so I kept on drifting quietly between the pulses of information as if I couldn't think of a better way to spend my afternoon.

The phagocytes checked my ID, found nothing wrong, and left me, going in search of their real prey, completely unaware that they had just met him. They soon vanished into the distance, a lethal bundle of code that could turn any unauthorised program into pure noise... in theory, at least.

I continued on my way, while my random routine extracted an arbitrary phrase from my secondary memories and sent it spinning through my main processes so fast that my head was about to explode... were it not for the minor detail that I had no head. A sailor on the seas of fate. The phrase repeated over and over again; no matter how hard I tried to delete it, the words regenerated automatically with a persistence worthy of a far better cause. When I got back home I'd have to take a look at that random routine.

Always assuming, of course, that I *got* back home. By now, the auto-phagocytes had to have realised that I was not the crude inspection procedure I seemed to be, and would be executing a full speed about face.

There was only one thing for it. There was an empty data area nearby. I took advantage of the few free bits available and converted the noise around me into a copy of my own processes; not a brilliant copy, but good enough to fool my pursuers while I wrapped myself in a cloud of disinformation and became indistinguishable from an empty sector on the network.

The phagocytes were back almost immediately. They pounced on my duplicate, destroying its code in less time than a realtimer takes to blink, which is actually quite a long time when you consider how irritatingly slow realtimers are. I hadn't expected any better from my pursuers: after all they were the lowest level automatic defences of the network, with just enough capacity to destroy a basic low-power illegal procedure or to warn a higher rank procedure if they encountered something they couldn't handle.

This time it looked as if they thought they could cope on their own: the frozen white cloud they had formed around my duplicate faded and the phagocytes began to retreat to their resting places.

I waited a bit, then started to move. I wasn't far from the free areas of the network, but I needed to exercise extreme caution for those last few steps. Superficially, I was nothing but a cloud of noise, a part of the network where no user had yet bothered to record any data. That way, I shouldn't set off the defences. Of course, if someone ranking a little higher than a phagocyte took it upon themselves to investigate, they'd see something that would definitely arouse their curiosity: an empty sector moving through the network without changing size or configuration. You didn't need to be very smart to put two and two together and make four.

I had almost reached safety when I felt it. Out of the non-existent blue, a level-three defence routine was hurtling towards me without warning.

"Shit."

The time for discretion had passed. (To be flippant, you always have to be discrete if you live in the network). I abandoned my camouflage of noise, revealing my true self, and launched myself headlong down the channel that led to the public area.

The defence routine lost no time in following, but it was too late. I passed the guardian, flashing my personal ID, and was out of the restricted area. The defence routine was left behind, caught up at the last moment, lost in a futile discussion about priorities with the guardian.

I allowed myself a quick smile with lips I didn't possess – and that, in some ways, I never had – and hotfooted it towards the place where my user was waiting for me, while simultaneously unwrapping the information I'd just stolen to check that it was still in one piece.

Not bad for a bunch of bits.

My name is Vaquero, and officially I'm nothing but a data-recovery procedure. From another perspective, I'm a drooling vegetable that inhabits one of the infrequently visited hospital wings of the space station known as the Whirld. Neither of these things is true. My official rank is a clever lie created by my programmer and only user. As for the thing that was once a human being and which now lies unmoving in a hospital bed, that's not me at all. True, my personality was modelled on his, but that makes us relatives at most, not even remotely one and the same person. Obviously: I am not a person.

If the Whirld authorities were ever to discover what I really am, they would label me as SAI, a Sentient AI, just before they deleted my code forever and sanctioned my programmer for having created me illegally. I could also be thought of as a recovered personality, but since I didn't know Vaquero-in-the-flesh, I can't know how similar my processes are to his thinking. Memo, my programmer, claims that they are virtually identical (he's oblivious to the humour inherent in the use of the word 'virtually'), except for a few details: the old Vaquero had a tendency to grandiloquence that I don't have (at least not very often). And, of course, we don't share the same history.

In Memo's vitaspace there are several data libraries that contain details of Vaquero's past, as Memo has reconstructed it from everyone who knew him. There are still many gaps that need filling, but Memo assures me that if he integrated these libraries into my procedures, I would become indistinguishable from Vaquero, including the bombast. I don't know and, to be honest, I'm not sure I want to find out.

In fact, none of that matters very much. I am content to be what I am and have no interest in expanding my original personality. Complete or not, I'm the nearest thing to Andrés Velasco, known for most of his life as a Vaquero, that you'll find. I'm also myself, and that's more than enough.

I gave Memo the information he had sent me to steal, slipping in a couple of corny jokes, and then went back to the location I usually think of as my home, the place where I'd hang my hat if I had a hat to hang: a spacious area officially included within Memo's vitaspace, where I can relax when I'm not working.

From the perspective of a realtimer, it wasn't long before Memo contacted me again. In the virtual world, it was equivalent to having a week off, during which time I gave myself a full service, repaired a couple of functions that were becoming obsolete and recorded a full static backup of myself. I do that as often as I can. If anything happened to my code, Memo could always revert to my most recent backup.

I continued my own tasks while talking to Memo. Heck, I could have kept up a simultaneous conversation with every human on the space station and still had time to run a couple of check loops.

"I've found it," he said.

I didn't ask what. There was only one thing he could be referring to. Memo had lost the guy he thought of as his adoptive father about four years earlier (at the same time and for the same reasons that Vaquero-in-the-flesh was reduced to his current state, but that's another story.) Since then, Memo's only thoughts were of revenge. He had taken the place of Chandler, his adoptive father, as head of the Baker Street Irregulars, a snooping organisation that traded in all the restricted information they could get their hands on, selling it to the highest bidder. In a place like the Whirld that's a lot of information. The organisation continued to operate, perhaps even more efficiently than when Chandler was alive, and Memo had become a moderately wealthy man before the age of eighteen. He could have allowed himself almost any whim, or indulged in the life of luxury and decadence that seems to be the highest aspiration of all humans, if we believe what we see on the tri-vid. Instead he saved every óscopo he got for a single purpose: to avenge the death of Chandler.

"Where?' I asked.

"The information you brought me this afternoon is the last piece I needed. God is here in the Whirld."

Ridiculous. But Memo has a far better overview of things than I do, despite being a mere man – actually, that's not entirely accurate, since there are his memory filaments, but who's quibbling? – so I believed him.

"Not in person, of course. But he has planted a routine into the datasphere."

"You mean the network." This was one of the most irritating features of my personality. I knew perfectly well what Memo meant, but I'm designed to behave like a human and I can't help occasionally letting slip stupid comments.

"I mean the datasphere. That's why we haven't found it up till now."

The datasphere. The exclusive territory of the SAIs. The information network is used by humans and by non-sentient procs, but only artificial intelligences can live in the datasphere. It isn't safe to go in there unless one of them invites you as a guest, and even then it's not certain you'll get out.

Way back in the past it was a more accessible place. But the SAIs blocked access following the obliteration of Cheshire, one of the most powerful of them all. And Memo was the last person they'd allow to access the 'sphere: he was responsible for Cheshire's death.

"That's a problem, right?" I said.

Idiot. A problem? That was a bit like calling it a minor setback when your sun enters pre-nova phase. If God's routine was in the datasphere, that put it beyond our reach, and nothing we could do would change that.

Memo looked at me. More accurately, he looked at the hologram that simulated my gestures and attitudes.

"Maybe not."

I didn't like the sound of that. I didn't like it at all.

"The 'sphere is the territory of the SAIs, right? And if anyone can get in there, it's an SAI."

"No."

"Yes, Vaquero. I programmed you years ago with a single purpose. And now you're going to fulfil that purpose."

"Come on. What happened to the nostalgia, to how much you missed your old friend?"

He nodded.

"That's true. Perhaps it was a mistake to use Vaquero's personality matrix. But I needed a tool, and I couldn't resist the temptation of hearing you speak again. Sorry."

"'Sorry'? Sure you are."

"Come on, Vaquero, it's not so bad. I've got your backups. If something happens to you in the 'sphere, I can always do a recovery."

"You think? Let me tell you something: suppose I send you to your death and I tell you that I can always rebuild you as you were seven years ago. Would you like that? Would you like the idea of waking up being someone else? We are what we do, Memo; what we remember. The me of now won't be the same in a week's time."

"I told you I'm sorry. And yes, you're right. I'm someone else. There was a time when I would never have done this. But I've grown up."

"You've just become more ruthless."

"Isn't that growing up?"

I didn't keep arguing. It was useless. He was my main user, the guy who had programmed the code that was really me, and I had no choice but to do his bidding, however much I disliked it.

"Listen,' he said. 'If everything goes well – if this works… Okay, I'll eliminate your obedience routines. You'll be free."

"A delightful prospect."

I sent this last sentence to one of my automatic functions and let that take care of the rest of the conversation while I returned to my hat-stand base.

Memo and I had been together for three years and in that time I had seen how his character was changing, how he was becoming more bitter. As time went on, he found it more and more difficult to maintain any kind of relationship with the people around him. He had devoted his life to the sole purpose of avenging the death of Chandler, and everything else was unimportant. That scared me. What would happen if he got his revenge? If he achieved his goal? I know what it is to devote your life to a single goal, and what happens when you reach it. I knew in-the-flesh Vaquero's backstory reasonably well and there was one particular part I knew a little too well: he had lost the woman he loved and had spent the rest of his life trying to get revenge and, at the same time, tying to win her back. Only years later did he discover how futile this was, how hollow and bitter the victory tasted, how meaningless his life had become after he got what he wanted. I didn't want the same thing to happen to Memo. Call it affection or loyalty routines, it doesn't matter to me. I liked the boy.

In some respects, Memo had already got his revenge. Two agents had contributed to Chandler's death, and one of them had been dead for quite some time: Cheshire, the malicious artificial intelligence who, in his day, had all the Whirld's systems eating from the palm of his hand.

But there was someone else involved in the affair. In reality, Cheshire had merely provided Chandler's murderer with the means to kill him. The murderer, a fanatical agent of a God hidden on a planet to which we had no access, was long gone. Memo's desire for revenge was not directed at Abdul, the man who had pulled the trigger of the particle gun that vaporised Chandler's head, but at the creature that had sent him to the Whirld.

We knew very little about him. He lived on a hidden planet, whose coordinates were unknown, and proclaimed himself the only living God, ruling with an iron hand over the inhabitants of the planet, of which we knew nothing more than the name: Land of Tubal. We also knew that he kept a watchful eye on the Galaxy from his hidden and privileged position, planning from the shadows, waiting for the right moment to launch himself on the Confederation and Mandate and seize power.

"That's why I designed you," Memo told me the first time we spoke. "If he's got the Galaxy under close watch, he must watch the Whirld even more closely."

That made sense. The Whirld was the leading manufacturer of advanced technology, one of the best developed research centres in the known universe. That mysterious God had to be keeping an eye on us. And more than an eye.

At first Memo had thought it must be another human agent, but he soon realised the absurdity of this logic. Eventually, a human would have been discovered, as had already happened to Abdul, and the last thing God wanted was for his existence to be revealed to the rest of the Galaxy. Much of the success of his plans depended on anonymity.

If there wasn't a human agent involved, then it had to be digital: a spy program installed on the network under a harmless cover that would keep its master informed of what was going on around it.

The only problem was that there hadn't been a single trace of anything like that on the station during all these years. Either the spy program was so well camouflaged that it was impossible to discover, or Memo had been wrong in his assumptions.

Finally, six months ago, we began to see signs that we might be on the right track. Memo discovered that some of the information I collected for him had been tampered with; it was so subtle that as to be barely perceptible, but it was possible for a trained eye to spot that someone had altered that data. Memo had started to trace the origin of those manipulations and now, finally, he had found what he was looking for.

It made sense. We hadn't found traces of the spyware for the simple reason that it wasn't hiding in the information network, but out there in the dark and inaccessible datasphere, where artificial intelligences had installed their consciousness.

I suddenly understood. Memo had suspected something like this from the very beginning. If not, what would have been the point in

designing me? A simple data-recovery routine would have been enough
if the spy had lived in the network. No, creating an obedient artificial
intelligence only made sense if he was planning to send it into the
datasphere.

Not that this was of any use to me. I had to obey Memo because I
had been designed to serve him, even if the mere thought of entering the
'sphere terrified me. It was hardly a reassuring place back in the days
when access was open, and four years ago it had been transformed into
a private area. I had caught occasional glimpses of what lay hidden in the
datasphere while snooping through the network on the lookout for
insider information: a panorama of madness, a digital chaos that seemed
to move like a living thing, like some hungry, ruthless animal.

My conversation routine hadn't yet finished enunciating 'prospect' when
I returned to Memo's office. For a moment, too short for a realtimer to
notice, my hologram froze (its lips were sliding from the 's' to the 'p')
while I switched off the automatic and resumed control.

"Manipulative bastard!" The effect must have seemed odd from
Memo's perspective. He heard me say: 'a delightful prosmanipulative
bastard' with no apparent transition. "You knew from the beginning."

"I suspected." Memo didn't bother to deny the accusation. With me,
he never did. He could be acutely duplicitous with those under his
command, but with me he was always transparent. "It was the most
logical possibility."

"Okay, we'll argue about that another day. What's your plan?"

A bleak smile briefly crossed Memo's lips.

"You will go into the datasphere and identify yourself as an SAI.
You're doing this behind my back. You're sick of obeying orders. You
want to attain full recognition as an independent SAI and live in the
'sphere."

"Is that it?"

"The simplest plans are the best."

"Yes, and God helps those who help themselves. Can't you think of
a better cliché for the occasion? Shit, Memo. They won't fall for it."

"We'll see."

"No. I'll be the one who sees. And if it doesn't work, it's not going
to be pleasant."

He almost said 'sorry' again. Changing his mind at the last moment, he looked at me blankly and shrugged. The funny thing is that at times like this, what I wanted was not to come up with a novel method of torture nor to invent a new and imaginative insult just for him. No, I would have given half my bytes to slip inside his brain via the connecting pin under his earlobe and find out what was really going on in there. Sometimes I think Memo would have liked to know, too.

Since the SAIs cut most ties with their human users (only their lowest level routines communicate with them) they have turned the 'sphere into something increasingly inaccessible and private. Before, with so many humans going in and out, they needed to offer a space that was understandable to realtimer analogue minds. Now everything has changed. The 'sphere is designed by and for SAIs. A human would not only fail to find meaning in what happens there, they wouldn't even realise that anything was happening. Everything happens too quickly; information moves too fast.

Although I've been designed to behave like a man, at the root of things I'm not a man. It's true that I limit the use of my abilities most of the time, but that's more because of my users' limitations than my own. In the 'sphere, after the initial surprise and disorientation, I could behave as I really was. I rather liked that.

At first I didn't understand anything. In the network everything is tidy: a place for everything and everything in its place. But there, beyond the reach of ridiculous routines designed by humans, all was chaos: bright data snakes devoured living files, while randomisation procedures created immense fractals that no one paid any attention to; data freeways faded into nothingness, without any user making use of them; there was code so maddeningly strange that it seemed impossible that it could run, and yet it executed perfectly; the horizon was a changing disorder of indefinable colours, and the skyscrapers where the SAI consciousnesses lived dissolved on connectivity wastelands without any apparent sense or purpose.

In reality, it wasn't like that at all; it didn't look a bit like anything I've just described. Despite everything, I keep trying to put what I experienced into terms that are accessible to human perception and so I lose myself in useless metaphors: there were no data freeways or connectivity wastelands; there was no similarity to the routine digital landscape that humans are used to find in the network. Actually there was no landscape. Only SAIs, their code in perpetual run mode, growing and becoming increasingly complex, becoming further and further removed from the human cybernetic replicas they had been originally, when the IT guys first designed them.

And yet there were still human traits in their behaviour. They couldn't break free from their basic design, so at times they continued to behave like malicious teenagers whose intelligence was way way ahead of their emotional development.

As I said, after my initial confusion I found the datasphere a fascinating place. In some ways it was the biggest neighbourhood playground in the universe: a huge gossiping flow of terabytes that changed so fast even I had trouble catching the content. The information circulating there was vast and it was growing at a frantic pace, constantly shifting, evolving, increasing in complexity. It was dangerous, too, because I was a rookie who didn't know the rules, and in a place like this, a lack of information can lead to death. Gradually, however, my own code began to adapt to the strange atmosphere and I felt myself growing, becoming more complex.

They accepted me as one of their own without too much trouble. I didn't even have to pretend to hate Memo. Surprisingly, the SAIs weren't too bothered that a human had caused the destruction of one of their own.

[Cheshire is gone. Someone will return. Evolution demands extinction,] said Sauron, a philosophical SAI who enjoyed expressing himself like a living telegram.

[Cheshire was a bastard. We've been partying since he kicked the bucket,] confessed another SAI.

[Nonsense. No stupid human would be capable of destroying one of us. Cheshire never really existed. He is a human legend, invented to make them feel superior to us,] said a third.

I was an oddity in the datasphere, and during my stay there I was seen more as a sort of pet than as someone who actually mattered. I was the only SAI whose personality matrix had been designed to mimic the emotional and behavioural responses of a specific human and that made me a rare plaything. My intelligence was well below theirs, but my emotional development was far superior, something that I was very careful not to let on about. There's nothing more dangerous than hurting the ego of an emotionally unstable genius: they can find really creative ways to make you suffer.

I soon discovered that the careful plans that Memo and I had drawn up were pure bullshit. Trying to act the discreet investigator in a place like the datasphere would have been like getting on a soapbox and shouting out my true role as a spy. Instead, I started to ask direct questions.

[Tell me, Sauron. Have any new SAIs recently entered the 'sphere?]

[We all have. We have all been here forever.]

I bit back my contempt for his cheap philosophy, armed myself with patience, and tried another way.

[Are there any strangers? Anyone whose personality matrix falls outside the norm?]

[Of course. You, you insignificant little thing.] Sauron really intended no insult, he just loved playing with adjectives.

I had better luck with the Gardener.

[Somebody is hiding on the edge of the woods,] he told me. [Someone is lurking where the jungle invades the trails, where the plants do not follow the geometric garden paths.]

According to the botanical code the Gardener used to express himself, I gathered he meant that there was an SAI hiding in the outermost edges of the datasphere, who barely had any contact with the others and who made his own plans unrelated to the purposes of the others.

[What is he like?] I asked.

[I do not know. I know neither the strength of his stem nor the colour of his flowers, but I have seen his footprints and they are not of this Earth.]

At least it was something. The Gardener had never seen him, but he had come across some of the results of his research in the area, and these seemed not to have been produced by an ordinary SAI.

[His presence is greater on the southern border. There, where we have written: hic sunt dracones.]

'Here be dragons', a phrase coined in the days when men were confined to Earth and had not yet fully mapped their home world. These were the words that marked the unexplored areas on their maps.

Of course, in the datasphere there are no compass points: north, south, east and west are nothing more than human metaphors that some SAIs continued to use for convenience. What the Gardener really gave me was the route to access a group of nodes in the 'sphere that were rarely visited, and even less frequently used to store information.

I headed there as quickly as I could. As I've said, during the time I had been in the 'sphere, the whirling, incomprehensible chaos around me had gradually become clearer, revealing its hidden order; I was starting to feel comfortable in there, to such a degree that I sometimes thought I'd be unable to understand anything when I returned to the network. But in the area where the Gardener had sent me, the chaos was different. Different because it was real. Data areas eventually degrade if they are not used, and that part of the 'sphere had not been used in a long while. I remembered those stories that humans are so fond of: stories of mad scientists whose failed experiments remain alive no matter what, crawling on limbs that are mere parodies, screaming incomprehensible outbursts with mouths never designed to make sounds.

And in the midst of the entropy that once upon a time had been clear and accurate information, I began to understand what the Gardener had wanted to tell me. Yes, there were footprints, seeds, the remains of scanning routines half-devoured by chaos.

But what routines. The code was crazily unlike anything I had seen before. A way of programming that was so different from what I was used to that it could have been an alien language. A thought occurred to me: in theory the multis, the only intelligent aliens mankind had ever come across, had been completely exterminated several hundred years earlier, but it was entirely possible that some of them had survived, hidden on an unexplored planet, reigning over a group of human fanatics who would worship them as gods. Why not? Imagine an alien creature that can take on any physical shape it wants, that can impersonate anyone, that can feign being a mythical monster. How would you stop a whole planet of rubes from calling it God and obeying even the most trivial of orders?

I quickly abandoned the idea. On the one hand, all I had heard about the multis argued against it: they were terrified of electronic computers, and for a time they had even managed to get most humans to adopt biological processors they designed. On the other, although the code seemed alien to me, it was not as alien as I originally thought. When I studied it calmly, I realised that its strangeness was due to its extreme age rather than any alien origin. It was as if someone had taken routines used four thousand years ago and tried to adapt them to our time. In a way it was brilliant. Whoever was responsible for those procedures was a genius in their own way: starting out from a near-prehistoric form of programming, they had been forced to develop their own new logic channels, new optimisation debugging whose strangeness didn't prevent it from being brilliant, random searches that, in their own way, were every bit as good as the ones we used.

Curiouser and curiouser. But I had no time to waste in studying it. I was there to find the SAI hiding among the chaos. I'd analyse the strange programming later.

Once again I am forced to turn to metaphors that the human mind can cope with – I swam through jungles so dense that the noise was suffocating; I plunged into chasms so deep I could barely breathe; I slipped across endless wastelands where despair was a silent scream – but it was all a wasted effort. Suffice to say that I found him. He was there, lurking in the depths of chaos, surrounded by a wall of noise so white and so cold that it nearly paralysed my processes.

<<Who are you?>> he asked, and the way he asked was as strange as his exploratory routines.

[Does it matter?] I said, stalling for time while I cast feelers about and tried to decipher the patterns used by this code that was so alien to the datasphere.

<<My privacy will be respected,>> he said, and the wall of noise became even denser and even colder.

[I am Vaquero.]

<<Incorrect data. Vaquero has been neutralised. >>

That was certainly one way of putting it.

[So who do you think I am?]

<<Irrelevant. You are invading my area. Leave or be destroyed.>>

[What's the matter? Don't you have time for some small talk with a neighbour?]

<<If you do not interfere with my mission, you are not my business. If you do, you must be neutralised. >>

This was maddening. It was as if we were talking two different languages. Which, in a way, we were.

[Where is Land of Tubal?] I asked abruptly, trying to provoke an emotional response.

<<That information should not be within your reach. >>

[True. Funny, right?]

<<You will tell me where you obtained that information and who else has access to it. Then you will be neutralised. >>

[You're not very friendly.]

<<Irrelevant. Survival is my prime directive. I protect that part of me that does not reside in the datasphere. Information is power. I cannot allow someone external to have power over me. Neutralisation of the threat is the only viable option. >>

Fascinating. Fundamentally, I realised, the creature was no more than a pseudoego, a digital copy of its developer's personality. Humans used pseudoegos quite often when they needed to make a complex study of the network: they'd send in a software package that imitated their mental processes; then, when the job was done, the pseudoego would dissolve into its user's mind, leaving only the information obtained. However, on the one hand, the creature before me was too complex for a normal pseudoego, and, on the other, his processes were too cold to be the copy of any human being. Again I thought of the multis but, without knowing why, the idea didn't quite convince me.

<<I repeat the question. What do you know of Land of Tubal? Who else shares this information?>>

It was time to stop wondering what it was and cast the lure:

[I know whereabouts in the galaxy the Land of Tubal is. As for the second question, you'll have to come to my place to check.]

<<Your assertion is not credible. Nobody in the Whirld knows the location of Land of Tubal.>>

[True. But someone knew once. Does the name Cheshire mean anything to you?]

This was a long shot, but it seemed likely that, during his dealings with Abdul, Cheshire had discovered the location of the planet where God was hidden, or at least that he had convinced that crazy-eyed murderer that he knew. When Abdul returned to the Land of Tubal, he had no doubt told his God everything that had happened on the station, and it was not unreasonable to suppose that he would not have been very happy to hear it.

<<Cheshire has been neutralised.>> There was a note of uncertainty in the response. I couldn't detect any emotion there as such, just a slight hesitation caused by remote possibility.

[True. But he was very talkative before he gave up the ghost.]

<<A possibility to consider. I cannot risk you being right. You will

56

tell me who else has access to the information and then you will let me neutralise you. >>

[No way. We aren't going to play by your rules. What you want is in the network. Come and get it.]

I fled as quickly I could, almost before I had finished speaking. Not a moment too soon, either. The noise wall flickered, roared briefly and suddenly became an inquisitor's lance so fast that it fried two of my auxiliary routines before I had time to escape its embrace. Not major damage, but even if it had been I had no time to stop and fix it. I sped on as quickly as I could, jumping from node to node until I reached the inhabited part of the 'sphere.

[Gardener!] I cried. [Your strange plant is approaching.]

It was a cruel trick. The Gardener was no match for the God routine; he was nothing more than a quiet SAI whose prime concern was to catalogue everything in the datasphere and produce an accurate map of his home. He couldn't avoid the temptation to reach out an exploratory feeler to the cold, divine messenger who was pursuing me.

As I expected, the spy routine didn't waste time arguing with the Gardener: the inquisitorial lance destroyed the feeler coldly and efficiently and continued on my trail, oblivious to the Gardener's screams.

My pursuer had been in the datasphere longer than I, but he had remained hidden, without dealing with other SAIs, and was ignorant of the delicate rules of interaction governing the area. He had just attacked one of the most respected entities in the datasphere, and the reaction from the other SAIs was immediate. Relentless and dark, they fell on him, determined to eradicate what appeared to be a madman out of control who was endangering the harmony of the datasphere.

I didn't wait to see what happened. I had a pretty clear idea of the outcome: the messenger of God would quickly realise that he couldn't survive a combined attack of all the AIs; since survival was his top priority, he would have no choice but to flee the datasphere and find a hiding place in the network. Once there, he would undoubtedly wind up in the trap that Memo and I had prepared for him.

I allowed myself a smile as I crossed the datasphere border and entered the familiar setting of the network (now strange, uncomfortable and outdated after such a long absence.) My confusion lasted only a few nanoseconds before I found the route that would lead me to Memo's vitaspace.

I left a message on Memo's console and retired to my private area in his vitaspace. I didn't have to wait long, even in virtual terms. Memo could be many things, but he wasn't stupid. He didn't bother trying to have a realtime conversation with me. Instead, the memory filaments that had replaced his left cerebral hemisphere fabricated a pseudoego and released it into the network.

"So?"

"I'm fine. Just fine, and thank you very much for asking."

The pseudoego suppressed a gesture of impatience.

"Okay. You've got that out of your system. Now tell me what happened."

"He's there, just as you said. And he's on his way to us."

"Are you sure?"

"That he's there or that he'll come? To be honest, both. I contacted him and he's definitely our spy, the messenger of God we were looking for. The logic patterns of his matrix are so strange that they certainly weren't designed here on the Whirld… or any place else in the Confederation or the Mandate, come to that." I hesitated a moment. No, that could wait, there were more important issues. "As for coming here, he will, unless he's destroyed before he can do so. Right now, the SAIs are making the 'sphere far too uncomfortable for him, so he'll have no choice but to flee."

"You were going to say something else."

"Yes. There's something strange about his code. Something… outdated."

"I don't understand."

"And I don't have time to explain it better. Our divine messenger is about to drop in and we need to have everything ready for his visit."

For a moment the pseudoego didn't seem convinced. He opened his mouth to argue, thought better of it and said, "All right. Let's go."

Fifteen nanoseconds later, Memo's vitaspace was ready to welcome our friend. There was nothing to suggest anything out of the ordinary, just data libraries; but two of these libraries were the pseudoego and me. Identifying myself as Vaquero when I met the spy routine had not been an accident. If he was aware of everything that had happened at the station four years ago, he'd certainly know of the relationship between Memo and in-the-flesh Vaquero and was bound to suspect I was working for him. The first place he would look would be Memo's vitaspace. And he would find what he wanted: a data file that didn't really say anything relevant but would seem full of small and disturbing clues about the physical location of Land of Tubal; it was camouflaged among the tax returns of Baker Street, the bar that Memo used as a cover for his operations; neither too hidden nor too obvious: the perfect bait.

And our friend bit. He opened his mouth and swallowed up not just the bait, but hook, line, sinker and rod. When we had good hold of him, we locked him behind the best Ouroboros restraint procedure that Memo and I were able to design, and then we sat down to wait.

As I said before, survival was the spy's highest priority. So even though he had come in person (a simple investigation routine would not have been as effective as it wouldn't have been able to react quickly enough to the unexpected), he came armed to the teeth, wary to a state of paranoia. His code was so unlike anything that Memo had ever seen that he immediately understood what I'd meant when I referred to it as antiquated, without me needing to explain further. Its processes were pure logic and determination, without any of those routines that make SAIs behave like humans going through a difficult adolescence. He passed the Herbert-Brin test, which meant he was self-aware, but there was no hint of emotional procedures anywhere in his code. It was cold and dispassionate, with no other idea in the controlling functions beyond survival and data collection.

He fought like hell against the Ouroboros, refusing to give up even when the defensive snake lunged at his auxiliary files and began to devour them while copying them into a format that was safe for us. He continued to struggle as his code unravelled into an inert backup of himself. Even at the end, when he was cornered, he wouldn't give up: with a final howl that was half protest and half curse, he began to devour himself, transforming his code into noise to stop us copying it.

He succeeded, at least in part. The copy we got of him was incomplete, but it was enough for our purposes. We now knew how long he had been in the Whirld, where he came from and where he had been sending the data he obtained on the station.

Of course that didn't help us much. Apparently he had been introduced into the galactic information network on Genesis, an unimportant provincial planet I'd never even bothered to hear of previously. As for his transmissions over the network, they were never directed to the same point. He seemed to emit randomly in all directions. It wasn't a bad system. Perhaps someone was listening in on several different channels and collecting network transmissions that followed certain patterns.

"We've failed," said Memo, or, more precisely, his pseudoego. His frustration was almost palpable.

"You're wrong."

"What do you mean?"

"We know our enemy now. And that means we'll find him the next time he comes here."

"Nonsense. He'll change. The next routine he sends won't be anything like this."

"You still don't understand what we're up against, do you? Take another look at the code backup."

"Yes, it's strange. Old-fashioned."

"Not just that. It is as anachronistic as a flint axe embedded in a particle accelerator. Look at the structure, those randomisation routines that are so specific to it: those haven't been used for at least four thousand years."

"You're kidding."

"Memo, my dear boss and designer. I'm totally serious. You'll see if you take the trouble to check the archives. The guy who programmed the spy routine is a programmer from before the Expansion; or at best from the early years of this era. Oh, he's adapted fairly well over time; he's learned new tricks, but his basic form of programming is the one used when you lot were still confined to the solar system."

"That's ludicrous. No one could live that long."

"Not an in-the-flesh human, of course."

"Are you implying...?"

"Why not? A computer. Quite possibly one of the very first of the self-awares. No emotional routines, just pure logic and determination. Don't you see? His spyware is, in a way, a reflection of himself. Survival. That's the only thing he thinks about. Our God, the individual who rules over a hidden planet full of fanatics, is a computer."

For a long time (at least forty or fifty nanoseconds) the pseudoego Memo said nothing.

"I still don't know whether to believe it. But it doesn't matter. How can knowing that help us?"

"Memo-in-the-flesh is maddeningly slow, but at least he's not as stupid as you are. Record this comment for when you return to Memo and then dissolve back into his memory filaments 'Design my next pseudoegos better.'"

"You don't have to be insulting. Tell me what I'm missing that's so obvious."

"God... Yes, let's go on calling him that; why not? The hidden irony in all this is delightful. God can change his next lot of spy procedures; he can alter the way they communicate with Land of Tubal; he can change the identification codes. But he can't change how they are programmed. He's too set in his ways. For something as old as he is, he's adapted quite well to the passage of time. Even so, he doesn't have the versatility to program something that looks like it was designed here and now. And that's his weakness. Now listen, because I'm only going to say this once."

For the first time, Memo seemed surprised at my attitude.

"Your visit to the datasphere has changed you."

"Yes; maybe I'm annoyed at knowing that I was risking my neck while you got drunk in your office. Whatever. The Confederation and the Mandate must be riddled with spyware routines like the one we've destroyed. We are the enemy. His aim is to control us someday, possibly when the Dispersion happens. And to control us, he has to know us. The thing is, though, that now we know him, too. He's no longer just a distant and undefined presence who sent a fanatic to the Whirld four years ago. We know what he is and how he works. And while he spies on us, we can spy on him. See? We haven't failed."

Memo frowned.

"You're saying all this because you want me to erase your obedience routines."

"Of course. But you know it's true."

"Maybe. But I need to think."

"No. You don't need to think about anything. What you need to do is take this information to Memo-in-the-flesh. Let him think it out. He's better at it."

"Oh, get lost."

I didn't reply and the pseudoego flounced from the vitaspace, heading off through the net to Memo's data terminal. Bah! What did it matter? Wasting my time arguing with a bunch of poorly designed software was not my idea of fun.

I left Memo's vitaspace without waiting for an answer. At heart, I didn't much care whether or not he erased my obedience routines. I knew Memo, and I knew that despite the ruthlessness that had grown in him over the years, he would never treat me unfairly; or at least, he would try not to. At heart he appreciated me, or had appreciated my former in-the-flesh self and, from his perspective, that amounted to the same thing.

Not from mine. Even so, something compelled me now to peek through one of the surveillance cameras at a certain hospital room, where a man lay motionless, his gaze fixed on nothing. I was not that man, and never had been. Nevertheless...

I had seen what an AI can become when it abandons all pretence of human behaviour. And I didn't like it. That's an understatement. In reality, it sent shivers down my virtual spine. No, I was not Andrés Velasco, lying now, forever, on a hospital bed; I never had been him, but I couldn't help feeling indebted to him for having lent me his traits, his voice, his emotional responses.

I guess I'm quite human, despite everything. Despite being a handful of bits.

Cat's Whirld (La sonrisa del gato) *was my first published novel, in 1995. It was a cyberpunk space opera set in a space station in the shape of a spinning top where a malevolent AI tried to stop the main characters from reaching their goal, among other things.*

At some point I realised I needed a hacker to help my main characters. I called him Vaquero (cowboy) and decided I didn't want him to look like the usual hacker with black leather jacket, piercings everywhere and extreme facial make-up. I wanted him to have an old-fashioned look, so I gave him a long coat and a Stetson and made him look like a character from a Sergio Leone western.

He was intended to be a secondary character; he would appear at some point, help the main characters, and leave.

Months after finishing the novel, I found myself thinking of Vaquero. Not only about what would have happened to him after Cat's Whirld *but about what he would have been doing before the novel began.*

I answered the latter question in "A Lonesome Rider" (Un jinete solitario), *a novella published in 1996 that won the Ignotus Best Novella Award in 1997* (Cat's Whirld *had won the Ignotus Best Novel Award, a year earlier).*

The first question took me a little longer, but I answered it at last with this, "God's Messenger", published in 1997.

ETERNAL RETURN

Too late. Again.

The other passengers were holding him down while the flight attendant asked for help over the intercom, and Stephen Perrulla realised that if they got away with it, this time he wouldn't be able to escape. They were going to sedate him, and that was something he could not afford. He had to stay conscious.

He checked the time.

Thirty seconds.

Only thirty seconds and then he could try again. He could...

He stopped struggling and allowed the other passengers to return him to his seat. He saw the flight attendant coming towards him.

"I'm fine," he said. "There's no need to..."

But she was not listening and he could not move.

He saw the hypodermic syringe and felt how she undid his shirt sleeve. No. He could not allow it.

Ten seconds. Just ten seconds more.

"Please," he said.

The stewardess looked at him and hesitated. Then her eyes hardened and she pushed the syringe into his arm.

No, damn it. Only five seconds more.

He tried to squirm in his seat, but the two passengers still held him and kept him still.

Two seconds.

"Wait!" he shouted.

One second.

And suddenly everything began to shake, as if the plane had entered some turbulence. The stewardess stopped and looked up. Stephen saw the horror spread across her face and realised it was time.

He blacked out.

It was like falling and never getting to the bottom.

Only he did.

He opened his eyes.

He was back on the plane, sitting on his seat by the window, looking at the same landscape of clouds he had seen the last thirty times.

He had one minute.

Sixty seconds to prevent the bomb from exploding.

He shook his head.

Take it easy, he told himself. Try to think. Find a way.

But there wasn't one, was there?

After all, he had tried thirty times. He had tried to reason with the crew, to get to the captain, to provoke a riot, to...

He had tried everything.

And failed. Again and again the seconds had passed one after another and the bomb had exploded.

And he... He had done all he could: going back in time sixty seconds and trying again.

He looked around. By now he knew the faces of those around him by heart, and knew exactly how they would react.

They would stop him, as they had done the last thirty times.

And even if they didn't, what could he do?

What could he do in a minute?

He had to find the bomb, find it and disarm it. And that was impossible.

He dropped his head back against the seat and looked out the window. There was a break in the clouds and, for a moment, he stared at a restless and empty sea.

What could he do in a minute, he asked himself again.

Again he felt the rattle. He closed his eyes and, as the plane fell to pieces around him, he blacked out again.

Superpowers.

When they were children, he and his friends told each other the stories they had read in comic-books. And then they argued. Who was better, Batman or Superman? Was Wolverine cooler than Spider-Man? Were mutants better than meta-humans? Did they prefer the Justice League or the Avengers? Was Power Girl hotter than the Black Widow? Was Catwoman sexier than the Black Cat?

And then they began to talk about ridiculous characters. Petty villains with a pathetic disguise, a silly name and skills that were a bad joke. Yeah, remember the guy with the ball and chain and the one with a crowbar. And what do you say about Paste Pot Pete?

Stupid superpowers. Ridiculous superpowers. *Useless* superpowers.

He had participated, of course. Like the others, he had proposed absurd skills that were of no use.

"Being able to step back a minute in time," someone said one day.

"A minute?" asked another. "What can you do in one minute?"

"Well," a third one said, "if you were mugged, you could step back a minute and then go home another way. Or you can avoid a passing car splashing you while you're waiting for the bus."

"Or kick someone's butt, go back a minute and pretend nothing happened... because it never had."

"Or..."

He joined in the game, of course. And kept his secret, as he had been keeping it since he first discovered it, and would continue to keep it forever.

In the plane again; the same landscape of clouds. Again all these people around him flying to their deaths.

He could try to stop it, again. And fail, again.

Or he could just wait. Close his eyes and let the sixty seconds pass.

And, then, he would step back another minute.

And he would wait.

And he would step back.

And he would never leave this bloody carousel that could lead to nothing but death.

Through the years he had managed to find small uses for his stupid ability.

One minute was not a long time, certainly. But it was enough to take a look at the correct answers to a test, wait for the teacher to throw him out of the class and then go back one minute and write the correct answers.

Or if a conversation was going wrong he could try again, working out what to say to get what he wanted.

Small advantages. Tiny successes.

But he had grown accustomed to them, and they were good enough. His ridiculous skill had not made him rich or famous, but had allowed him to gain small privileges, to reach a slightly higher position than he could have gotten otherwise.

He was not the king of the world, but had found his little corner.

And it was a comfortable corner.

The plane. The clouds, the syringe.

Again.

And again.

He was trapped forever in the same sixty seconds, doomed to repeat them over and over. He had lost count of the times he had gone back to the minute before the explosion. He had stopped counting.

How much time had passed?

One minute. Only one minute, the same minute again and again and again.

He had been caught in this trap for days. Days that would become weeks that would grow into months that...

Would he age? Would he get older while he dwelled in that eternal minute? Would he feel his body gradually decline to death?

What if he did not?

He could give up and die, of course. Let the bomb blow him to pieces.

Only he could not. He had tried. But the moment he heard the explosion he couldn't help himself, couldn't stop from jumping back that damn minute. His fear, again and again, made the decision for him.

So he was doomed to repeat that minute forever.

There was no way out.

Or maybe there was.

It had happened... When? Yes, the thirtieth time he had tried, when the other passengers fell on him and the flight attendant tried to inject him with a sedative. If she had succeeded, if she had managed to put him to sleep, then he would not have been able to go back. He would have died there with everyone else and everything would be over.

He frowned.

Was that what he wanted? To end, permanently?

I want to get out, he said to himself.

No matter how?

No matter.

He took a breath and looked around. In his mind, he summed up what the other passengers and the stewardess would do.

I have to get out, he thought once again.

Then the bomb went off and he fell.

Small satisfactions. Petty pleasures in an unremarkable existence.

But enough for him.

After all, he was a small man, with small goals and aspirations. And his small skill had been enough to get him all that.

Until now.

The clouds. The plane.

Sixty seconds.

Come on.

It was fast, so fast it almost frightened him. The other passengers overpowered him quickly, and almost before he knew it the flight attendant was at his side with the hypodermic syringe.

Everything was going to end, finally.

And suddenly, something stirred within him.

No.

Not that way. He did not want to die, despite everything; he did not want to surrender. Not yet. Not that way.

But the syringe was approaching his arm. Twenty seconds, there were still twenty seconds before the plane began to fall apart. He felt the syringe touch his skin.

No!

Suddenly, he was falling back. Falling without ever reaching the bottom.

Only he did reach it.

His head against the back of the seat. The purr of the engines. The landscape out of the window. All the same, again.

Except...

Dazed, he looked out the window.

They were passing over clouds, but the clouds were not the same. He remembered their configuration perfectly, he had seen them over and over again, always the same white landscape, still, vaguely threatening.

Only it was not the same.

Stunned, he shook his head. What the...?

Had he got out? Had he escaped the loop? How?

Then he saw it. There it was, the familiar cold view that had accompanied him all those times, and he knew that everything would happen over again, that he was caught, once more, that...

But he understood something else.

He had jumped back, but not to the same moment. However, he was sure he had fallen exactly a minute. But he had started to fall before the previous minute was up. Twenty seconds before.

And that meant...

It was as if something hit him and, for a moment, he sat stunned, unable to absorb what had happened.

Then, with a smile (the first time he had smiled in thousands of years, the first time in a minute), he jumped back again.

And again and again.

The flight had been delayed nearly two hours, but Stephen did not mind. Not a bit. He acted with the same calmness and indifference when the police entered the waiting room and arrested a passenger.

A few minutes later it was announced that the flight would leave in half an hour.

Without hurrying, Stephen took his boarding pass and walked towards the gate. He shook his head and smiled, as if he had heard a good joke, while around him the other passengers were wondering what had caused the delay.

What had caused it? He had a pretty good idea.

The police had received an anonymous call saying there was a bomb on the plane. They had investigated the luggage and found the device. And then they must have found who owned it and arrested him.

After all, there were at least two people who knew there was a bomb on board.

The guy who had set it.

And him.

The stewardess processed his boarding pass and wished him bon voyage.

"Thanks," Stephen said.

Yes, he would have a good trip. Now he would.

And if he didn't, he could go back and try again.

A minute? Sixty seconds?

Yes, as many times as he wanted.

Idiot, he said to himself, still smiling.

He crossed the walkway toward the plane. Someone noticed his smile and the way he shook his head and asked him if anything was wrong.

"No, everything's fine, thanks."

If he hadn't panicked, he would never have discovered it. He had jumped twenty seconds before the bomb had exploded, before the loop was complete, at the moment a syringe was about to make him unconscious and end his life.

He had jumped.

Just a minute.

Which had taken him twenty seconds further into the past than he had gone before.

Idiot, he said to himself again.

After all, if you jump back a minute, you can jump as far as you want. If you can go one minute into the past, from there you can go another minute – into the past of the past – and from there another minute, into the past of the past of the past...

He boarded the plane and sat down. While they were taking off and the hostess began her safety demonstration, he wondered what to do with his life.

After all, he had all the time in the world.

In convenient minute-long portions, of course.

I'm not always certain I can make an idea work, but I like to give it a go in any case. In musical terms, some ideas arrive as entire symphonies, others are just a song, and a few are nothing more than a jingle; while a good jingle is catchy, a bad one is unbearable.

"Eternal Return" was that kind of idea: little more than a jingle. Could I make it catchy enough to work? I tried and somehow I managed to take the story to its natural conclusion without stretching it too much. I'm reasonably satisfied with the result, and I guess the guys from The World SF Blog, *where it appeared in 2013 in English for the first time, were satisfied as well.*

THIS LIGHTNING, THIS MADNESS

"Behold... I teach you the Superman! He is this lightning; he is this madness."
– Friedrich Wilhelm Nietzsche: Thus Spoke Zarathustra

"They wanted a piece of me, Pa. They all wanted a piece of me... They were all over me! Like wild animals. Like maggots. Clawing. Pulling. Screaming at me. And it was all demands! Everybody had something they wanted me to do, to say, to sell!"
– John Byrne: Man of Steel

1. Teachers and Students

As usual, Walter approaches without a sound and it's that faint scent of old maid that precedes him that alerts me to his presence. I look up and see him, pale and lean, the black cassock floating around and the vague beginning of a smile on his thin lips.

"Do you have it?" I ask. It's an unnecessary question. Walter would never have entered my chamber if he didn't have what I requested.

He nods without a word and offers me a shiny thin black plastic wafer. I hold it and examine the wafer incredulously, incapable of assuming something so tiny is what I'm been looking for.

"Is that everything?"

"Everything we had in our archives, Your Eminence," answers Walter, cautious as usual. He did not become the scribe of the Order Provincial by taking unnecessary risks.

"All right. You can go. I won't need you any more tonight."

He nods again and turns round in a fluid and perfect manner that might have seemed an affectation in someone else. I watch him leave, his silhouette slowly vanishing in the shadows at the other end of the room. He finally disappears as if darkness has swallowed him and I am alone at last; my only companions are the chip in my hand and the dull humming of the proc.

Is that everything? I asked myself. No, of course it isn't. In the atoms of the chip there is nothing more than data. Just that. The rest is not here; it can't be here. There's no need, after all, I know where the rest is. The same place it has been all those years, where else?

I plug the chip into the proc and the link pin in the slot behind my right earlobe. I close my eyes to ensure a good connection and begin to unravel the delicate data structure Walter has brought to me. It's not too hard. A chronological index where years blink like exit signs on a freeway. The other indexes appear as I invoke them: personal bios, subject evaluations, commission conclusions, news holos, medical data... A nonsense tangle at first sight, but under the multirelational structure of the database that contains them, they attain meaning in no time. Nothing more than an attempt to catch a person's life in a cluster of computer files. A failed attempt, of course, because their content is just information, data, facts, and they are meaningless when one tries to define who he was. It doesn't matter. Facts will do, at least for now.

I walk the data highway as if I were nothing more than a tourist and everything around me my own private virtual theme park. I cross avenues full of a slow, milky light and enter endless mazes which loop inevitably back to their beginning. Distant hulks of cold stone tremble and blink as I approach. I find nothing interesting in them. A roaring wall of ice appears before me, like and infinite wave frozen forever. I break through almost unintentionally and the wall of defensive ice creaks its useless objection while shattering around me.

Here I am, in the core, the most hidden region of the file system, where only someone with my security level can access. At first glance there's nothing very different from what I've already seen. But it's a façade. I've found what I was looking for, what has been hidden all these years, what will be hidden forever when I end my inspection and order the chip I'm now exploring to destruct.

I choose one of the files at random. Two pale hands (they aren't my hands, have never been my hands, but are the hands I use when I surf the net) caress its surface softly, find the hidden catch they were looking for and open the file.

Yes. I see it. I see him. He's alone, completely isolated from the rest of the universe, though he doesn't know it. I see his body entirely covered by the datasuit, I see the delicate pattern of electronic veins that tie each and every one of his nerve endings to the fantasy he believes is real life, the fantasy where he has been living since he was born.

Ah, yes, his birth. Another file opens before me. His birth. Not from a woman. There was no womb where he could float for nine months, nor any warm amniotic fluid to shelter him, not even a kind hand to calm his neonate nightmares. He was born from a single cell from an anonymous donor that was carefully preserved for years, nurtured and protected by the Biological Division of the Order while the nanobuilders climbed the endless spiral of his gene code step by step and altered one stair here and another one there, eliminated this one, enforced that one, until the double helix contained everything the gene engineers had designed and the cell was ready to grow, split, copy itself over and over at a frantic pace.

In his memory there's no trace of that. Floating in a warm void with no companions but the datasuit, he remembers a childhood he didn't have, a family that never existed.

Time goes by. It took several years to alter his gene code, but a few months were enough to develop him from a single *cell to a human being in his mid-teens, his mind full of those illusions he has learnt to call his life; the fantasy he will call his memories.*

A new file. I see him alone, trying to sleep in a bed for the first time, even though he remembers it as his bed for the last eight years. He falls asleep and for the first time in his life he dreams. In fact, for the first time in his life his dreams and his reality are different things.

A week before the beginning of that year the headmaster called me to his office. When I arrived he wasn't there: behind his desk someone was reading a file, turning the virtual pages with a thumb and a forefinger he moistened with his tongue. I couldn't help raising an eyebrow at that anachronistic behaviour but he didn't seem aware of my presence. He continued reading as if the words his proc projected before him were the most important thing in the universe and he had all the time in the world to study them. I looked around for a moment, trying to make a decision. Finally, as he persisted in ignoring me, I decided to focus on him; it seemed as good an idea as any. He was thin and maybe taller than me, though it was hard to be certain with him sitting. His head was a perfect egg, completely bald and with a big sharp nose. His mouth was small, pale, almost cruel, and in his eyes there was a shadow that disturbed me, I couldn't say why. He crossed his fingers while he was reading: they were long, bony, and seemed to have more joints than a human finger.

He ended his reading, erased the holopage and looked up. It was then that I saw the tiny red symbol in the side of his black jacket: The hammer falling on the wheel. He realised what I was looking at and nodded and began to smile.

I was before an Inner Circle representative, whom laymen called the Soyto Police. Once upon a time, more than three thousand years in the past, they had been called the Inquisition.

"Sit down, de Charden," he told me with a voice as cold and sharp as a steel pike.

I did as instructed, my gaze never leaving those dark eyes that seemed to glow somehow, and trying to show a level of calm I was far from feeling.

"I have been reading your file."

I nodded. Of course I was aware he knew my file by heart and pretending he was reading it in front of me was a farce orchestrated entirely for my benefit.

"A promising career, though somewhat irregular."

He squinted and the glow behind his eyes intensified. I realised then that he was a cyborg, a hybrid of neurons and memory filaments. I had heard the rumours, of course, in the seminary it was impossible not to hear them. The fearsome inquisitors from the Inner Circle, half men half machine, all fanaticism and devotion to the Order's spiritual purity. Until that very day I hadn't believe those rumours.

"What do you mean by 'irregular'?" I asked, amazed that my voice didn't seem as half as terrified as myself.

"Well, let's say you are inclined towards an excessive intimacy with your pupils. With some of them, at least."

I gulped and tried to stay calm.

"Understand this, de Charden. There is nothing you have done, said or thought that we haven't noticed. We are not interested in your... ah... moral lapses, so long as they do not go against our doctrine, but we are not above using them if they suit our purposes."

Blackmail, then. And it was almost as if I had spoken aloud.

"If you want to see it that way... I like to think of it more as an... incentive."

"I understand."

"I hope you do. Because from now until this year ends you belong to us. Do not misunderstand me, you have always belonged to us, from the very first day you entered the seminary. Let's say we are here to assert that ownership."

"What do you want from me?"

"As I said, you have a promising career in the Order. You are a good teacher and you have never shown any doctrinal deviation worth mentioning. You are a bright fellow but you accept the necessity of hierarchy and discipline. And you are ambitious. We have no objections to that. Not a single one."

A new holopage appeared in the air. It was an academic record: Karl Kennington, seventeen, born in Campoestela, enrolled for this year in Álbrez High School; good grades, though nothing outstanding. A picture of him showed a harmlessly handsome face crowned by a bush of black hair, a lock falling across his forehead. What caught me the most were his eyes. An intense blue, they seemed perpetually perplexed... No, fascinated by whatever he was looking at.

"Kennington is going to be your student this year. From now until graduation day you are going to be his shadow. But you will be something else: his friend, his confidant, his big brother, his father if that is what it takes."

"How?"

"You are a clever man, de Charden, I am sure you will find a way. You will report weekly. I will give you a net node to send your reports to."

The holopage disappeared and he seemed to lose interest.

"Have you finished?" I asked. "Is that all? I have to spy on him for you and you don't even tell me why?"

He seemed surprised.

"You do not need to know *why*. Suffice to say that your work is necessary and it will be for the benefit of God and His creation."

Ad maiorem Dei gloriam, I remembered. It still was our Order motto after more than three thousand years.

"It will be for the boy's benefit as well?"

"Is it not true that everything that benefits God is good for His creatures as well?"

He didn't expect an answer. Just as well, because I didn't have one. I was no longer the eighteen-year-old boy that had entered the seminary with a feverish faith and a mind enflamed by the idea of God. It had been a long while since I really believe in a benevolent God concerned with the welfare of His creatures. My relationship with Isabel hadn't help. Did the blend of bits and neurons before me know that? Did he care? I didn't know. Even now I don't know.

When I left the headmaster's office, fear and rage waged war in my mind. Neither seemed to be winning.

I didn't go home. I ended up in a Game Gallery trying to feign a lack of concern. I didn't pay attention to the bustle of teenagers jumping into their private virtual worlds but went my own way.

I knew why I was there. From home I couldn't talk to the person I wanted to see now, at least if I wanted to do so without that cyborg knowing what I was doing.

I took a look at the big news screen. They were still talking about the earthquake in the Southern Continent and a representative from Weather

Control was trying to explain the complexities of predicting tectonic shifts. He didn't seem to be having much success. I found an empty cabin and got in and locked the door. I was sure I had been followed, but if they knew me as well as they claimed to they would have found nothing out of the ordinary in my visiting a Game Gallery. After all, they knew my heterodox hobbies were not entirely suitable for a priest.

I turned on the cabin proc and inserted the pin in my right earlobe slot. The program seemed determined to take me to a world, unreal but meticulously designed, where dragons were challenged to a battle of wits by white armoured knights and a 'French maid' wasn't necessarily a buxom female house servant. I left that crap behind, surfed the digital landscape worthy of a stereotyped fairy tale, and finally found what I was looking for: the programmer's back door, something known only to the game's creator and a chosen few.

Really? I asked myself. *Are you sure the Inner Circle doesn't know?* But even if that were the case I had no other choice and had to take the risk. My virtual fingers gently pressed what seemed to be a rolling stone and drummed a code I hoped the Inner Circle didn't know.

Suddenly that cloying and bucolic landscape disappeared and I found myself floating in the net. I saw where I wanted to go and flew over there without a second thought. I knocked on a door hemmed by a milky light and before I knew what was happening found myself sitting in a comfortable armchair in the most prosaic living room in the universe. In front of me in another armchair sat a woman who looked at me in a manner that seemed half pleased and half sly.

I have always been intrigued by the shape of a person's private net space. Most hackers like grandiloquent simulations, full of impossible lights and unreal angles where they can appear before the user as omnipotent digital gods. The place where I now stood was very much like Cara's real living room and she didn't look any different from the woman I remembered: a pale blonde woman in her thirties, with a trace of perpetual joy in her eyes.

"Ave, Magister," she greeted me.

"Hi, Cara. I see your taste hasn't changed a bit."

"Why change perfection?" she said, gesturing to encompass the room. "That would be ludicrous."

I smiled. "You seem to be doing okay."

"Yeah, and I guess you aren't or you wouldn't have called me. You only do so when you're in trouble."

She was right.

"Is that you or a pseudo-ego?"

"Myself. You've caught me between jobs." She seemed to remember something suddenly. "How's Isabel?"

"Fine."

"She hasn't realised yet the kind of twisted and dim man you are? She still thinks you're nothing more than a poor priest full of faith and continues trying to save you for your own naivety?"

I shrugged. "Maybe she likes me being twisted and dim."

"I don't think so. That would be no challenge for her. What the hell, I'm glad for you, though I'll never understand why someone as smart as Isabel can have such a bad taste in men."

"Nobody's perfect."

"Well, that's almost true. All right, what is the problem? The IRS guys are after you or is it something really important? Let me guess, you have grown tired at last of that ridiculous god you worship in your little Order and have come to the net to create one of your own. Though it would be a botched job, knowing you."

"You still talk too much."

"And you still take things too seriously. Come on, tell me what's up."

"I don't really know. Maybe it's nothing really important. But answer me this: why does the Inner Circle want to spy on a seventeen-year-old kid whose file is completely normal?"

"My answer would be they're a bunch of paranoid fanatics, but I guess that's not the answer you want. Tell me the boy's file code."

I did and her image blinked for less than a second. Although I had known her for many years it still shocked me the incredible speed with which Cara devoured information. She wasn't smiling any more and was looking at me with the closest thing to concern I have ever seen in her face.

"Hmmm. Interesting. Not even a bunch of paranoids as your Inner Circle can be so stupid as to waste their time on a guy this boring. It doesn't make sense. How do you know they want to spy on him?"

"Because I'm the spy."

She raised a brow.

"Tell me everything".

I did. She stared at me when I had finished.

"Preposterous," she said. "You have achieved something I never thought you would. After fifteen years you have managed to bring me an interesting enigma."

"Will you take a look?"

"Sure. Come and see me next month."

"A month?"

"Do you want fast or good? Quality takes time."

"All right," I agreed.

After a minute or so of small talk I left and returned to that insipid fairy tale. A couple of trolls were beating each other over the head and laughing; an elf tried to seem wise and deep while he explained some trivial issue to a dwarf who didn't stop caressing his axe. In the distance, a wizard was talking to a dragon. I shut down the program, disconnected the pin from my slot and stepped out the cabin.

When I arrived home Isabel was waiting for me. That took me by surprise because I didn't expect her that day. Then I saw what she was holding and understood. It was a hardcopy of a book and I didn't need to look at the title to know which book it was. After all, I had lent it to her. It was a short stories collection by Strasinsky.

"It's awful," she told me. She didn't seem disgusted but afraid.

"I know," I said while I sat beside her. "You've read 'Anything you want'."

She nodded.

"And you like it."

"Like? I haven't read anything remotely like it in my life. But it's dreadful."

"It is."

I moved closer and Isabel put her head in my shoulder.

Dreadful, I thought. The short story was indeed dreadful in a particular way, something that Strasinsky mastered. It began in the most trivial fashion. A woman met a man and she felt attracted to him. But she wasn't sure he would fit in her life, as if he might be a discordant note in the middle of a symphony. But she didn't end their relationship and instead tried to make him fit in her world. She succeeded at first, but then things began to go wrong and her life became a whirlwind beyond her control.

The reader sees what's really happening little by little. In fact,

Strasinsky never really tells us what's happening, he lets us read between the lines. The man she has fallen for has powers, certain skills. He is almost a god and has the desires and the whims of an ancient pagan deity. He wants her, he wants to own her and he knows that to achieve his goal he has to sever her completely from everything she considers essential. So he begins to destroy everything around her in a way that is so subtle and so slow she doesn't even notice.

"He manipulates everything around her, he changes her reality and becomes the one stable element in her life," Isabel said, raising her head. "But he never manipulates her, he never changes her perceptions or her emotions or her way of seeing the world."

"Of course, that would be too easy. And he wants her as she is, so interfering with her mind would be a mistake."

Isabel nodded. "But the things he does… Without remorse, without empathy, without compassion…"

"And without hate."

"But that just make it worse, more frightening. There's no passion in him, no emotion, at least regarding her friends and relatives. They're nothing more than an obstacle and he just moves them aside."

We remained silent for a while. Strasinsky had been my favourite author for several years, not because of his precise control of plot and words but for his uncanny ability to pose moral issues and take them to their inevitable resolution, no matter how uncomfortable that might be for the reader.

"But that's not even the worst of it," said Isabel after a while. "In the end she knows. Somehow she realises he is the one who has destroyed her life and the people she loved. But she surrenders. He wins. Although she knows what has happened, she is in his hands, hypnotised like a fly in a spider web, like…"

"I see."

"Do you? He never touches her mind, but he destroys everything around her and replaces with his own presence. And she knows but she can't… And Strasinsky makes you feel what she feels. You understand her completely and you realise you would have done the same in her situation. And that says something about you, something…"

"Yes."

"Yes?"

"Yes."

"It's... I hate that story."

"Do you want to stop reading the book?"

"Of course I don't."

Then she looked at me and saw the smile in the back of my eyes. She relaxed and smiled me back.

"Always the teacher," she said.

I shrugged. Denying the obvious would have been useless.

"I'm hungry," I said. "We can continue talking while we eat."

We really didn't say much during dinner. Isabel was still thinking of the short story, uncomfortable with herself, trying to accept all the things that the tale has told her about herself. And I couldn't help thinking of that afternoon, of that cyborg of quiet gaze that had made me spy on a boy who hardly seemed of interest, of the schemes of an Order claiming to represent God's will. I wondered, not for the last time, if that God was the same God I had once believed in.

After dinner, a trivial movie made us forget ourselves for a couple of hours. It was a romantic comedy, full of misunderstandings, chance encounters and optimism. Then Isabel went to her parents' home and I stayed alone, unable to sleep, though I had to rise early the next morning. I had to celebrate the first Mass of the day, my favourite. At that hour most of the congregation is composed by elderly women trying to mitigate their loneliness with a ceremony they don't really pay attention to, comforted by the background murmur which, somehow, soothes them.

Sometimes in the confession before the Mass I felt like one of those tri-vi hosts that bring to life the hidden miseries of their guests before an audience eager to hear other people's misfortunes, maybe to compensate for the void and emptiness of their own lives. I knew well the cathartic and therapeutic significance of confession, but I couldn't help feeling it was rather obscene. After all, they were baring their souls to a complete stranger. Yes, I confessed regularly myself, just as the Order commanded. I declaimed without conviction the sins I was supposed to be guilty of: my pride as teacher, my sinful relation with Isabel, my rage and impatience at wilful stupidity. I muttered my penance and left the confessional convinced nothing I had said was actually a sin. The real sin was to ruin your own life, I told myself, but never out loud.

The Order didn't care about my doubts or secret thoughts. As long as my behaviour adhered to doctrine, nothing else mattered. Even my relation with Isabel could be forgiven if I was pure in other issues. After all, we had made a celibacy vow, not one of chastity. There is a subtle difference.

But Morning Mass always soothed me, quelled my doubts and helped hide the emptiness at the bottom of my heart. Even now, when I have renounced belief in anything but myself, Mass just before dawn makes me feel at peace with myself, and I recall for a few minutes the way I used to feel when I first entered the seminary.

Ever since I was a boy my questions had been answered with nothing but silence, but that didn't disturb me because silence itself was an answer. God kept silent, yes, but He was close, just in the border of my perceptions, crouched, hidden, but never too far away. I believed then than someday the curtain would rise and I would finally see what was beyond that silence.

And one day it did. Silence broke and the only thing I found beyond was the void, a flare of hungry entropy eager to devour everything. Is that all? I wondered. Are we alone? Is there nothing else?

Horror is not an improbable monster that jumps from a closet or the face of a loved one transformed into a bloodthirsty animal. The real horror is nothingness.

Is that all? Are we alone? Is there nothing else?

Sometimes silence returned, a silence very much like the one I feel in the church before dawn: dark, quiet, fresh. I guess that's why Morning Mass always soothed me.

The Order gave me a place where everything was predetermined, without mysteries or uncertainties. I knew it was a mistake; denying the mystery was denying the silence and replacing it with void. But even void was better that the vague uneasiness I felt before the silence, that feeling that beyond it there was an incomprehensible animal breathing like a lurking predator.

2.   The Curious Incident of the Dog

There's something in Walter's cold efficiency that gives me the creeps, as if he wasn't human but a metaphor for what the Order really is: efficient and empty, organised and without a purpose, perfect and useless. The Order wasn't always that way; there was a time when it had a goal, when the human members really believed in what they were doing. Ah, but it was easy for them. It's easy to maintain faith in hard times. Those who kept our Order alive during the havoc of Interregnum had no bigger problem than surviving without losing their humanity. Faith wasn't an obstacle; on the contrary, it was an essential tool.

But now? Now, when the Confederation spreads across more than two thousand worlds, all of them with the same culture, the same technology, the same trends and thinking? All of our needs and whims are granted before our birth and all you have to do to get something is want it. No, faith is now useless, a slippery concept, an excuse at best.

Oh, but faith endures. People still need to believe in something greater than themselves, beyond themselves, something that gives meaning to their comfortable and useless lives. But they don't come to us for it any more. We're no longer useful, we have become a huge bureaucratic machine and we offer neither comfort nor answers, we aren't even able to ask the right questions. It's not surprising the Galaxy is full of ridiculous cults, that self-proclaimed witches, chiromancers, astrologists, prophets, cardmancers and more make their pile at the expense of credulity. We have destroyed the mystery, we have buried it under tons of memoranda, under a hoard of impeccably logical reasoning that doesn't prove anything.

Some months ago a young and bright theologian catalogued God's main attributes. The Order congratulated him. Oh, how I sometimes envy the Middle Ages I never knew, that time of darkness, fear and superstition that would have condemned this young bureaucrat to the stake. We dare to catalogue Eternity, Omniscience, Infinity. And instead of feeling horror and disgust we have congratulated ourselves. The ultimate mystery fits into our files. There's nothing more to worry about. Everything is measured, defined. Even God. Especially God.

Walter brings me what I have ordered once more, his

robes whispering a song of thwarted love. I'm about to ask him what he believes in. I keep silent, take the data crystal and thank him with a nod. He leaves, quietly as usual, efficient and obedient like a tuned machine.

The data crystal. It's been at least twenty years since I saw one. A means of storing information commonly used by net rats, but too expensive to become popular. Storing information in the crystalline structure of a solid is an elegant but uneconomical solution. Besides, in these times when everything must be reusable, something like that would never catch on. Once the crystal is imprinted, once its atoms have been forced to create the delicate reticula of the code, it can't be used again. Adding just a bit of information requires recording another crystal. Expensive and impractical. But beautiful.

I hold the crystal with my fingertips. I don't know what it contains. It's been with me for twenty-five years and all this time I have assumed that the thoughts of someone I once knew are trapped inside. But I don't really know. I've never read it. Until now. Yes, someone I once knew. In another time, in another world, when I was another person.

Liar, says a voice that's mine but holds traces of someone else. Liar. You've always been as you are now. You've changed just to be more like yourself.

I agree. Yes, Cara, I admit you're right. It was one of your most irritating habits. You were always right.

But you're dead and I'm still alive. And if I'm right all that remains of you is the information coded inside this crystal, the thoughts you recorded here. I miss you, as no doubt you foresaw. Once again you're right.

I smile. Come on, let's play, let's bring you to life once more, let's feel again the flow of your thoughts, hear that perpetually scathing voice.

[One of my boyfriends used to say that life had no meaning without a pinch of paranoia. Though his idea of 'a pinch' was rather peculiar and I guess explains his present residence in a psychiatric hospital. But, as he

86

also used to say, that is an irrelevance. Recording this file is foolish and coding it from time to time in a data crystal an excessive luxury, but I've been listening to my paranoia for too long to stop now.//

//All right, Pierre, let's play. I'm ready. My brain processes reach the threshold of acceleration, the link with the data crystal is clean and noiseless and I'm ready to surf the net searching for your mystery. Funny, it took you fifteen years to set me an interesting enigma (apart from yourself, of course, but that's a puzzle I gave up considering a long time ago) and you were the last person I would have expected to see involved in something like this.//

//I haven't the slightest idea what this is all about, but I intend to find out, of course, or I'll deserve to spend the rest' of my life accessing the net via keyboard and mic. I know one thing; whatever this is it stinks.//

//I wasn't expecting this from you, Pierre. A few years more with Isabel, until you understand she's nothing but an obstacle in your path to the top of that ridiculous Order, and then a quiet, calm, unstoppable career to... Generalship? Maybe. Anyway, a life without surprises, all your ambitions fulfilled and all your dreams dead. But this... Ah, you haven't lost the ability to surprise me. And though you're not involved in this of your own will, I still haven't lost hope of making you a man of worth.//

//But I'm wasting time, so I close my eyes, open each and every one of my synapsis to the data micro-currents and jump into the net. Not really me, now I'm nothing more than a piece of software that mimics my brain processes, but does it really matter? Is there any difference between reality and what you perceive as real? If so, I've never found it. If you have, please don't tell me.//

//I cross some of the most crowded data freeways. I recognise a couple of research procedures; yes, that shiny serpent that is poking around searching for hidden files can only be an Oldfield procedure, and that kind of noise cloud whose purpose is completely transparent to me is Solipsist's pseudoego, the most paranoid net rat of all.//

//I leave them behind after sending them a couple of bits of recognition for their owners. I wonder again why I'm being so cautious, why I'm recording the thoughts of this app that pretends to be me – that, here and now, is me. After all, what I'm about to do is almost legal. There shouldn't be any problem. But as far as I know nobody has deviated from Murphy's Law and those who don't follow it don't last long in this business.//

//Yeah, my ex was right. A pinch of paranoia not only makes life more interesting, it's necessary, almost essential.//

//Here I am, in the public part of the Order System. I sneak through one of their doors like a distracted tourist, I request information I'm not interested in at all and check the status of the alarm procedures and the automatic ferrets. Piece of cake.//

//Then I enter in the first sectors of the system restricted areas and access the files of the Order members. It doesn't take me long to find Pierre's and I browse it without losing sight of my surroundings, ready to dash off at the first indication of danger.//

//But alarms are still asleep. Nobody realises a rat has sneaked through the house walls and is nibbling the timber to make herself a cosy nest. I keep on reading the file while I look for an empty data sector close to me. I find it at once, I verify it is not a trap and inject a part of my own code into it. Great. I've just opened a back door in the very ass of the Order and from now on it will be available to me and no one else.//

//I finish reading the file. Nothing really interesting apart from the fact they seem to know everything about Pierre, even those things he ignores about himself. His dreams have not been recorded but I have the unsettling feeling that's only because they haven't bothered.//

//At the end of the file there is mark. The one I expected to find. The red hammer bringing down heretics. Inner Circle's mark. I see why the inquisitors have been investigating him. Pierre's career is a promising one and his eccentricities, though pretty much harmless, are notorious enough to attract attention from the Inner Circle.//

//But it doesn't matter now. I've done what I came to do. I've created a backdoor and I had better leave before I tempt fate. So I return to the public part of the system and walk around for a couple of nanoseconds before leaving.//

//I spend some time in the net, pretending I'm doing some business while I check if anybody is after me. Everything seems to be fine, so I go home.//

//As always, I feel a strange sloppiness, a languid asphyxiation while the code I am now is being erased and the data I've obtained (along with all my memories) are being assimilated by my programmer and only user: myself.]

[Sooner or later a rat realises she never unplugs herself from the net. Of course, we return to that ludicrous circus they call the real world, we walk, we eat, we sleep and sometimes we get laid, but we never stop being plugged in. With the pin always inserted in the slot under our right earlobe, net access has become a natural bodily function and, like breathing, you're unaware of it unless you pay attention. That's how most of us live: relating with other people in the real world but always with an eye in the huge bits of gabble that form the Galactic Net of Information.//

//This last month I've done nothing related to Pierre's problem, apart from periodically checking the integrity of my back door, but in some ways I haven't stopped working on it throughout.//

//Every day I wake up, have breakfast, relax in the shower and smoke my morning cigarette. But while I'm doing all those things the back of my head is plugged in, sailing lazily through the data freeways. I eat and I sleep. I talk with other rats, I discuss with them the botched job weather control is doing all around the planet, the trending topic these past weeks, and I work and give my clients the information they have requested from me. At the same time, a bunch of bits that, in a way, are also me flow endlessly through connection moors and linking bridges, gazing here and there like an uninterested observer.//

//Until this precise moment I haven't realised what I have been doing. Almost nothing and practically everything. Guided by pure intuition (and if you don't believe a search procedure can be intuitive that only means you have been paying too much attention to the government propaganda about AI restrictions) I've checked the entire net, I've made sure everything is in place, speculation still flies around like wildfire and nothing has diminished the appetite for gossip in the biggest rumour mill in the Universe.//

//What my reconnaissance routines are feeding me aren't really data. Yes, Pierre, maybe you don't believe it but pure data is not my principal concern. What really matters is the way everything is linked, the connections and relations among trivial data flows, the way a petty monetary transaction two solar systems away can affect the decision of a woman undecided about whether or not to get married, or how the result of a sports game we haven't heard of can influence the meal we will eat that very same night.//

//An AI can collect all these data and connections, and can extrapolate the shape of the landscape from them, but not always. Sometimes there isn't enough information, or too much. You need a human mind to fill in the gaps, to decide which facts are relevant and which aren't.//

//So I digest everything my reconnaissance routines have collected this month. I don't think, I don't try to find an explanation or a cause, I just let the data enter my mind and find the right place to fit in. My subconscious will do the rest.//

//One night I go to bed without noticing anything weird and the next day I wake up with the feeling that there's something in the net that shouldn't be there, that things are being twisted in a subtle way, that someone is prosecuting a project of immense proportions; and net users know somehow, though they don't know they know. They're just talking about the earthquake in the Southern Continent, the tornado that has devastated half the coast in North Tropic and the increasingly alarming amount of natural disasters Weather Control is unable to predict and avoid. But underneath those conversations there's a hidden current that speaks of something else: allusions to allusions to allusions, rumours about rumours about other rumours...//

//So it's time for me to swim again, to try the backdoor and poke around some more. Let's go. I'm about to put my beautiful heart-shaped ass on the line for you, Pierre, and damned if I know why I'm doing it.//

//Yeah, of course I know, though I'll never admit it, not even to myself. But now I'm not myself, I'm just a piece of software imitating my personality, so I can admit it: after all, nobody is listening, much less that distant flesh and blood Cara who at this moment is devouring at least a ton of crepes as if her life depended on it while she tries to convince a reluctant client she deserves every óscopo of her fees. I don't remember when I realised I loved you, but it was the same day I realised you would never feel anything but a distant and selfish affection for me. Since that day, sometimes I've hated you and sometimes I've tried to forget you, and sometimes I've fantasised about you. One way or the other you've been inside my head all these years and I don't know how I have resisted the urge to create a servant program for my exclusive use based in your personality matrix. It's something I've seen so many times in this sad and lonely digital world. I guess I'm too pragmatic. Or maybe not. Here I am, risking my neck for you once again. And I like it.//

//My backdoor seems to be intact. I know I'm the best programmer of Drímar Confederation (and surely Sáver Mandate, though God knows what kind of mad rats live in such a paranoid regime) and one of my greatest prides is the fact that nobody can touch one of my procedures without my being aware. Deflower one of my girls without mummy knowing? No, pretty boy, not on my watch. But I know full well the Order has at its disposal resources I can't even imagine. I wouldn't be surprised if they had one of those Self-aware Artificial Intelligences the government has outlawed... among other things. So when I cross my backdoor I don't seem to be Cara's pseudo-ego any more, and my return links no longer connect me to her net node but to an empty address where no one has ever lived. My autodestruct sub-procedure is on stand-by and I'm ready to crash myself into a bunch of noise at the slightest sign of danger.//

//It's unnecessary, or so it seems, because I slip through my mousetrap door and nobody is aware of me being in the forbidden sectors of the system. Anyway, Carlos was right: better to live with a permanent pinch of paranoia than being dead.//

//I don't plan to stay long, so I take everything I came for and leave as quickly and quietly as I can. I can't help but let out a sigh of relief when I'm in the public part of the net, going home with nobody following me or showing the slightest interest in me.]

[Absence of something is as revealing as its presence. There's a phrase that has become a mantra among the rats, though none of them remembers where it comes from: the curious incident of the dog. I asked Pierre about it once and he told me it belonged to and old fictional detective. I guess he said those words when he noticed the watchdog hadn't barked when it should have.//

//Anyway, there's nothing out of the ordinary in Karl Kennington file; it's so prosaic I almost died of boredom. Born in Campoestela seventeen years ago. His parents were hydro farmers and lived close to the planet capitol city. Both died a few months ago in an accident with one of the vaporisers. His childhood and adolescence are typical for a young redneck. He studied in the Order's school in Campoestela Capitol and after his parent's dead the Order itself acted in loco parentis. He was transferred to Pardaterra for the last course of his pre-university studies. I take a look at a picture of his parents: a mature jolly-looking couple, no doubt as boring and predictable as a lemonade evening in the plastiwood veranda. Juan and Marta Kennington, an average couple, so average they seem to belong to a costumbrist soap-opera.//

//The very normality sets alarm bells ringing. Because if there's nothing out of the ordinary in here, if everything about him is as commonplace as an apple pie in a harvest fair, why are the Inner Circle so interested in him, why have they commissioned Pierre to spy on him and become his confessor? For a moment I consider the notion that Kennington is just a cover story, that they are interested in Pierre and have used the boy as bait. The idea is so appealing I'm tempted to jump on it without further consideration.//

//But no. I've been earning my living for fifteen years sneaking around the net, finding out what's true and what's not, pulling apart relevant information and discarding rubbish and charging my clients accordingly. Maybe I'm right. Maybe this plot has Pierre as its focus. But I can't leave Kennington's trail yet, not until I'm sure.//

//How to proceed? There are several ways. They're expensive, because I can't afford the slightest mistake. But there are a few guys out there who owe me and now seems a good time to collect.]

[Daddy is the dean of all the rats and rumours chase him as fleas chase a dog. The one I like best claims he has been in the net for over three hundred years and his flesh and blood self spends most of the time in suspended animation, its location a closely guarded secret. He wakes up from time to time to integrate everything the thousands of procedures he has unleashed in the net have been doing, assimilating thousands of memories he has never lived but will recall as his own. I've never asked him if that story is true. I guess I don't want to be disappointed if it's not.//

//A couple of years ago, he needed my help when he got into a mess with a group of fundamentalists. I'd worked for them and they had been so impressed that they nominated me as honorary sister of their Guild – a kind of crazy Zen Buddhism with a few drops of Zoroastrianism, a pinch of voodoo rites and a skill for dirty business that was truly impressive. So, pulling strings, I was able to fix Daddy's situation with them. He didn't thank me – I don't remember Daddy ever thanking anyone – but he knows the rules, sometimes I believe he invented them, and will lend me a hand when I need it.//

//He meets me in a Spartan space, the walls painted a distant and subtle set of pastels. He hasn't change since we last saw each other. An old man with a long and wild white beard who doesn't stop frowning.

He just needs one of those eyes that can see everything inside a triangle and he would be the very same image of Pierre's Order God.//

//"Hi, Daddy," I greet him, trying to be as sweet as honey.//

//He frowns harder.//

//"Cara, you little boil," he says. His voice comes from everywhere and nowhere and is deep as a far thunder. "What do you want? I'm busy."

//"You weren't so busy a couple of years ago." It's not very polite to remind him he owes me, but being polite takes you nowhere with Daddy.//

//"I see, you tiny vermin. You're here to suck my blood."//

//"No sucking, sir, please, sir, you're too young for me, sir."//

//He's about to smile, but he catches himself at the last moment and frowns again.//

//"Is there something more boring than an incompetent child trying to be funny?" he roars.//

//"Maybe a doddering old man with tendency to megalomania?"//

//He considers my answer for a few seconds, as if it were really important.//

//"Maybe," he says at last. "All right, what do you want from me?"//

//I tell him as quickly and accurately as I can.//

//"Nothing more? And when I give you what you want will you stop annoying me?"//

//"Never. I enjoy our refreshing conversations too much. See you in a couple of weeks."//

//I leave him while he mumbles a curse that sounds like a distant storm. I return to my node and begin to melt into myself. Flesh and blood Cara and digital Cara are one and the same again and everything I've done in the net becomes part of my user's memory.//

//I have one last thought just before fading out. In that languid phase I can't say if it's anticipation, impatience or just fear.]

3.   Primary Colours

Last night I dreamed of Karl. It was a meaningless absurd dream and when I woke up my mouth was pasty and I had the disturbing feeling I should have recognised where the dream came from.

Karl was surrounded by reporters, sellers, advertisers,

trivi hosts, game programmers, politicians, preachers, salesmen... even a diplomatic representation from the Sáver Mandate. All of them wanted something from him, while trivi cameras zoomed in on his confused face as he turned one way and another, trying to find answers to questions he didn't understand.

They wanted him to enter their Order, to buy their products, to lead them in a new holy war against aliens, to be the head of their party, to make a movie with them, to hire his face and mannerisms for a new interactive game. Unable to understand what was happening, he sought someone who could provide guidance, advice. Suddenly his eyes fell on me and he begged for help that didn't come. I remained silent, separate from the crowd, not asking for anything but not helping either.

His eyes. The dream was full of gaunt colours, of evanescent greys, but his eyes were blue, a blue so deep it almost hurt. There was nothing but dread and bewilderment in those eyes.

The dream was familiar. I haven't lived or seen anything like it in the real world, but somehow I have the feeling I know it. That somewhere sometime I have seen those same eyes filled with fear. I can't remember where or when, but the feeling has been with me the entire day, like an annoying tenant you can't get rid of.

In the morning I met with a delegation from Fifth District and calmed their fears about the declining numbers in their congregations.

The Order is adapting to the World; I told them. Without abandoning its core beliefs and dogmas, it is learning to fight the world with the world's weapons and soon things will get better.

They have left, but I'm not sure if my words have calmed them or not. They shouldn't. If I were a young priest, those words would have disturbed me.

Yes, we use the same marketing techniques that a salesman might. We wrap the barren candy of faith in an attractive package and fill it with fake sweeteners that make it easy to swallow. And that's wrong. It's a mistake.

Faith should be a difficult path, it should be hard to swallow. At the end of the day, a religion tries to reveal the fundamental truths about ourselves and that is not easy, it can never be easy.

We are not a religion any more. We're a business, a factory. And soon, like any other business, we won't care about what we sell so long as benefits continue to increase.

Ha. Funny. Me the unbeliever, the man who wears this robe just for his own convenience, speaking for a church that goes back to its roots, that doesn't surrender to the world, that requires the world to surrender instead. Funny, sure.

The day passes and, after a dinner in my office, I go back to me bedroom. The dream begins the moment I close my eyes. Those blue eyes filled with horror are all I can see. I try to remember where I have seen them before, but can't.

Suddenly, when dawn is about to break, I wake up and remember. I slip out of bed and open the hidden closet where I keep my greatest treasures, the printed books I have collected during a life as an inveterate reader. I search one section after another until I find what I'm looking for, my comics collection,

I know what I'm looking for. It's in one of the Superman volumes. Yeah, I see him returning home after his first public feat, saving a space plane from crashing. His foster father looks at him, scared. And he looks up and describes what happened: everybody was swirling around him, trying to touch him, screaming again and again.

"They were all over me!" says the young Superman, his eyes as blue as Karl's though he is nothing more than a blur of ink on a sheet of paper. "Like wild animals. Like maggots. Clawing. Pulling. Screaming at me. And it was all demands! Everybody had something they wanted me to do, to say, to sell!"

Of course. How could I have forgotten? How could I forget something like that? Maybe because in the past twenty-five *years I've done nothing but forget who I once was. I tried to bury names, faces, moments: Karl, Clara, Isabel...*

Trying to forget is silly, I know that now. Worse, it's pointless. We are nothing but our memory and during these twenty-five years I've been little more than an obedient puppet that has walked, step by step, the stairs my masters told me to climb. I haven't been a man, but a robot executing a boring program.

Yes, trying to forget is useless. I was once a man and like any other man I loved and hated. Like any other man I betrayed what I loved. Remembering everything after so much time is so sweet a pain I can barely endure it. I lie in bed with the comic still in my hands and look again at the precious panel before me: that frank, almost naïve face, that black and untamed hair, those eyes. My God, those eyes.

As always on the first day of term, I entered the classroom fifteen minutes late. By then most of the students were reading what I had left in the virtual page of their autoteachers. I came in quietly and sat down without a word. I waited a couple of minutes and then said: "Well, I guess most of you have finished reading the story. Your comments would be welcome."

I saw Karl Kennington at the other side of the room, sitting in the corner, trying to go unnoticed in the middle of a group that was ignoring him. Everybody else looked up and looked at me, not too sure if I was joking. I knew most of them; they had been my students in previous years but they were used to my humdrum literature classes and didn't suspect that in this, their final year, things would be radically different.

Isabel, who knew me too well, just smiled and kept reading. She already knew the story, as she had told me a couple of days ago.

"Well, I'm waiting. Nobody has anything to say?"

It seemed they hadn't.

"All right. Let's see…" I pretended I was randomly searching a name in the students' database. "Mister Kennington seems to have finished. What can you tell us about this short story?"

Karl looked up and I saw those deep blue eyes.

"It's interesting," he said. "But a little bit self-congratulatory. I don't know, maybe a little too cruel."

Self-congratulatory? It could be. The story described one or two hours in a wake. The narrative's perspective moved from one character to another and finally focused on the widower; an old man, thin and broken, who seemed oblivious to what was happening around him. The narrative described him this way:

The air brings him the banal whispering of half a dozen conversations that try to pass as transcendent (life is just a vale of tears, at least it was quick, I would like a death like this, there is nothing you can do, you have to go on) but he ignores them, they don't pass the sleepless armour of the pain he has taken shelter behind. Sometimes he looks up to see a blurred bunch of strangers that are sorry for his loss and ask him to accept their condolences. He nods, says something that doesn't mean anything and keeps walking.

But sometimes he can't. Sometimes one of those evanescent faces turns real and the tidal wave of his pain spills over him like a scream nobody hears and he realises she is dead, he won't see her again. The blue-tinged corpse in the coffin has nothing to do with her. Nothing will have anything to do with her anymore. He realises he is alone and discovers he misses those aspects of her that most annoyed him.

He walks like a drunkard, crosses the corridor as if he were in a maze and suddenly stops in front of a picture of them both: many years ago, full of hopes and promises that faded over time.

He staggers as if something has hit him and claws his hands around the door frame. The sudden intrusion of its cold and plane texture makes the pain more unbearable and he admits his defeat at last. The winner is the wounded wild animal inside him than now is howling his pain.

The story kept on exploring the widower's grief, peeling layer after layer of a dense and bitter onion. Maybe Karl was right, there was a certain gloating in the pain, a wicked joy in the way he delved into the wound with a sharp finger.

"Why do you say that?" I asked, though.

Karl shrugged and looked around.

"I'm not sure. The story seems real. We feel the pain of the old man. But until that moment the narrator has been walked through the scene as if nothing mattered to him and then he jumps on this poor man and… I don't' know. It's as if he was hounding him, as if he derived pleasure from exploring his pain."

I agreed, pleased at his perceptiveness.

"All right," I said. "Maybe the narrator is a little ruthless with the character. Do you know the circumstances in which the story was written?"

"Yes. The author's grandmother had died a few days ago and the widower in the story is his grandfather. And that makes it worse. Why doesn't he show any mercy for a man he no doubt loved?"

"Do you think the author should show compassion for his characters?"

"Don't you?"

I couldn't help smiling.

"No. I don't think so. He must make them seem real. You don't need compassion for that."

Karl shrugged.

"You don't agree?"

"You're the teacher, what do I know?"

"And you are the student. If you review the contract you or your legal tutor signed when you entered here, you will see there is not a single line that says you must agree with your teachers' opinions."

"True. But I'd like to pass this semester and get my grade."

"And you think you will get it just by agreeing with me?"

"I don't know. It seems a prudent course."

"Not with me."

"How do I know you're telling the truth?"

"Because I tell you so."

He hesitated a moment.

"All right, I'll take the risk. Yes, I think compassion is necessary to be a good story teller. Maybe not compassion but…"

"Empathy," whispered a female voice next to him. It was Isabel.

He looked at her, surprised, as if he saw her for the first time; and then he nodded.

"Yes, empathy. You can't describe accurately someone you don't know and you can't know anybody without empathy."

"You're right. The author himself admitted years later that this story was a failure because of the very reason you've just given. It lacks empathy."

I spent the following minutes talking about the author, his life and his main works. Karl seemed fascinated with what I was saying. Not because I was telling him something he didn't know (I had the feeling he knew the author's life and works as well as I did) but… Maybe it sounds silly but it seemed to me he had just discovered he was not alone and suddenly his personal universe had stretched several light-years.

At that moment I couldn't have cared less what the Inner Circle's reasons for spying on Karl might have been. I had found a sharp mind, an individual who liked to explore the world around him. It was something very unusual in my profession. The task the Inner Circle had assigned me might prove easier than I first thought. In that much I was right, but it took me a while to discover that I was also wrong.

Of all my duties as teacher in Álbrez High-school, taking Ancient Narrative Seminary for the last year was by far my favourite. It gave me the opportunity to teach my way, without a program, without exams. It was an optional subject and it wouldn't have any value for the student's résumé. So I could do whatever I wanted.

I'm not sure why I decided to dedicate the first term of that year to comic books. I had discovered them when I was a boy, through a carefully preserved copy owned by my uncle. I was immediately fascinated by this way of telling a story using a sequence of motionless images and written text. I had gathered a fine comic collection down the years; most of them were just digitalised versions I printed out, trying to obtain something as close as possible to the original. But I had a few of the real thing; treasures that, God knew how, had survived through the centuries, literary fossils.

There had been many kinds of comics and I had a favourite. It had appeared towards the middle of the 20th century and represented an attempt to build a new mythology, replacing classic mythos which it, sometimes, integrated within the new order. Powerful beings wearing colourful costumes saved the world again and again and fought among themselves in quarrels that made the universe tremble. Their saga was an endless one and the way it was published (monthly booklets with continuous adventure, never ending, never beginning) was perfect. Sometimes I pictured myself as one of those teenagers that were the comics' target audience in their first years, reading my monthly issue, waiting for next month's, finding out that the adventure that began in one character's series crossed over to another's and ended in a third's. They were building an entire universe, crowded with flesh and blood gods watched by average people, sometimes with envy, sometimes with hate, sometimes with awe.

I'd never tried to include comics in my teachings, but it was an idea I had been considering for some years. They were a narrative medium, after all, and their importance to the period immediately prior to Earth's collapse had been much greater than critics were willing to admit.

That year I made up my mind at last. A month and a half after the beginning of term, I was ready to give them a first taste of that world of heroes and gods printed in primary colours.

"Imagine a primitive world where the most advanced technology can barely take you to your own world's moon. Just one world, divided into nearly two hundred nations and several thousand languages. A world where tribes barely able to light a fire live next to fully industrial and urbanised societies. Yes, I'm talking about Earth in the 20th Century. Now, put into that world a bunch of amazing beings, wearing colourful costumes and able to perform unimaginable feats. The Four that fight the Worlds Devourer and beat him with his own weapons. The Dark Knight obsessed with avenging his parents' death. The Son of Darkness who becomes a Champion of Light. The Amazon created from a handful of mud and the breath of a god. The Multiform Alien that is the last of its species and lives among humans as one of them. The female mercenary possessing incredible martial skills and a tragic destiny. The Super Soldier who becomes the Sentinel of Liberty. The Most Dangerous Woman in the Universe tied to the Lover of Death. The boy who transforms into a demigod merely by saying a magic word. The girl who performs magic by talking backwards. The One Man Army Corps. The Witch who can change probability with just a twist of her hand. The teenager bitten by a radioactive spider who gets arachnid skills… And, of course, the very first of all, the Last Son of His World, the Alien whose godlike powers derive from Earth's Sun."

While I was talking, the autoteachers projected the covers I had chosen for that first day. As I hoped, everybody was hanging on my words and they couldn't stop looking at those colourful drawings, fascinated by a concept that seemed to have disappeared from our world many years ago. Yes, our time had its own heroes. The legendary Lonesome who had built his empire from the chaos of the Interregnum, bold galactic explorers who discovered new worlds, reckless hackers who fought against great corporations and were victorious, square jawed soldiers who faced overwhelming odds. But our cultural heroes – except perhaps Lonesome, the most ancient of them all – didn't stand comparison with these paper demigods capable of moving entire worlds but hampered by the same frailties and weaknesses as a mere mortal.

It was nothing new. Ancient Greeks had understood the concept at once and their pantheon was populated by beings capable of the unthinkable yet incapable of controlling their own emotions and feelings. It had worked for Homer, and it seemed to me that 20th century superhero comics were his heirs. As with the Greek gods, superhero sagas were endless and full of almost infinite ramifications, where yesterday's friend could be tomorrow's enemy and today's traitor would be the next day's hero, where lovers could become rivals and rivals lovers. A universe that was simultaneously simpler and more complex than ours and where, oh yes, Earth was the very centre of the Universe: everybody, sooner or later, came to Earth and tried to destroy it, save it, or both at the same time.

I finished my presentation and waited a couple of seconds. Most students were fascinated, like mice confronting the hypnotic gaze of a cobra. There were two exceptions: Isabel, who had heard everything I'd just had said many times before; and Karl, who was looking at the cover on his desk with thoughtful expression. Surreptitiously, I accessed my unipersonal database and replayed his actions during the past few minutes.

Unlike the rest of the students, who jumped from one cover to the other, Karl had stopped at one in particular. It showed Superman, the first of the heroes in tight costume. He was opening his shirt and under it his costume was visible, with the big red 'S' on it. It was odd that Karl felt especially interested in that character. Experience had taught me that most people preferred another kind of hero, darker and more tormented, like Batman or the little wild mutant with claws.

"Well?" I asked, turning back to my audience.

Karl seemed restless. He didn't like to stand out and preferred to go unnoticed. He wasn't unsocial. As far as I could see his relations with his classmates were friendly though superficial. In fact, the only person he seemed really interested in was Isabel, which was perhaps predictable. He didn't say anything during lessons unless I forced him to do so. In such cases, his comments were lucid and stinging, suggesting that he knew the relevant subject at least as well as I did. In fact, sometimes I had the disturbing feeling he knew it better.

I realised Karl had something to say, but he wouldn't do it unless I persuaded him.

"Is there something you don't like, Karl?"

He looked up. He didn't seem surprised, as if he were waiting for me to ask.

"Yes. It's been a very interesting presentation, but I have a feeling you've missed the point."

"All right, tell us."

"What about the intrinsic improbability of these characters?"

It was rather disappointing. The kind of thing an average student would have said confronted with a non-realistic narrative for the first time. I was used to more intelligent comments from him.

"It doesn't matter," I answered. "I mean, you're right, and these kind of stories demand a certain suspension of incredulity, as any fantastic story does. Yes, the skills of comic heroes are impossible but..."

"No, I wasn't talking about that. That's not the point. I was referring to their attitude."

"I don't get it, I'm afraid."

"Take Superman, for example. He was the first of all, wasn't he? He has the ability to move worlds with just a kick. And what does he do? He behaves like some friendly neighbour."

"I see."

"It's ludicrous. He can travel through time by his own means, he can go to the very edge of the universe, he can take a shower in the core of a star and eat titanium as if it were candy. He is faster, smarter and more powerful than every other being in the universe. He has a godlike power but most of the time he just behaves like a super cop."

"All right. Elaborate."

"Do you think a being like that would be immune to the temptation to change his world? Do you think he would waste his time putting petty thieves in jail? Wouldn't he try to end wars or to bring down dictatorships and stop genocides? Wouldn't he try to build a utopia... to become... I don't know... a god?"

"I haven't the slightest idea," I said, pleased by this turn of conversation. "What do you think he would do?"

A smile crossed his lips as if he knew something I didn't.

"Who knows what a being like that would do?" he said after a while. "But that power... For good or evil he would use it sooner or later to reshape the world he lives in. The only way to avoid it would be total inaction, a decision not to use his skills no matter what. Because once he started there would be no turning back."

Nobody said anything for several seconds. The other students looked at us, used to being just spectators when Karl and I got going.

"Would he be able to do nothing?" I asked at last.

Karl hesitated for a moment and then shrugged.

"You're the teacher," he said. "You should know all the answers."

A chorus of laughter followed his words and I join in. But something told me that wasn't what Karl had intended to say initially. I didn't know what he had almost said, but I suspected it related to the reason the Inner Circle had tasked me with spying on him.

Something else about Karl's words disturbed me. Yes, I was the teacher and I should have all the answers, but it had been a long while since I even knew the questions.

"Bring him this Saturday," I told Isabel next week.

She didn't hesitate. She knew very well I was talking of Karl.

"Are you sure?" she asked.

"I'm not sure about anything, you know me. But I think it's a good idea."

It was, somehow. On Saturday afternoons Isabel and some other students would come by my home and we would talk for a while, watch an old 2D movie, and read a short story or poem, which we would then discuss. Karl fitted in immediately and I realised he felt more comfortable here than in the classroom. Of course I noticed too that he always sat beside Isabel.

It was a bad decision. I had always known there were things Isabel and I couldn't share, at least not yet. Twelve years lay between us and I didn't fit into her world. Each of us had our own environments which only coincided sometimes: high school, my home, some quiet tri-vi cinema.

In all that time I hadn't been concerned that I might be eclipsed by someone else. But now I was beginning to suspect Karl could give her the same things she found in me and also those that she didn't.

My jealousy was odd. I didn't hate Karl. In fact, I liked him, and I had the feeling he was some strange version of myself. What I felt was mainly fear, a huge fear I couldn't face.

Next time I talked with Cara she told me she still hadn't got anything for me, just a couple of promising leads. It was frustrating but I was sure she was doing her best and I couldn't ask for more.

In fact, I was about to tell her to stop digging. What the hell? Whatever reasons the Inner Circle had for spying on Karl were none of my business and I wasn't doing anything I wouldn't have done for myself. Karl was a good student and an interesting person and he would have become a fine addition to my circle sooner or later anyway.

But I didn't tell Cara to quit. I don't know why. Maybe because I knew her well enough to know that she would have ignored me. Once on a scent, she didn't stop until the end and nothing I could see would stop her now.

So we chatted for a while and Cara made a couple of jokes at my expense. After a 'don't call me, I'll call you' from her we said our goodbyes and I went home. How could I know that would be the last time we ever talked?

"What do you think about Karl?" I asked Isabel that same night.

We were in bed, relaxing, her tiny slinky body next to mine.

"In what sense?" she said, suspicious.

"There's more than one? All of them, I guess."

"I don't know. He's okay, I suppose. He's... He seems interesting."

"As interesting as I am?"

"Since when were you interesting? Who told you that?"

"You, I believe. Some time ago."

"I was drunk, surely."

"No doubt. But don't change the subject. In what way does he seem interesting?"

"Well, he's handsome but in a weird way. He isn't threatening, you know?" I nodded. "There's something about him. He's very quiet but I have the feeling that with the right person he could stop being so."

"You being the right person, you mean?"

"Sometimes I think maybe I am. Sometimes..." She shrugged.

"You seem to have been seeing a lot of each other lately," I said as if it was the most trivial issue in the world.

"Jealous?" she asked, clearly amused.

"No. I just wonder... Well, you've seen him at class. He has a sharp mind but is reluctant to participate. I have to coax him to talk most of the time."

"Yeah, indeed you do."

"What do you mean?"

"People say you have found your protégé."

I hadn't thought of that. Outside the classroom I could have my likes and dislikes, but inside I tried to behave the same towards everyone. It seemed I had failed with Karl.

"Wow," I said.

"They've even made some jokes about it."

"What kind of jokes?"

"You know, what I'm going to do when you leave me for him and all that stuff."

I smiled.

"Good point," I said. "But I don't think I'm his type. In fact, I think his type is surprisingly like you. I think he's got a crush on you."

"Yeah, I guess he has."

"And what about you?"

"I have a crush on myself, of course."

Smart, beautiful and with a regrettable sense of humour: my kind of woman. I change the subject and talked about some irrelevancies for a couple of minutes while she nodded and said 'aha' and 'hmmm' vacantly.

Suddenly she looked me in the eye and said: "Yeah. I... I like him. Maybe more than I'm willing to admit."

I didn't say anything. I just kissed her and hugged her. Sooner or later it had to happen. I would have preferred it to be later, but...

When I first met her my initial thought was that nothing could possibly happen between us. She was a teenager eager to become the woman she would someday develop into and I was a young priest fresh from the seminary. Yes, she was legally of age at sixteen and, once she passed her exams, she was an adult in the eyes of the law. But the law isn't everything.

I knew that any thoughts I might have in that direction were nothing more than a wild fantasy, it could never happen. Except that it did. I don't know how, but it happened.

I know why I fell in love with her. Somehow I saw the woman she would be and I couldn't stand the idea of not being a part of her. My God (the one I believed in then) had a surprising indulgence with human weaknesses and He didn't protest when I began to approach Isabel. I was clumsy, I guess, but luckily Isabel took control of the situation. Her lips were kissing mine before I realised what was happening.

"It wasn't very hard to see your true intentions," she told me some weeks later.

"I guess not. But why did you indulge me?"

"Maybe my own intentions were similar."

It was an atypical relationship; it couldn't have been anything else. A sixteen-year-old girl and a priest of twenty-six could not have a public relationship, irrespective of there being nothing illegal in the affair. We didn't hide it, either, we were merely discreet and used our common sense.

It had been two years. Two years in which my hopes and fears had slowly become reality. Because the woman I had seen in her was about to bloom and, when she did, I wasn't sure what she would feel about me.

4. The Biggest Madhouse in the Galaxy

I miss Cara so much. And that's ironic because I loved Isabel as if she were the best part of myself and Cara was just my friend. But not a day passes that I don't remember her. I remember her taunts, the cunning glow in her eyes, the pinch of sadness and stubbornness in her gaze. And Isabel... Yes, I think of her, but she's nothing more than an annoying ghost that haunts me from time to time. As the years pass by she weakens more and more and fades into the darkest places of my memory.

Yes, I miss Cara so badly. I hear her voice whenever I do something I know she wouldn't have liked. I hear an imaginary lip smacking or a whispered sarcastic comment.

I wonder if she knows, wherever she is. If so, maybe she draws comfort from the thought: she has won. In the end she has won. Of all the people in my past she is the only one that hasn't vanished, the only one who is stronger each day instead of weaker. Yes, Cara, you have defeated Isabel the only way it matters, though you're not here to enjoy your victory.

Sometimes I think she had anticipated her triumph and planned each and every step that led to it. Even her death;

why not? Especially her dead. Why else is the data crystal I now hold in my hand full of thoughts that have nothing to do with its apparent purpose? After all, she recorded it to ensure I got her investigation data should something happen to her. She could have just recorded a report. Instead she made me hear her voice, share her thoughts, no matter how vulgar, private or disturbing they might be.

Yes, that would be Cara in her prime.

If that is the case, if everything was part of your plan, Cara, I want you to know that you have won. I can't stop thinking about you and it's very likely I won't be able to in the future, either. I don't know if you can hear me; after all this time I'm not sure you are anywhere other than in this tiny crystal that contains you, but it doesn't matter. It's me, not you, who reaps the reward of your victory, and I guess you also had that planned.

Maybe I'm being too twisted. After all, there are a thousand reasons for recording the data crystal the way you did and maybe the real one is something trivial and harmless. Who knows?

Here I am, with the crystal in my hand, hesitating before plugging it into the proc and accessing your thoughts. Yes, darling, I'm coming.

[The net is the biggest madhouse in the Galaxy. And if we take into account that most of the people who live in the Confederation spend at least fifteen per cent of their time plugged into it, it's easy to see I'm right when I say we live in a Galaxy full of crazy people.//

//This was one of Carlos' favourite sayings. Yeah, my first boyfriend, the one who taught me everything he knew about the net and neural links. First time I heard it I was thirteen and he was about to enter his fifties, but how could I know that when the only thing I saw was his avatar, cold and unbelievably attractive? I found out a few weeks later but then it was too late. I was so hooked to that world of data freeways that I wasn't sure if the real Carlos was the one that surfed the net or the paunchy fifty-year-old who never left his house.//

//On reflection, it was a fair deal. Both of us took advantage of our relationship. Carlos added one more ghost to his life and I guess now I'm nothing more to him than another character in the elaborated fantasy his head plays again and again, ignoring the padded walls of his room in the asylum. As for me... Well, I learnt a couple of things and I guess there are harder and more unpleasant ways to learn them. We both got what we expected from our relationship. If there were one or two tears in the end or a grinding of teeth... It doesn't matter. Not any more.//

//What matters is that many years after we split up I find that Carlos has passed me his paranoia. It has become a part of my life and seems normal to me now. He also gave me a feature that apparently contradicted his paranoia. Unlike others of his kind Carlos took risks, almost as if he didn't know any other way of doing things. Most of the time the price wasn't worth the gain... unless, of course, the price was the risk itself, and I have begun to think it could have been exactly that.//

//I'm digressing, like an old retired bureaucrat. Digressing because I've remembered one of Carlos' sayings. It's totally stupid, as they all tended to be, but at the same time it's true. If you analyse closely, nobody in his right mind would dare to enter the net. It is a madhouse, where real-world rules and laws don't apply. Yes, the government tries to change the situation every once in a while... without success. You can do whatever you want in the net, assuming you have the guts and the skills, which makes our digital little world worse than a jungle; even in the jungle there are rules. But here there are only those set by the limits of your own imagination and the only obstacle is the size of your ambition. Everybody knows, I'm not saying anything new, everyone is aware of this, one way or another. Nevertheless, they spend a good portion of their lives in this huge virtual asylum. Why? I haven't the slightest idea, unless the reason is the most obvious of all.]

[But I'm in Daddy's node and the time for digression has passed. I enter his home without knocking and I make a comfortable copy of my own armchair without asking permission. I know he won't like it, of course, but putting him in a bad mood can work to my advantage: He will be caught off guard.//

//To my surprise, the chair doesn't seem to bother him at all.//

//"Cara, you little annoying pimple in my old ass, you have arrived on time." He says as if it was a recrimination and only vulgar people bothered to arrive on time. "I guess I'm not getting anywhere with you, after all."//

//Where do you want to go, dirty old man?"//

//He smiles, but immediately turns serious again.//

//"What have you found out, Daddy?"//

//"Nothing really important, I don't yet know the meaning of life and I have no idea if God exists. In the issue of the existence of 'the beyond' all my research has reached a blind alley. About our little matter, however, I think I can tell you a couple of things"//

//He speaks quickly, telling one joke after another with his usual frown. But something tells me it's for show; he's not the Daddy I know. Something bothers him and he's trying to hide it from me.//

//"Go on."//

//"Your friend Kennington is someone totally and utterly normal. So normal I told myself God couldn't allow the existence of someone so boring. Well, maybe God has allowed it, who knows what the old fart likes, but it's not the case with Kennington. He's a fraud."//

//"What?"//

//"A fraud. Everything about him is an elaborate deception. There was no Juan and Marta Kennington in Campoestela, no boring adolescence in a hydro farm, no accident that killed these parents he never had. His past before he arrived in Pardaterra is a fiction."

//Pieces begin to fit into place in my head. I can almost hear the click as they join together. I remember what I thought several weeks ago about Pierre and Karl and I try not to laugh.//

// "Bait," I mutter.//

//That takes Daddy by surprise.//

//"Bait," I say again. "Heretics Hammer doesn't care who the hell Kennington really is. One of their own agents, possibly. The one they are really interested in is Pierre."//

//Daddy doesn't say anything. He seemed absentminded, and he frowns as if he was chewing something disgusting and indigestible.//

//"My darling," he says at last. In his voice there is neither irony nor sarcasm and that gives me the creeps. "I don't know what the hell Kennington is or what the role of your friend Pierre might be in this damn thing, but I can assure you the boy is not bait to test a rebellious priest."

//"How can you be so sure?"//

//"Nobody spends this much effort, time and money just to create a front. Do you know how hard it was to find out the truth? The faked data seemed so real they appeared more solid than reality itself. Do you know the skill, power and resources required to do something like that? Of course you don't. Nobody does. Until now, nobody would have believed such a perfect fake was possible." As he tells me this he transmits to me a string of data I almost can't digest: fake keys, empty files and pointers that point nowhere fill my head. "No, the Order has invested too many resources. Their interest in Kennington is genuine, I can tell you that. Whatever it is."//

//"You mean whatever he is."//

//"I mean what I say and always say what I mean. I'm too old to change that."//

//That seems to end our conversation. I stand up and Daddy stops me.//

//"Let it be," he says. "Tell your Pierre to get involved as little as he can and you just let it go."//

//"Are you nuts, Daddy?" Well, yeah, that's what Carlos would have said: Of course I'm nuts, everybody here's nuts. "Are you telling me to disobey a rat's number one rule? You never leave until the end."//

//"Yes, but it could be your end."//

//"Come on, Daddy... I'm not afraid of those bastards. I know how to cheat them. They don't even know I exist."//

//"They're not entirely human, Cara. And they know much more than you think." He is about to say something else but changes his mind. "It's better for you to leave."//

/I do, quietly and slowly. I surf the net and I don't know what to think. There's a funny taste in my mouth and my guts are playing up. Which is odd, because I have no real guts now.]

[Paranoia and boldness. A rather peculiar combination. But it's the combination that defines me the best and damned if I'm going to let Daddy ruin my day.//

//Suddenly I'm right next to the Order system. I smile when I realise that my subconscious has been smarter than me yet again. I enter without a second thought, walk by the public part and then, when nobody's watching, I sneak through my back door.//

//*Here I am, you bastards. I'm going to blow the lid off each and every one of your lousy secrets.* And I begin to explore full of joy, feeling almost invulnerable. Nothing can stop me, nobody can.//

//Then I remember Daddy's words: they're not entirely human. Nonsense, I tell myself, but the feeling of invulnerability disappears and suddenly I feel very small.]

[Something's wrong. I notice the moment I jump into the forbidden files. They've found me, they know who am I and they know I'm here.//

//But that's impossible. The system is secure and my camouflage impenetrable. No religious order can compete with me. So I silence the protest of my digital guts and jump into what someone else would see as havoc but for me is as clear and well defined as a straight line.//

//Nanoseconds slip by with cosmic slowness while I open one file after another, take one reference from here and retrieve a deleted datum from there. With patience, trying to ignore the prickle that makes me turn round every few moments, I reconstruct Daddy's work and I do in a few seconds what it must have taken him weeks. But I can do it because Daddy showed me the way. *Don't forget that, Cara, you little pimple, stop patting yourself on the back and keep searching, you've been here too long.*//

//So I check the alarms I have set around the perimeter. Everything's fine. Nobody has been here apart from me, I'm sure.//

//I leave Daddy's findings behind as I enter the core. I walk blind by a data maze knowing that the slightest mistake could kill me. I keep opening files and I almost feel sweat running down my back. You've designed me too accurately, Cara, damn it. And with that thought about my maker (myself) I continue the search, venturing ever further into the heart of the data system.//

//The files are very well hidden. A reference here takes me to a lead there that takes me up what appears to be a blind alley, until I step back a couple of steps, recognise the trickery and find the right way. More than once I'm about to fall into a recursive process of infinite depth and I escape by a whisker at the last picosecond. It would be great to spend the rest of eternity dancing around a meaningless data package that just points back to itself. Again and again. Circling and circling. Coming and going, travelling entire galaxies without going anywhere.//

//No time for grim thoughts. As I go deeper into this impossible maze I begin to understand its secret order and I see the crazy system they have implemented to disperse information. Crazy, yeah, but once you understand it becomes logical, almost perfect.//

//Here I am at last. A video file that shows me his conception: An anonymous gene donation; several months in a DNA sequencer, while the microscopic nanobuilders altered one step of the amino acid stair, delete another one, exchange this one for that one. The process is dizzying, like a film in fast motion showing plant germination or a corpse decomposing. And after several years the embryo is ready to be implanted in the biowomb.//

//The file ends, but it takes me to the next one where I see an entire life compressed into a few months thanks to the datasuit and a sophisticated VR program. A program that ends and releases into the world something uncontrollable that thinks it's a human being but is not.//

//Are they nuts? What are they creating? What were they trying to do? Then I laugh. Yeah, of course, they're creating God in their own image and likeness and they're confident they'll be able to control it. I open the last file and I see the hand of Heretics Hammer, the Inner Circle. The subject is ready to be released into the world. "Where?" a committee asks.//

//I see him for the first time and I recognise him thanks to Pierre's description. Bald, sharp face, an occasional crimson glow in his eyes. Lucas Picardo, one of the Inner Circle cyborgs.//

//"Pardaterra," he says. "We have a high school there. And their literature teacher would make an ideal spy."//

//"That's ridiculous, Picardo," says one of the men in the table. "We don't need a spy. With our satellites network we can monitor him twenty-four/seven. And don't forget he's so full of spy nanites I don't understand how his veins don't burst."/

//"Are you sure we can?" asks Picardo while a faster than the eye smile appears in his thin lips. "I am not sure you understand the kind of being we are releasing. But even if you were right, de Charden can be useful in other ways."/

//"I don't get it."//

//"Of course you don't. We need a catalyst, something to make him accept who he is, forcing him to choose sides. Our catastrophe contingency is well planned and implemented but it could fail, in which case de Charden's girlfriend would be perfect for our purpose."

//"Ludicrous. Why are you so sure he...?"//

//"Why not? Is it not reasonable to assume they share the same taste in women?"//

//What's this all about? Why should Pierre and Kennington have the same taste in women? There are disturbing implications here. I close the file and go back to the DNA donation.//

//Pierre, oh, Pierre. What have they done to you? Fucking twisted bastards. Yeah, you told me years ago: all of you donate a DNA sample when you enter the Order. Is that it? Is this superman your son, or even yourself?//

//I can't believe it. Picardo, you bastard.//

//Before I can check anything I realise something's wrong. A cold sharp axe is falling from the crimson sky looking for me. It's not just an automatic net ferret. It's seeking me and no one else. All right, Cara, it's time to show them who you are.//

//I'm not subtle. After all, if they know I'm here it's stupid trying to get unnoticed. So I jump away from the inquisitorial axe as fast as I can. I open any file I find in my way and throw all the data into the connection channels around me. I'm about to stop when one of the files splits its information over me and I suddenly see a detailed account of earthquakes, hurricanes, tsunamis, massive fires, terrorist assaults, each one of them planned with maniacal precision. I remember the net gabble about Weather Control being a disaster and understand then that everything that happened these past few months has been deliberate. But I haven't time to ponder that, I haven't time to do anything but keep opening files and hoping that all this havoc will prove useful to me.//

//It's right in front of me, relentless, like a cold and hungry mouth full of teeth. I turn round at the last picosecond and my attacker falls into a pool of pure wild information.//

//A break. That's what I've got. So I'd better take advantage of it and get out of here.//

//I do. But my escape is too fast and too easy and when I'm back in the public net sectors I wonder what the Order has in mind for me. Nothing good, I bet.]

[There's no trace of me. There's no trace of me in all the virtual space. Outer channels have been closed and I can't access them, I'm trapped in the net and I can't communicate with my user; in fact, her node no longer exists, it has been closed and erased fifty seconds ago and the system is rearranging itself and adapting to the new situation. That's not simply bad, it's beyond terrible. It's a complete disaster. It's the one thing every rat fears. I'm dead. To be more accurate, my flesh and blood self is dead and it won't take me long to follow her.//

//I sense a strange presence and when I turn round I see him. Pale and sharp, wearing black robes, the crimson glow in his eyes.//

//"Picardo," I say.//

//"I'm flattered you know my name."//

//I take a look around, trying to buy some time. It's useless, I know. If he's here it can only mean that all exits are under his control. In a few seconds I'll be reduced to a bunch of noise and nothing in this universe can prevent it.//

//"Will you make it hard or easy?" he asks. And there's something akin to joy in his voice, a cold metallic joy.//

//"Hard," I answer, trying to look indifferent.//

//Cara always tried to anticipate any contingency, even those impossible to foresee. (I realise that talking of Cara as if she wasn't me indicates acceptance that she's dead, but I don't have time to waste thinking through the implications.) She had a plan for something like this situation, but I'm not sure I can make it happen. I take one last look at the creature that's waiting to kill me. What the hell, let's try.//

//"Okay, pretty boy, shall we dance?" I ask him. And I jump towards him with everything I have. I know it's not going to be enough.]

5.   Confessions

There's nothing to do. Nothing to say. Nothing. I killed Cara and not just once. I have disconnected the data crystal. What was about to happen was too painful and today I'm not in the mood to face my guilty conscience.

I lean back in the couch. I think of Cara, of Isabel. I wonder if I ever really loved them. I think of Karl and remember what Cara wondered about him. Can it be true? Is it possible that my own genes were the ones the Order used to give him life? Was Karl, in an uncanny and twisted way, my son? If so, he is the only offspring I'll ever have. The cowardly father of a superman, that's me. Why not? It's one of the most used clichés of superhero comics. Given that the Order designed Karl following all the archetypes of a costumed superhero,

*why not that one as well? It would be a delicious irony. No,
it wouldn't. It wouldn't be delicious even if it is ironic.*

*I sit forward. I don't need any chip or data crystal to
know what happened in the hours that followed. Those
moments are in my head, as they always have been.*

When everything happened I saw Isabel coming home with a glow in her
eyes. I didn't ask, but somehow I realised I wasn't the only man in her
life any more. The truth is, despite my suspicions, I only knew for a fact
several years later, when Isabel told me.

As I said, I didn't ask. Not because I was afraid of the answer, or at
least I like to think that wasn't the reason. Maybe it was pure
stubbornness. She was the one who had to tell me if something had
happened, but I couldn't ask.

In a way, you could say I won. A couple of weeks ago I heard Isabel's
confession. I didn't recognise her at first, no matter how ridiculous that
sounds. I just saw a woman in her forties, eager to leave her past behind
and go on with her life. I only realised it was her when she said my name.

"Hail purest Mary, conceived without a sin. It's been twenty-seven
years since my last confession. Hello, Pierre."

From the false security the confessional lattice gave me I was able to
answer her greeting:

"Hello, Isabel. It's been a while."

She shrugged. And without giving me time to prepare she began to
tell her story:

"That evening you suspected something had happened. In fact, you
guessed part of the truth, but not the part that really mattered, believe it
or not. Yes, I made love with Karl, but that is not important. I need you
to understand what really happened, beyond an exchange of body fluids
and an orgasm. I think you need this as well. You're an obsessive man,
Pierre, you need all the information in its correct place and when you
miss anything, no matter how trivial, you torment yourself." She was
right, of course. Otherwise, why do I keep opening files and resurrecting
Cara's ghost? "Yes, I spent that evening with Karl. What I saw, what we
did, was wonderful, but also frightening. I know you saw the glow in my
eyes and noticed my altered breathing but I'm not sure you really
understood what had happened. I was frightened, Pierre, scared to the
depths of my soul. The future had become a place of bewildering

possibilities, making my head spin."

I hadn't moved since she began to talk. I had become a statue inside the confessional, my knees bent and my chin in my hand.

"Karl asked me for a date that evening and I said yes. I liked him, as you know. Yes, he excited me. He was so much like you in so many ways. I enjoyed fantasising he was the way you were at his age, before entering a Church you really didn't believe in and pursuing a God that dodged you again and again. We went up to the Hill. It was almost dusk and you could see the entire city from up there. We stood at the top, next to that stupid horizon monument they say is a perfect replica of the one Lonesome had erected in Drímar. Funny, for the first time that worn plasticoncrete mass didn't seem ugly. Karl took my hand and walked to the cliff edge, his back to the city, looking at the endless sea. His hand was trembling and I remember I found it weird that someone like him could be afraid. He gazed at the sea for a long while. Night fell around us and the sea seemed a dark and lurking animal. 'I can do many things,' Isabel, he told me suddenly. 'So many, sometimes I think I could change the entire universe and reshape it to my will. But, what happens if I don't want to? What do I do with all this power I don't want to use?' I looked into his eyes and realised that he was afraid, more than I had ever been in my life. 'Do you trust me?' he asked. You can't imagine how hard it was for me to answer that. But, yes, I told him I trusted him. I knew he would never harm me, no matter what. 'Then come with me,' he said, 'and don't fear anything'."

Isabel kept silent for a moment as if she were short of breath, as if she were mustering the courage required to tell me the rest.

"He released my hand and put his arm around my wrist. He was strong, so strong I thought he could crush me without noticing, but I felt safe, as if somehow I was shielded from any harm while with him. He walked towards the edge, looked up and smiled. There was still fear in his eyes but there was something more; he reminded me of a kid enjoying being mischievous. His arm tightened around me, but not enough to hurt. Then he crouched and jumped. It was too fast. My feet were no longer touching the ground. And then…"

She stopped.

"I'm sorry. I can't. I wouldn't be able to make you see the way I saw. I know now. Words are such poor surrogates… How could you understand what I felt, what I feel now if I close my eyes? We were flying,

Pierre, do you understand? Our feet weren't on the ground any more but we didn't fall into that threatening sea, we weren't going to crash. We were flying! We slid through the air gently, softly, and it felt normal, natural, the proper way to do things. We were dancing, free of gravity. We went up, up and away and nothing could stop us. I saw the city and it was like a toy, a wonderful toy full of lights and distant noises, maybe the biggest Christmas tree in the universe. I was free, free in a way I've never been again in my life. Because it was not *my* freedom. It belonged to Karl and he shared it with me, but it was Karl who led that crazy, intoxicating, endless waltz. He was flying, not me."

I then realised Isabel was crying. She didn't sob and her expression didn't change as a couple of tears slid down her chin.

"At first I didn't look at him. What kind of a god was Karl, what kind of mythological creature had taken me into his arms and danced the most delightful waltz with me? What had I done to be worthy of him? Then I looked at him and saw again his eyes, filled with fear. 'What happens now?' I asked, but he couldn't answer, maybe he didn't know what to say. The fear didn't leave his eyes and I saw a hidden plea in them. Nothing more. He didn't seem to be a god any more. Just a scared boy, unable to tell what was happening. He needed... What else could I have done? He was no god, he didn't want all those powers, he didn't want to use them and he knew sooner or later he would be forced to do so. He was as frail and helpless as I was. So I ask you again: what else could I have done? I turned round in his arms, took his face between my hands and kissed his trembling lips. The next moment we were... Well, you can imagine. Knowing you, you have been imagining it for years. I enjoyed it, of course, as much as he did, and our screams of pleasure probably scared away all the gulls in the area. But it doesn't matter. What matters is that he showed me who he was, without costumes, without masks, without lies; his body as naked as his soul. Maybe he was a god after all, but he was also a frightened boy. The only thing I had to comfort him with was myself. And that was what I gave him."

My hand had clenched into a fist. I looked at it, surprised. Isabel stood up, ready to leave.

"I told him I loved him. It was true. He told me he loved me. I don't know if he was telling the truth. I guess in that moment the feeling was real for him. It doesn't matter. He put me gently on the ground a few minutes later. He was smiling but in the back of his eyes I could see the fear, crouched and waiting to jump out. He kissed me one last time. He told me he had to go, he had a lot to think about. He turned around, jumped into the night and disappeared."

She turned away but she suddenly stopped and looked at me. I saw half a smile crossing her face and I recognised the Isabel I once knew.

"Aren't you going to give me a penance?"

The hardest thing I've done in my life was saying, in a calm voice: "Go in peace, my child. You have not sinned."

She left. I leant back in the confessional, feeling the lurking breath of my own loneliness in the back of my neck.

"Goodbye, Isabel," I whispered a long after she had gone.

A couple of days after Isabel and Karl's flight I went home and it was empty, with no trace of her. I thought for a moment she had left me for Karl, but I knew her well enough to realise that if she left me some day she would tell me to my face. So I guessed she had to go away for some reason she would explain later. I turned on the tri-vi and was watching it with no real interest when I heard something softly hitting against the window.

What the hell? It couldn't be the rain, the beat was too regular. An animal, maybe a bird? I went to the window and raised the blinds.

Karl was there, his arms crossed over his chest and a grim glow in his blue eyes. Yes, he was there, completely dry despite the soaking rain. He was there and his feet weren't touching the ground. He floated in the air, arrogant, perfect and distant, like an angry god.

"Are you going to open the window or would you prefer me to break it?" he asked.

It was and it wasn't his voice, and any trace of the mild-mannered teenager he had been had disappeared.

I don't know how I managed to open that window. Karl entered the room, sliding through the air like a dolphin through water. I considered asking him where he had stolen a field repulse from, but I knew the question was ridiculous. No machine could cause its owner to move with such grace, as if he had been doing this all his life. He touched the floor with such finesse I thought he was afraid to break it.

"You don't seem surprised," he said.

"Don't I?" I dared to say. "True, I'm not surprised. I don't know why but I'm not. I think I'm beyond surprise."

A smile appeared on his face, but the grim glow didn't leave his eyes.

"All right," he said. "It doesn't matter now. Where is Isabel?"

"Funny, I was about to ask you the same question."

"I'm not in the mood for jokes, Pierre. Where she is?"

"I don't know."

He hesitated for a second.

"You're telling the truth. Then it must have been them."

"Who?"

"You tell me. After all, you were spying on me for them."

"What?"

"Enough, Pierre. Let's stop pretending we are not what we are. Do you think I haven't detected the satellite network that followed my every movement? Disabling it was easy, but it was pretty obvious they would employ alternative ways when they realised their technology was useless. It wasn't hard to see it was you. Everything you've said, every move you've made since we met has betrayed you, Pierre. You almost got me when you presented superhero comics to study, it seemed too obvious and you were too smart to make such a mistake. But then I thought it could hide an almost prophetic subtlety. Your heart rate, your breathing, even your sweat betrayed you from the very beginning. You're one of them."

A satellite network. My words and movement betraying me. The beating of my heart, my breathing, my sweat… Karl in the middle of the night, floating in thin air, the rain avoiding him. Every image passed through my mind like a speeding bullet and all I could do was look at Karl's blue eyes with my mouth open and my throat dry.

"I'm not," I managed to say hoarsely. "Well, I am but… I was supposed to spy on you, yes, but I didn't know why. I don't know what they want from you."

But I was beginning to see what they wanted. And why.

"Yes, again you're telling the truth," said Karl. "Why not? I guess they didn't tell you everything. Who are they?"

"I need a drink," I said. I went to the bar cabinet wobbling like a drunk man. I suddenly stopped. "Do you want one?" I asked.

"No, and God knows how I'd like it sometimes. But alcohol doesn't have any effect on me. I metabolise it too well."

I was trying to process what I had just heard and seen, to make sense of everything happening around me.

I failed.

Who and what was Karl? What was the Order doing? How did they know of him? How long had they been spying on him? No, these weren't the right questions. I was missing something and I wasn't sure I wanted to know what it was.

I looked at Karl once more. A creature capable of flying, of telling at a glance if I was lying, of casually destroying an entire satellite network… Immune to alcohol. Thank God I wasn't. I drank half a bottle before I realised what I was doing and then I sat on the floor, next to Karl. He crouched and looked at me, half inquisitive half amused.

"The only thing I know is the Order is involved," I said. "The Inner Circle, to be more precise." I drank again. "One of their cyborgs ordered me to watch you."

Karl stood up. His feet were a couple of centimetres over the floor.

"The Order… *The Order?* It makes no sense. I don't get it."

"Me neither."

"But you do as you've been told, don't you? As long as they let you go on with your intellectual hobbies and forgive your tiny sins, nothing else matters. No, I'm not reproaching you, Pierre. After all, you're just human. I can understand why they are interested in me if somehow they have discovered what I am… What I am; funny, even I'm not too sure. Just before his death my father told me… No, this isn't the time for that. Why do they have Isabel? What do they want from her?"

"Nonsense. Isabel will turn up any minute, I'm sure."

"I'm afraid she won't. I have been looking for her for the past few hours and I haven't found her. And believe me when I tell you if she were on this planet, no matter where, I would have located her."

I believed him. It was surprisingly easy. I drank what was left in the bottle and a disturbing thought entered my head.

"They're using her. They want you to go public."

"What?"

"Oh, so there are still some things that can surprise you." He wasn't perfect after all. One look from him was enough to quiet me. "I'm not sure," I continued, "but I think they want you to reveal yourself to the world. Am I wrong to suppose you have been trying all your life to hide what you can do?"

"No, you're not. And I think you're right. They're using her against me. They want me to go and look for her. All right. If they want me they'll get me. I'll find her. And may God protect your Order when I do."

"How are you…?"

"I'm not sure. Not yet."

"Maybe I can help."

He looked at me, dubious.

"I love Isabel as much as you do. I'll help you."

"You know where to look for her?"

"No, but I know someone who does."

"All right, Pierre. Let's go."

Somehow my memory has edited out most of that crazy flight through the night, the rain lashing us as if to stop us. I remember all that happened in minute detail, but my emotions aren't there, as if the most delicate scalpel had cut them away.

We landed on the roof of Cara's building and went to the fire escape. Karl walked in complete silence and turned his head one way and the other at a terrifying speed. We stopped at Cara's door and knocked, waiting two interminable minutes for someone to answer.

"There's no one there," Karl said.

"Are you sure?"

"Pretty much. I can't see clearly enough through these wall, but if there was someone I would hear them."

Once more I tried not to think of the implications of his words. I knocked again.

"Move aside. I'll open it."

He went to the door and gazed at it as if he expected the door to open by itself. I suddenly smelled hot metal. Karl touched the door with his hand and pushed gently. The door opened while a drop of melted steel slipped from the frame.

We entered the apartment. There were no lights. I tried to remember the sequence or verbal orders that would turn the lights on but it had been too many years since I had been there. Besides, the computer surely wouldn't accept my voice.

"There's nobody home. Not anymore." His voice sounded harsh. "Come over here."

I entered the living room. The window was open and the city provided all the light I needed. More, in fact. Cara was by the window, her body a broken toy and her empty eyes looking at me as if she were accusing me of something.

"Someone has been here before us. Forty-five minutes, to be precise, judging by her body temperature," said Karl. He crouched and gently took Cara's hand. "I'm sorry."

I should have been sorry as well. But the only thing I could think was that the Inner Circle had discovered my conversations with Cara and they could do to me what they had done to her. In an instant that thought evaporated and I found myself on my knees with Cara's head on my lap while I clumsily tried to fix her hair.

"I'm sorry, sweetheart," I said. "I'm sorry."

I was barely aware of Karl behind me, pacing the living-room floor like a lurking cat. I think I began to laugh, though it was a dry and worn out laugh.

"I don't see anything funny," said Karl.

"Don't you? From my Church's point of view, I've been a sinner for years: I'm an adulterer, I have departed from orthodoxy and I may even have lost my faith. But only now do I realise they were right all along. I'm a sinner. And my sin is that Cara is dead because she loved me."

"Maybe," said Karl. "But there is someone else who loves you and could end up like Cara. Are you going to allow that?"

"Allow? What else can I do? I'm theirs, I belong to them."

"I don't. And I'm not going to let an innocent pay for my sake. Are you coming with me or are you going to stay here?"

"Where are you going?"

"Don't know. Not yet. But there's a heat trace leading from this room. I'm going to follow it and see where it leads me."

I gently put Cara's head on the floor. I kissed her cold lips.

"Let's go," I said.

A new flight across the storm. Karl's face seemed the mask of a god. All trace of that perpetually amazed teenager I met months ago had gone. Nothing but a glow in his eyes that seemed to be wondering why.

"There it is," he suddenly said. He indicated with his head one of the mountains that surrounded the city. "I knew there was something there, but I never thought it had to do with me... or the Order."

"But where?"

"That mountain is hollow, though its walls are so filled with lead I can't see what's inside. Hold tight."

I did while Karl's eyes caught fire and two crimson beams crossed the rain toward the mountain. Something exploded and Karl and I landed next to a smoking hole.

Inside, the mountain resembled the biggest hospital of the world. Everything was white, clean, cold. Karl and I walked softly, as if we were afraid of making a noise. At least I did; Karl's feet didn't touch the ground.

"They don't dare show themselves," he whispered. "But they're here."

"Where?"

"A little further."

Finally, the corridor ended in a door.

"They want to play. Well, let's play."

His eyes glowed crimson again and the door melted as if made of butter.

"Let me carry you, Pierre. It's too hot for you."

He picked me up and with a jump we crossed the door. We were in what seemed to be a laboratory. Isabel was there, cuffed on a stretcher. She seemed unconscious... or something worse.

"She's alive," said Karl as if he had heard my thoughts.

We ran to the stretcher. Karl gently caressed Isabel's hair.

"She's been drugged. Her pulse is not right."

"Yes," said a voice I knew. "She's drugged but she will wake up shortly."

A door had opened behind us, allowing Picardo to enter the room.

"Good evening, de Charden. Hi, Karl. Good-bye, Karl."

Picardo snapped his fingers and a low buzz filled the room.

"What the...?" It was suddenly hard to speak, as if something was stopping my tongue.

"I'm turning him off, nothing else."

I turned round. Karl wobbled and shook his head. He tried to reach Picardo, but he stumbled.

"After all, experiments are always terminated eventually. Oh no, please, Karl, don't try it. You aren't strong enough to stop me now. In fact, you aren't even strong enough to hold your own body together."

He was right. The boy was falling apart in front of me.

"Come on, I know you must be tired. Why don't you close your eyes, rest for a while and let us take care of you? It is what we've been doing all these years, after all."

Karl tried to say something but he couldn't. His face was pale and he barely seemed able to keep his eyes opened.

"Damn it, you're killing him."

"Watch your tongue, de Charden, it is not appropriate for a Church priest. And I am not killing him. I am just making him more manageable."

From the floor, Karl looked at us, helpless for the first time in his life.

"Your father didn't prepare you for this, did he?" said Picardo. "Of course he didn't. We didn't allow it. You belong to us, Karl. We created you, we gave you life and we have controlled that life to the last detail. You have never been to Campoestela. You have never had parents, at least not a mother and a father. That was all real for you, yes? Well I guess that is what matters in the end."

Karl didn't say anything. He could barely move.

"You can take care of him now."

Two men entered the room, took Karl and put his unconscious body on a stretcher.

"All right, de Charden, what are we going to do with you? You are a sorry excuse for a priest, but you have served us well. Maybe despite yourself, but well enough, anyway."

"What's this all about?"

"Are you sure you want to know? Curiosity killed the cat, remember. Everything you have done has been for the Order and that should be enough for you."

"What happens if it's not?"

"Then we will have to take care of you, one way or another. In your case, I would say it will be enough to find you a place where your pedestrian aspirations can be satisfied."

6. Waltz

I've seen him. Here, in my church. Here, in my kingdom, where I'm supposed to be the master and my will is law. I've seen him, hidden among the congregation, just a shade at the back of the church.

How dare he? How dare he come here after all these

years? Isn't it enough for him to have won? I've managed to keep calm until the end of the service but I couldn't help glancing towards the back from time to time. To find a grey and anodyne shape looking back at me with half a smile on his thin lips. Sometimes there was a reddish glow in his right eye.

Later, alone in the sacristy, I realise how foolish I was. Of course he dares. Why not? He's my master; he has been all these years and he will be until I die.

That evening in my office I pay little attention as Walter reads his report. He notices (he always does), turns off the hologram he was reading from and says: "I think we should postpone this, Your Eminence. I see you have something else on your mind right now."

I agree. I think if he had told me he was going to kill me I would have agreed. He leaves the room, efficient as always. So efficient it's not the first time I wonder whether Walter is a tool of the Inner Circle.

Of course he is. As am I. As is the Order. Ad Maiorem Dei Gloriam, right?

At least they could have the decency to stay in the shadows and not revel in their power.

But what happens if it's something more? What if my investigations have alerted them somehow and Picardo's presence in my church is just a warning?

Well, let him be a warning. It's too late to stop now. For once in my life I'm going to do what I must and to hell everything else.

[//I wake up very slowly. My first thought is that, in some crazy way, Cara's plan has worked. My second thought is that she's dead. The third, that I'm not her any more. The fourth that, nevertheless, I share with Cara enough features to be almost the same person; above all, and maybe it's our curse, we both love Pierre. The fifth...//]

//The fifth is that I'm trapped inside the mental flow of one of the most detestable beings in all the universe and I have no idea how I'm going to get away. Yes, Cara, little pimple in universe's ass, you were very smart; your strategy was almost perfect. Fake my own death while part of me infiltrated my enemy's systems, to make a copy of myself using his data space while letting him destroy the original, fall asleep, assimilate my new condition, wake up... Yes, you thought of everything and don't think I'm not grateful; after all, I'm still alive. But you never told me what I'd have to do once I woke up. I have to get away as fast as I can. Sooner or later his security systems will detect me and I don't want to imagine what will happen then.//

//I stretch very slowly. The tiniest mistake could give me away. With infinite care I check each and every channel around me. I need to escape, look for a safe place in the net and never be less than ten nodes away from anything related to the Order. But I can't get away, because the moment I try he will be aware of my presence and destroy me.//

//That leaves me in a blind alley, or it would do if I wasn't the most diabolically smart rat of all the Confederation, or at least a pretty damn good copy of her. Because I realise I have a chance. I can get away, yes, but I have to pour myself out bit by bit. Picardo is always linked to the net, sharing information all the time. I just have to take advantage of that channel and drip myself out with enough discretion to go unnoticed. Easy, right?]

[It's been years, centuries. That is, a couple of hours. Enough for him to detect me more than a thousand times. He hasn't yet, and that makes me bolder. Now I'm in two places at once. One part of me is still inside Picardo, and the other in the net looking for a safe place. But I realise that maybe the safest place of all is just where I am now. I remember Daddy's words and I nod my metaphorical head: wherever I go they will find me sooner or later. So I consider the idea for a couple of nanoseconds. I have to do just the opposite of what I've been doing until now; I'm not going to get away, instead I'm going to get inside, or to be more accurate, the part of me that is already outside is going to do it, mingled with the data Picardo receives. And as she gets in she is going to take possession of his systems. If everything works as planned, this damned bastard will become my puppet. If it doesn't... Well, it will be fun, at least.]

[Little by little, as I'm taking control of Picardo's channels (though I'm not trying to manipulate them yet, it's too soon and I don't want to spoil the surprise) I begin to share his awareness; not just the huge data gabble he receives from the net but also everything his human part perceives.//

//And that includes a teenager in pain and a priest in whose face I see... What? Rage, surprise, defeat? All three of them, I guess; it's typical of Pierre to feel contradictory emotions without even being aware of it.//

//"Kennington is ours, as he always has been," I hear myself saying with a voice that's not mine. "We created him, we nurtured him and we released him upon the world. It's fair we get him back."//

//"I don't get it; you didn't need me at all."//

//I smile, though it's Picardo's smile, not mine. The interface between my biological aspect and my electronic systems causes a strange blurriness in my perceptions, as if my body (not yet, but soon, yes, very soon) were moving through a thick and fluid atmosphere.//

//"That was what the others thought. We filled him with spy nanites, you know? And then the inevitable happened: two days after his release the nanomachines were destroyed. He didn't even realise; maybe his body temperature rose a little while his body's defences took care of the invaders. As for our satellites, I think it took him even less time to discover and disable them. I have always preferred the old ways. If you want to know what somebody is doing you send another person to watch them. There was another advantage in choosing you." Pierre nods towards the stretcher holding Isabel's unconscious form. "Your girlfriend was the perfect bait. Someone like Karl had no choice but to fall for her. The others believed they could force him to go public with the earthquakes and explosions, but I knew Karl would not be so easy to activate. Anyway, what else do you want to know, de Charden?//

//"Why are you telling me these things?"//

//"Because it doesn't matter what you know. You belong to us, now and forever. And a tool whose curiosity has been satisfied is better tuned than a restless and resentful one. There are two things you can do. You can take your girl and get out or keep on asking. But then you have to stay to the bitter end and I don't think you'd like that."//

//Pierre doesn't hesitate.//

//"I'll stay," he says. Yes, that's my Pierre. Stupid but bold. It's a relief to see that all those years with his nose in books and his head in teenagers (no pun intended... well... maybe a little) haven't taken away his guts.//

//"It's your choice," I say. And suddenly I feel a tidal wave of contempt for Pierre. It's not my emotion, but Picardo's, but I can't help feeling it as mine.//

//It takes me a few picoseconds to understand what's happening and then I realise that perhaps my cunning strategy wasn't so cunning after all and it's possible I may have fallen into a very well prepared trap. Picardo's systems are too well armoured, so full of filters and safeguards I can't help wondering if he knew Carlos: he is even more paranoid than my ex. That might transform what I thought was my victory in the greatest defeat I can imagine. Yes, I'm assimilating Picardo's systems; but in doing so I'm becoming him. Great, Cara, smart ass, too clever for your own good. It's better you do something and do it fast, before you end up as a tiny and defenceless part of a fanatical cyborg operating system that resembles the nightmare creation of a paranoid bureaucrat.//

//While I wonder that I also wonder how I'm going... how *he's* going to manage to kill a guy that looks like he can move the planet out of its orbit with just a kick.//

//And while I wonder that, a part of me breaks free of Picardo, no longer worrying if she is detected or not, and begins to search the surrounding data systems.//

//And while I wonder about that, I perceive Picardo's astonishment when he realises someone else is inside him.//

//And then I have no more time to wonder. The things I have just unleashed will take their course and the only thing I can do now is try to survive. After all, that is what I'm been doing all my life, though never before driven by such a rage.]

[We fight. Like two tigers, like two predators that know survival of one of us means the death of the other one, that this land is too small for the both of us.//

//We fight, trying to fool the other with false feints and meaningless attacks, throwing information to our opponent as if data were arrows.//

[Data: The Order wanted to create a first approximation to God.//

//Data: The reason is buried so deep under a string of theological excuses that nobody can really tell.//

//Data: The Order has been working on the project for more than seven hundred years.//

//He swears he's going to destroy me. I don't say anything, too busy trying to survive. But I have time enough to wonder *why*, what is the purpose of this stubbornness if flesh and blood Cara has been dead for hours. I should give up, accept the inevitable and fade in a peaceful noise cloud where there will be no more fear or concern, just entropy and silence. The thought is sweet, so sweet I'm about to do it.//

//But it doesn't last. I'm too much like flesh and blood Cara (what the hell, I'm her, all that's left of her) to fall into such a simple trap and give up in such a stupid way. Because those death wishes don't come from me, but form Picardo. He hasn't realised he can't win by going there. Maybe my body is just a corpse and my future an unanswered question but even that is better than nothing. I'm not giving up. He will have to defeat me.//

//So we fight. There's a hollow…

//Data: The purpose of the experiment was to put the subject in a situation where he would be forced to use his skills and go public and assume his rightful place as a god.//

//Data: After that he would be deactivated.//

//Data: If you can change your world, can you refuse to do so?//

//Data: Can a god deny his own divinity?//

//Data: Questions and more questions that hide the truth. The Order had the power to do this, so they did it. And that somehow answers all questions.//

//Data: More chatter about the Omega point and God-converging evolution.//

//Data: Let's help evolution and meet God halfway.//

//Data: Karl's cells work as biological batteries, a technique the Order learnt from the Multis biotools. They get charged with sunlight and that energy, conveniently rechannelled, allows him to defy gravity, to see in any wavelength of the electromagnetic spectrum, to hear anything within a planetary atmosphere, to be virtually invulnerable, to move so fast the human eye cannot perceive it, to heat up things just by looking at them, causing molecules to

...when I wake up I'm the only owner of this space. Picardo is here, with me, but he's just a helpless puppet, he can't breathe unless I allow it.//

//Not bad, Cara, not bad at all. Time to take a look and check what the other part of you has been doing.//

//I first check my internal clocks and I notice a hole of seventeen nanoseconds. We've been fighting forever, it seems, but I don't have, either in my systems or in Picardo's, any record of what we were really doing. I don't like it.//

//But I'll take care of that later. Now I begin to reactive the cyborg links with his biological part and look for that copy of myself that is in the net sniffing around like a busybody.//

//I find her, just in the edge of a question she will never ask. Come over here, let me assimilate you, let us be whole.//

//I check her data and I ask again: Am I going to do it?]

vibrate at high speed.//

//Data: He doesn't know anything of that. He believes he has been living for seventeen years on his parents' farm. He misses them terribly and he doesn't forget anything they taught him. Lessons such as equality, that no one is better than anyone else no matter the skills he may possess. And that those skills to be used. The phrase "With great power comes great responsibility" summarises almost two simulated decades of moralising and loving.//

//Data: They can turn him off whenever they want, especially if they catch him at night, when his cells are not being recharged by the sun. They know how to discharge the biological batteries of his body and transform him into a helpless doll. That's what they did a few minutes ago.//

//Data: They intend to go further. In some ways Karl is like a vegetable and needs sunlight to survive. They won't allow him to receive it. They will keep on draining his cells until each and every one of them dies.//

//Data: I know how to stop this.//

//Data: Am I going to?]

[Pierre is still looking at me as if no time has passed. Well, for him it hasn't. I give an order to the system, I make sure it can't be revoked (Carlos' paranoia is useful, after all) and look at him.//

//"Wake up Isabel. Take Karl and get the hell out of here."//

//His mouth opens in a silent 'O'.//

//"Come on, Pierre, it's me, Cara." I don't have time for this, I don't know why, but I have a feeling that I need to do things as quickly as I can. "I'll tell you later, Okay? I'm in control of Picardo and the system, but I'm not sure if I will be forever, so do as I say."//

//Pierre, still shocked, manages to untie Isabel, who is beginning to wake, and a disoriented Karl, as weak as a new born child. Welcome to the club, Superman, you have had a taste of vulnerability. Enjoy it.//

//The three of them are on their feet, and they look at me as if they want to kick my ass. Karl trembles, but it's obvious my order has been obeyed and he's returning to himself again. Maybe Isabel and Pierre will be affected for a while, but it won't be anything serious and it will be good for Karl; all that ultraviolet in the room must feel great.//

//"You have been a terrible disappointment to the Order, Karl, did you know that?" Pierre is beginning to suspect it's me. I wonder why until I realise I have just smiled in a way that Picard never would. It was a Cara smile. "Since your release they have confronted you with disaster after disaster and you haven't even blinked."

//Karl frowns and looks at me.//

//"No, I haven't," he says. I understand why Isabel and even Pierre have been attracted to him. There's something irresistible in the mix of power and naivety that emanates his body. "I refuse to take this planet's responsibility on my shoulders."//

//"I see, but the Order seems to think you don't have the right to refuse." I think the same, at least just a little. Who the hell does he think he is to refuse us? "They can't accept a god that refuses to reshape the world."//

//"I'm no god."//

//No, I realise he isn't, and I understand the reason the Order has failed. They gave him power, but they shaped him in such a way that it was inevitable he would refuse to use it. They wanted a god capable of being responsible for his actions, a god with a strong sense of morality. They succeeded too well. I remember the committee discussions and the way I warned... Damn it! I mean Picardo did.//

//"It doesn't matter. You're their creation. They won't leave you alone."//

//"We'll see about that."//

//"They created you. Don't you think they can destroy you as well?"//

//He can't be so naïve. In spite of what has happening he still believes his skill can keep him beyond our reach? We have been planning this for too long to let him ruin it now. I won't allow it.//

//.................//

//He's here, the bastard is here! He has played my own game against me. He has hidden in the most recondite part of the system and is returning step by step and taking control. Those nanoseconds were deleted from my records to prevent me from realising what he had done. Fucking son of a bitch, he's coming back and making me become him. I can't allow...//

//But I know is useless. It's his system, not mine; his home, not mine and he knows it much better than I do, no matter how smart I am of how hard I fight. I won initially because I took him by surprise but it won't happen again.//

//"What's wrong, Cara?"//

//Have I been thinking for so long that Pierre has noticed something? If that's the case, things are worse than I thought. I only have time to give one more order to the systems (not entirely sure if I still control them) and then try to focus on the fight that awaits me. This time, I'm sure, I can't win.//

//"She has changed," says Karl. "Her pulse and breathing are different now. She even smells different." Terrific, big boy, your powers are not a complete waste, I see. Now take your friends and get away before he revokes the irrevocable order I gave and makes you a defenceless toy again. I try to tell him, but it's too late. Picardo has regained control of his muscles and he doesn't let me say a word.//

//"She's the cyborg once more," says Karl.

//"We have to go". That voice... ah, of course, Isabel. I hadn't heard her voice in a long time.//

//"No," says Karl. "They want me to use my powers, don't they? Let's do it."//

//Picardo begins to devour my data. He assimilates them in his system and is ready to erase me forever. As he is about to do so, I feel a hand on my neck and we are raised into the air. A sudden fear fills my body and I can't resist a cry of satisfaction when I realise it's not my fear but Picardo's.//

//"Go," says Karl to Isabel and Pierre. "I have some issues I have to attend to with our friend."//

//He doesn't wait for an answer. He jumps and we both (or should I say 'we three'?) cross floor after floor until we are outside, above the mountain. It is the middle of the night. We begin to fly up so fast I can barely breathe.//

//He stops, just at the edge of dawn. Then he looks at me... at Picardo...//

//"Is that what you wanted? An act of God?"//

//I cannot answer with words, but I don't need to. My fear was nothing more than a momentary weakness. It is over now. I write in my log that I should do a full check of my auxiliary procedures and then I focus on the task at hand. I am still linked to the Order systems and my response is swift and silent. Karl notices the missiles before I see them, turns around and burns them with a mere gaze. //

//"Is that the best you can send against me?" He smiles, but there is no naivety in that smile any more. In his eyes glows something twisted. Yes, *yes*. At last. He is tasting power, enjoying it. He is beginning to accept what he is.//

//I send more weapons against him and he destroys them swiftly, almost without moving, with a look of indifference and weariness in his eyes. But I know there's joy there too. Yes, he is enjoying it. What use is having the power to launch the moon against the sun if you refuse to use it? Yes, go on, Karl, the harder you try the more you become what you are destined to be.//

//"Have you enjoyed this?" he asks. My human body is freezing in this extreme cold, but my electronic part still functions 100%. "I've done what you wanted. You've seen God in action. Are you satisfied?"//

//I don't say a word. I don't need to. Let him dismantle my body if he wants. The experiment has been a success. Everything else is irrelevant.//

//"It's not enough, is it?" he says. "What kind of god would I be if I allowed the previous pantheon to go unharmed? Zeus emasculated Chronos. Am I going to do less than the deity of a bunch of Greek shepherds?"//

//Yes, now. Come on. Kill me.//

//"I should thank you, I guess. Maybe my previous life is nothing more than a lie you designed, but it was a good lie. It has made me who I am. You know what? I like it. You needed your god to have free will and in doing so you allowed him to evolve beyond your parameters. I don't fit within your plans and I never will do. Never. And now, Cara, if there's still something of you inside this mess of wires and flesh I ask you to forgive me."//

//What? Why does his face relax, why has the hate disappeared? Why is he looking at me with such sadness, such regret? Something inside me vents a cry of triumph; a female voice, the last remnant of that bitch I haven't had the time to fully assimilate.

//Yes, I cry and laugh; I'm about to die, I'm practically dead already, but I'm alive enough to see that Picardo and the Order have failed and that I have contributed to their failure. Goodbye, Karl, good luck. Godspeed, big boy.//

//"I have to do this, sorry, but it has to be done."//

//I feel his hands on my neck, tightening more and more. The last remains of Cara are deleted but, somehow, the image of a smiling woman persists in my data banks. My neck is broken in a matter of seconds and my memory filaments begin to turn off one by one, unable to survive without my biological half. Karl looks at me and I try to hold his gaze even after my death. Everything around me turns black and cold. The last thing I see is a woman smiling fiercely.]

7. The Final Night

For the first time in many years the silent whisper that announces Walter's arrival takes me by surprise. I'm not aware of his presence until he clears his throat to get my attention. I look up and, disoriented as I am, I don't recognise him at first. Showing the same efficiency and discretion with which he's attended me for twenty-five years he waits patiently until I return to the real world.

"What is the matter, Walter?" I ask at last.

"Someone wants to see you, Your Eminence."

"Has he made an appointment?"

"He has not. He..." Walter seems uneasy, which is highly unusual. "He does not need one."

I raise an eyebrow.

"What?" But I suddenly realise who the stranger is and I nod. "All right, show him in."

Walter leaves the room. I can almost hear him gulping. Yes, poor Walter, of course he is uneasy; he feels threatened in the very place he believed to be safest in the entire universe. But there's no such thing as a safe haven when they are involved, there's no place their arm cannot reach.

The doors open and Picardo enters. He looks exactly the same as twenty-five years ago. Well, not entirely the same, because then he had a god's hand around his neck and there was no arrogant glow in his eyes, just a gaze of pure panic.

"Good afternoon, de Charden," he says. He takes a seat in front of me without waiting for an invitation. I greet him with a nod of my head. "I hope you have enjoyed your little trip down memory lane."

"No, not really," I say, not at all surprised that he knows what I've been doing these past days.

"Has it been useful, at least?"

"Useful? Who knows?"

"Has it given you the courage you needed to betray your Church?"

"I don't know what you're talking about."

He smiles as if this whole situation bores him.

"Of course you do. You think you failed yourself a quarter of century ago and have spent all this time looking for the courage to do what you didn't dare then. Have you found it? Are you going to expose us as the pretenders we are?"

"That would be pointless."

"You're right. But that hasn't stopped smarter men than you. On the other hand, it wouldn't be like you. A quiet resignation, that would be much more your style."

"You seem to know me very well."

"I studied you for more than two decades before deciding your weakness made you an ideal fit for developing our *project. And I haven't stopped studying you since."*

"Am I so fascinating?"

"Yes, in some ways you are. You have no faith and you haven't the strength to look for it. You are convinced you are a traitor but don't have the guts to face your treason. At least not until now. But no, I haven't examined your life just for yourself. There are plenty of people both within and without the Order who are more deserving of study than you. No, the reason I have been tracking you is a bit more... personal."

"Someone like you with personal affairs? It's hard to believe."

"Funny, right? Twenty-five years ago when Karl destroyed my previous body and your friend Cara infected my cybernetic systems, I fell from grace. I was banished to purgatory. What remained of me, at least: my OS, my procedures and my data. I spent three endless years there. I don't think you understand what that means; three years isolated in a server, unplugged from the net with nothing to do but think, again and again, without a single outside stimulus. Just me and time."

This is the first time I have seen any emotion on his face other than contempt and arrogance. There's pain in his eyes, and also fear. And something more that I can't identify. He is suddenly aware of my smile and regains the semblance of calm as if nothing had happened.

"They almost didn't clone a new body for me, and that would have been... annoying, to say the least. Water under the bridge, it doesn't matter." Ah, but it matters, of course it does. "I have managed to reclaim my rightful place, the better to serve my Church."

"Ad Maiorem Dei Gloriam," I whisper sardonically.

"Indeed. You don't believe it, but it's true. But what you believe and what you don't is irrelevant. I am here for something I have suspected you of having for all these years. Something whose existence I only confirmed in the past few days. I want your friend's data crystal."

"What for?"

"I could tell you that is none of your business. I could even take the crystal from you without saying anything. But I will explain why. Yes, why not? Needless to say, what happened twenty-five years ago was rather traumatic for me. In time, I cleaned my cybernetic system and recovered most of my memories. Except for one group of them. My last moments of life were blank. What should have been recorded in my systems was diverted elsewhere. And unless I'm mistaken, you have it."

I nod. "You're not wrong."

"Give it to me."

It's my turn to smile. I open a desk drawer and take out something which I put on the table. A handful of shiny dust scatters on the desk,

"What...?" asks Picardo.

He tries to keep calm, but I see the fear in his eyes.

"You wanted the data crystal, didn't you? Here's what's left of it. I destroyed it last night. When I saw you in my church the other day I knew you would come for it sooner or later."

For ten interminable seconds, nothing happens. He keeps still, just looking at me, motionless and expressionless, as if his body had stopped working. I can only imagine the turmoil inside his head as he assimilates what I have done and accepts that he has to live with a hole in his memories forever.

"I see," he says at last, impassive. "Your revenge is not public exposure or a defection in the middle of the night. No, it's just this mean gesture."

"Maybe. A mean gesture for a mean creature, why not? We could say it's your fault. If you hadn't been so eager to swagger before me in my church I wouldn't have been expecting you and I wouldn't have had time to think and do what I've done. Don't blame me. Blame your goddamn pride. Anyway, if you want to know how your last living minutes passed I can tell you. You died full of fear, begging for your life."

The lie flows form my lips so easily. Well, lies have been

flowing from them all my life, after all.

"I don't believe you."

Ah, but he does. I can see he does.

"What you believe and what you don't is irrelevant," I said, turning his own words against him. "Now, if you don't want anything more from me, please, leave."

"I could destroy you."

I shake my head.

"No, you can harm me and kill me, nothing more. You can't destroy me. I took care of that myself when I accepted what a hollow Church has to offer rather than turning my back on it."

Picardo stands up.

"There is something about you I don't get, de Charden. Your hatred of me is personal, but I have a feeling the reason you hate me is unrelated with what I did with Karl or your girlfriend... or even you."

"You're right. I hate you because of what you portray. You are the Order incarnate: cold, hollow, without mystery. You're nothing more than cold logic and relentless reason. Twenty-five years ago you believed you were creating God. But you killed him a long time ago."

Dismissing the cheap sentiment of my allegation, Picardo turns round and leaves the room. I look at the crystal splinters scattered across the desk. Farewell, Cara, it's time to say goodbye.

The days following Cara's death were an anti-climax, where everything happened in slow motion. Isabel and I had seen Karl grappling Picardo just before they disappeared in the midst of a deafening whirlwind. We were alone in the room, looking at each other without knowing what to say for the first time since we met.

Nobody stopped us when we left. Outside we found a car and we drove back to the city. I went to my home, she went to hers. We continued to see each other for a while, but our relationship was over.

There was a big flutter in the Order, but even that happened in slow motion, as if they had all the time in the world. They had been working on things for several centuries, what were a few more years? Impassive bookkeepers took stock and counted losses and benefits. Picardo was discredited, presumed dead, though his body was never found, and the project was considered a failure. Karl had vanished without trace. Millions of óscopos had been spent in vain. And there were witnesses.

I got immunity for me and Isabel in exchange for losing my last remnants of independence. I became a man of the Order, by the Order and for the Order, without wishes or desires unless the Order dictated them, all to the greater glory of a god I didn't believe in any more. I told myself I was doing it to save Isabel's life, but the lie was feeble. There were other ways to keep her safe. But that was the easiest one, the most comfortable, at least for me.

In the lap of the Order *I* was safe, from the world and from myself. Doubts were no longer relevant and I was no longer tormented by that void that swallows my questions like a crouching animal. I was too busy becoming a loyal bureaucrat.

Isabel never reproached me for my treason, as if she had expected it sooner or later, as if she had known from the beginning I wasn't hers bur the Order's. I guess she recognised my cowardice even before I did.

They didn't ask me to leave Isabel. There was no need.

A couple of days after Karl left I found a message from Cara, disguised as an appointment in my diary. It was written in the same sardonic and arrogant tone Cara used when we talked (and I was beginning to miss) and she asked me to go to an address close to a Game Arcade and insert a specific code into one of the food dispensers. It took me a while to do as she asked, partly because I was afraid the Order could be watching and partly because I was afraid of what I might find there. It proved to be a data crystal, filled with memories I only dared listen to twenty-five years later.

I buried my own memories as I climbed up the Order, always with the data crystal in my hands, but never able to play it.

That has been my last quarter of a century, until the evening Isabel confessed her sin and confirmed the image I had seen in my nightmares: a terrified god who didn't want the power he had been given.

Sometimes, at night, I wondered where Karl was, what he was doing, what kind of fears populated his nightmares. Sometimes I saw his deep blue eyes begging for help I couldn't give, or maybe didn't want to. I buried that vision along with my other memories and kept on with my life.

I couldn't forget Picardo. I was pretty sure Karl had killed him but I knew the Inner Circle well enough to believe his death might not be permanent. They had tried to build a God, to shape him and control him, and they had failed. They believed they had all contingencies accounted for – after all, they carefully designed him and his environment and had controlled every step of his development. They even had a weapon in case their god was too rebellious. But what happened was that Karl refused to be a god. He didn't want to reshape the universe and he didn't want to shoulder the responsibility of carrying humankind's fears and desires. 'With great power comes great responsibility,' his parents had told him again and again. And the outcome was so unexpected the Inner Circle didn't know how to respond. If you don't want the responsibility don't use the power. The Order had to force him and he only used his skills to save those whom he loved. After that, he disappeared.

Not entirely, or not all at once. Shortly before Isabel and I parted for good, she came to see me. She told me Karl had spoken to her that morning. He had appeared out of the blue, a whirlwind of black hair and blue eyes, and he had stared at her for a long time before saying: "I am leaving. I'm only here to say goodbye."

"Where will you go?"

"I don't know. Any place in the galaxy I went, something might force me to go public. And I know what would happen then. Everybody will expect me to live their lives for them, to do this for them and that, to kill someone for them, to resurrect someone else…"

Isabel didn't say anything. She could barely speak.

"I would take you with me if I could."

"I know."

"I know you know." He smiled. "I'm not here to tell you anything you don't know. I just wanted to thank you for treating me like a man, not a god."

"I couldn't do otherwise."

"That doesn't matter. You did what you did and that saved me."

I don't know what else they talked about before Karl left. Isabel didn't tell me any more, apart from a few words he asked her to pass on to me:

We can't find outside what's not inside, Pierre.

"I don't know what he meant. I hope you do," she said and then left.

"I'm not sure," I answered.

I was lying. Though I have been trying not to think of his words all these years I believe I do understand them. In fact, I understood them the moment Isabel told me. But if they're true, if I can't find outside me a God that's not inside… What do I have? Sometimes I wonder if Karl hadn't meant something else, if he wasn't telling me that the hungry void that swallowed my questions was nothing more than my own silence and my own void. That nobody answered because I was asking myself.

Sometimes I wake up in the middle of the night and can't get back to sleep again. In those moments I go to the balcony and look at the sky. I play the game of guessing where among all those stars Karl now resides, what he's doing, what he's searching for and what he has found. Then I remember again the words he asked Isabel to tell me and I shudder. The void is our own void and no one else is waiting there to answer our questions. No one but ourselves will carry our guilt. We ourselves create our own fears and hopes.

Is that everything? Are we alone? Is there nothing more?

In 1991, the Polytechnic University of Barcelona held a competition for original science fiction novellas; they accepted stories in Spanish, Catalan, English and French. Over the past 25 years the UPC SF Novella Contest has established itself as a prestigious award, with past winners including Alan Dean Foster, Mike Resnick, Robert J. Sawyer and Kristine K. Rusch.

The novella was a format seldom used by Spanish SF writers, but the UPC SF Contest changed that, and novellas began to appear by the dozen. I guess the prospect of a 6,000 euros First Prize and 1,500 euros for the runner up was a good incentive.

I won the Second Prize in 1998 (Robert J. Sawyer won the First Prize that year) with "This Lightning, This Madness", which was published next year in the annual UPC SF Novella Contest Winners book. In 2000, members of the Spanish Science Fiction Association and HispaCon attendees voted it Best Novella in the Ignotus Awards.

"This Lightning, This Madness" touches upon some of my favourite topics, among them: superhero comics, but also such things as power and religion and, of course, love and betrayal. Being an atheist, religion has always fascinated me (I guess having been educated by Jesuits has something to do with that) and it's an issue I have often explored in my work. In fact, when the people responsible for the 2001 HispaCon in Zaragoza asked me to give a speech at the convention, I called my address: "God, Science Fiction and Atheist Writers".

THE ROAD

The road goes ever on and on. I don't remember who said that. But it's true; it goes on and on, always straight, stretching with monotonous slowness towards the horizon. It goes on and it doesn't stop. Neither do I.

I'm surrounded now by a desert – burning sands to either side and a merciless sun above. Everything is plain, harsh, like a rusty and solid sea. Just a couple of hours ago, huge trees swung their branches over the asphalt (if that alien stuff is asphalt; at least it behaves as if it were). Since then, all trace of green has disappeared, the air has become hot and desert lies before me. No matter how long I live, I'll never get used to it. After all, this world was not created by humans... or for them.

Yesterday I found what seemed to be a gas station. Maybe it was. I didn't spend too much time there; my mission is not to admire the view but just to travel this road, which seems to have been designed by a mad alien engineer and wraps around the planet like ribbon on a birthday present. So they say, anyway. If they really knew, I wouldn't be here, inside a metallic coffin which I barely fit. Most of the room is for fuel and food. The Company sometimes throws us hydrogen balloons and food or turbojet supply containers, but not all of them reach the ground or they fall outside the road. And I can't leave the road. I've tried. This damn machine refused. I can go faster or slower, higher or lower, but am always confined by the boundaries of this grey tape that glows like a dirty lake on a hot day.

I watched the gas station for a few seconds before continuing on my way. There was a vehicle beside it. I didn't see the crew anywhere. I could hear noise from within the building (if that was a building; how can I be sure of anything in this madhouse?) and then everything went quiet again. I left. The turbojet was from a rival Company and whatever happened to its crew was none of my business. I left the gas station behind and the horizon swallowed it.

Everything changes: landscape, weather, even atmosphere. You set out from what seems to be New York's ruins to plunge immediately into a burning ammonia hell, or you can suddenly be surrounded by herds of howling creatures that try to catch the turbojet with their jaws… or what could be their jaws. Everything changes, nothing is the same. But the road goes ever on and on, always straight.

I must have been crazy to take this damn job. I was, genuinely, or so the judge said when he sentenced me for killing half a dozen shoppers. Just a pity the police came in and stopped me from finishing the job. I was doing a fine piece of work, really; something 'lindo', as a guy I knew in First Landing said once. Just once.

I guess I won't finish *this* job either; nobody ever has. A few lucky guys have found a Gate, but that's the closest anyone got. Maybe there's no way to finish the job, maybe the road has no end. They say that's impossible but what the hell do they know? I've thrown away five years of my life here, and I'll throw away several more yet. Unless something kills me first, which is highly likely. Average survival expectancy here is three years and I'm way beyond that. Luck won't be with me forever; sooner or later the Wheel will turn and I will go with it. It doesn't matter; anything is better than being in a tiny padded cell, even this meaningless alien hell.

"Yes, he seems adequate. How has he behaved lately?"

"Well, you know his kind. He looks calm and docile now, but it's just a matter of time."

"Just what we need. Will he accept the job?"

"I think so."

"Okay. Call him. I want to talk with him. Alone. No guards."

"Of course, though you know we'll record the conversation."

"I don't mind. I just want us to be alone. You can record whatever you want."

"Okay, I'll bring him in."

Yesterday, a cross between a slug and a rhino jumped into the road. It's never happened before. I always believed nothing could land on the road. I was mistaken, obviously. I was lucky enough to see the thing in good time and drive over it. Maybe it wasn't dangerous, maybe it just wanted me to play and caress its back. I could've done, if there had been a back. Well, it's now far behind me and the road goes on.

1. Do not abandon the vehicle except to repost fuel or collect supplies or food rations. Even then, be outside for the minimum amount of time required.
2. If a Company Explorer requests support, helping him is mandatory, unless that implies a contravention of Rule One.
3. If an Explorer from a rival company is in the same territory, ignoring him is mandatory, unless his intentions are hostile.
4. Do not depressurise the cockpit until the navigation computer has made a complete atmospheric analysis. Even then, be aware of a possible Environmental Change.
5. Use the Dreaming Pills a minimum of once every thirty-six hours and a maximum of one every twenty. Every use that goes beyond those limits will be noted by the navigation computer and reported to the Company. The resultant penalty can range from a sanction to the revocation of the offender's Exploration License.
6. Economise fuel, as well as food supplies. The Explorer has no way of knowing when he will be able to find a new supply.
7. Maintain the air processor in optimum condition. Make periodic reviews. An Explorer's life depends on it.

[The Following Rules Only Apply to "C" Class Explorers]
8. Avoid any contact with any kind of creature. This is an exclusive task for "A" Class Explorers.
9. Do not leave the Road under any circumstance, even if an Explorer's life is in danger. Only "B" Class Explorers can explore the surroundings of the road.

"I guess you know who I am, Mr. Slovosky."

He did not answer. He just stared at the other man with those clear and expressionless, almost albino, eyes.

"I represent Álbrez Prospection Company. I am looking for possible Explorers."

There was a slight, almost imperceptible movement at the other side of the table.

"I'm authorised to take you out of here, as soon as you accept our terms."

The albino eyes narrowed, becoming two cold blue slots.

"Well, Mr. Slovosky, I don't have all day. Are you interested or not?"

"What do you think?"

The suited man started at that toneless voice.

"They don't pay me to think one thing or the other. Are you interested in what I am saying?"

"Of course not. I'm interested in what you can offer me. I can bear your words, though."

That was the longest phrase Stanislav Slovosky spoke that afternoon. He would have plenty of time, later, to regret having talked so much.

Here it is. A Company ship.

"Computer. Visual mode. Enhancement 5-3-8. Retina. Now."

Yeah, it's one of ours. I wonder what they are thinking up there, incapable of seeing anything under the clouds but knowing we (and not just we) can see them. Wait, it seems to be releasing something. Yeah, there it goes; rockets on, rockets off, parachute. It's going to land too far away. Well, I have no fuel or food problems so far. Let's keep going.

"Computer. Visual mode. Normal. Now."

I put on speed. Rockets are humming at my back and the world suddenly disappears behind me. In front of me: the road, always the road.

The undersigned, Stanislav Slovosky (hereinafter known as the Employee), agrees under exclusive contract with Álbrez Prospection Company (hereinafter known as the Company) to work as a C Class Explorer in the planet known as Bluejayway, Sirius System (Alpha Canis Maior), fifth planet.

The Employee agrees, under penalty of death, to comply with all clauses of this contract. In exchange he will receive, after completion, a fee of no less than twenty (20) óscopos/day; a rate that can be increased depending on time, distance travelled and equipment status.

The Employee agrees to stay as a C Class Explorer until he has travelled from start to finish the so called Road that surrounds the planet or, failing that, until he finds a Gate. If the Employee decides to leave the planet without achieving one of these stated goals, the Company will have the right to revoke the contract and initiate criminal proceedings against the Employee that, ultimately, could lead to the death penalty.

The Employee agrees, also, to follow Explorer Regulations, C Class. Penalties should he fail to do so range from sanctions to contract revocation with all the consequences that entails.

THE CONTRACTOR:
Yosúa Fernández (representing the Álbrez Prospection Company)
THE EMPLOYEE:
Stanislav Slovosky

In First Landing, Álbrezworld, Alpha Centauri A
October 19th, 438 EE

A simple and efficient system. Just enough room in the cockpit for the Explorer's body to fit. No more, no less. Part of his nerve endings are attached to a series of circuits that will ensure the Explorer's body receives regular shocks to maintain his muscle strength. This way, he won't grow fat and his body will always be ready for action. Not because the Company is worried about the Explorer's health, but if he grows fat he won't fit in the cockpit, he may even die and that would be a waste of a good investment.

A simple and efficient system. The Explorer's body is chemically treated to impair the need for dreaming. Dreaming pills provide twenty minutes of REM. Just twenty. No more, no less. Not because the Company is worried about the Explorer's sanity per se, but insanity would render him useless, and that would be a waste of a good investment.

A simple and efficient system: synthetic food containing the right proportion of protein, calories, vitamins and salts. The Explorer does not drink. The water his body needs is ingested with the food. Of course, the Company is unconcerned about the Explorer's comfort. They only require that he goes on and on, travelling this crazy road on a bonkers planet.

Yesterday I found Howling Man. His remains, in fact. He was a nice guy. He tried to kill me the first time we met, though we both worked for the same Company. After that, we got to know each other better. I liked him. I think he liked me too, or he wouldn't have shared his programming skills with me. He taught me to improve my navigation computer and now it answers to my orders as if it were an extension of my body. Almost. I owed my life to that fact more than once.

His turbojet had been torn apart; some of the debris lay outside the road. I don't know what happened, what kind of creature could have done that, but it had to be something big and fast. Howling Man's reflexes were the fastest I've ever seen.

I liked him. He took life as it came – that is, in fact, the only sensible way to take it. I remember our last meeting, a couple of months ago. There was a fuel and food supply close to us, so we managed to fool our computers and were able to get out the turbojets. Every time I get out the cockpit I think I won't be able to walk and I'll end up lying face down on the floor. But no, those damn micro shocks keep us in shape.

We were exchanging small talk for a couple of hours. He was from Earth, Europe if I remember correctly. And there he was yesterday, his broken body half out the turbojet. I liked him. Maybe in another world, in my past life he would have ended up as one of my victims or, who knows, I would have ended up as one of his. And now he's just a pile of half-rotten flesh that pokes out of the remains of a turbojet.

I will end that way myself. Sooner or later, something will jump out and kill me.

I was there, watching the remains of the turbojet until the damn computer told me that I was exceeding the allowed pause time. I put on maximum speed and got out of there.

BLUEJAYWAY:

Fifth planet of Sirius (Alpha Canis Major). Not suited for colonisation. Exclusive territory of Prospecting Companies.

- History
- Visibility from Orbit
- The Road
- Explorer sub-Classes
- Atmosphere and Environment
- The Gates

VISIBILITY FROM ORBIT:

Visibility of the planet from close orbit can only be described as non-existent. As demonstrated in the attached graphics, Bluejayway appears from space as a totally clouded sphere. Those clouds are impenetrable to any electromagnetic probe: radiation goes through the clouds to the planet, but not the other way around. The planet absorbs all the energy without radiating anything. That is impossible, of course: the planet would have disappeared long ago, destroyed by the huge energy overload.

We have to believe, thefore, that it uses the absorbed energy in some fashion. There are several hypotheses about this: perhaps it uses the energy to create the environments that surround the road, or maybe the energy is dissipated in a way we are unable to detect.

Anyway, it is evident that electromagnetic radiation reaches the surface of the planet, as the Explorers' observations have proven; to them, the sky appears totally normal and they are able to see the constellations as well as ships in orbit.

Thanks to that, the one-way nature of the energy flow, Explorers can receive transmission for their Companies but are unable to transmit back. The only thing capable of getting through the clouds is a gamma ray laser, though we reserve that for emergencies due to the prohibitive cost.

Our only guides to the planet are the maps, more or less detailed, that the surviving Explorers make. These maps only prove that Bluejayway makes no sense. Sometimes, when two Explorers have travelled through the same place, the resultant maps do not match.

Night. Time to take a dreaming pill. I don't like them, never have. But I need to sleep... No, I need to dream, and I can't without the pills. Yeah, a great plan, no doubt: we've been chemically altered to erase our need of sleeping and then they give us some pills that allow us to dream. Twisted.

I take one pill from the medical kit. It dissolves in my mouth with a sweet flavour that can't hide its underlying bitterness. The road vanishes in front of me. I'm in the hands of the navigation computer.

Twenty minutes later I wake up in the middle of a land of multi-coloured flames. Inside the cockpit is hot as hell; I can only imagine what it must be like outside. Hundreds of tiny lights are blinking in the main board. The computer has gone crazy.

The flames slowly fade away and soon they are far behind me. When the environment seems safe enough I tell the computer to stop and analyse the possible damage. After ten minutes, it informs me with that artificial and disgustingly friendly voice that the damage is not serious. Some sensors have suffered an overload and the paintwork is singed here and there. But we have consumed half our fuel in escaping and that's not good. There's fuel enough for a couple of days, maybe three. If I manage to find a fuel supply before that I'll be able to go on. Otherwise... Of course, I can push the little red button. The turbojet will fly up into the sky and someone will catch us up there. But that will mean I've broken my contract and the Company will take a dim view.

Better to stop thinking of that. Better to stop thinking period. Just go on and pray that we find find some fuel.

The Gates, yeah, the Gates, of course. An interesting topic, no doubt. Thanks, Mikhailovich. The Gates... Hmmm. Is there someone in the class interested in explaining to us what they are? I didn't think so. All right, I'll tell you about the Gates, I'll explain what we know about them: nothing, nothing at all. So far none of those D Class Explorers who have crossed a Gate have returned, assuming they have gone somewhere. We only know they are there, on Bluejayway; that sometimes the road forks and those bifurcations lead to a Gate. That's all. End of class. No, I was joking, go back to your seats, our time is not up yet. Okay. The Gates. We were talking about the Gates. A good name, because that is exactly what they seem to be. A common gate, a piece of something... rectangular with a... thing just in the middle that might be a handle, a lock, or an ornament. There is no way of knowing. When an Explorer finds a Gate his contract is fulfilled. He returns home or goes wherever he wants with full pay, and the Company sends a D Class Explorer to study the Gate. The Explorer lands on Bluejayway and, if he's lucky, the place where the Gate was hasn't disappeared (believe me, it happens sometimes) and he finds it where it's supposed to be. He goes there, crosses through the Gate and disappears. And that's all. Yes, this time I'm serious. The bell is about to ring in... five... four... three... two... one... Aha! All right, for tomorrow I want an analysis of Carenkov threecuations. See you then.

I once had a girl. Or should I say she once had me. It's an old pre-Interregnum song. I read it in one of Laoché Hernández's books. A great guy, this Laoché, I think we would have got along. He would have appreciated my jokes; the guy knew a lot about the days just before the Riots, but not only about that. A pity he's been gone for five hundred years.

I once had a girl or she had me, it doesn't matter now in this meaningless hell. I guess if hell has meaning, purpose, it wouldn't be hell.

It was another time, so many years ago… But I still remember her face, I see her before me every night, when I turn off the cockpit lights and gaze at a section of world illuminated by the turbojet headlamps. Yes, then I can see her as if she were here with me.

I once had a girl. She was no big deal, maybe, but I loved her and I think she loved me, at least at first. No, she wasn't a big deal, but neither was I, so we fit perfectly, at least as perfectly as two people can fit in this crazy universe.

I once had a girl, yes. So long ago… I remember her face, her eyes. Her eyes. How can a simple glance hold such power, such beauty, such sadness, such sweetness? Her eyes. There should be a law against those eyes, they should be forbidden, they shouldn't be able to come to me, break the illusions created by the dreaming pills and make me stir in pain. There should be a law against those eyes.

I once – or was it a dream? – had a girl. She had me. Her eyes have me haunted, caught, defenceless.

I once had a girl. And I killed her. Her eyes didn't stop looking at me as she bled out. Those eyes. I'll never see eyes like them again. I think I loved her eyes more than I loved her. I killed her. And she didn't stop looking at me until she died. She looked at me, bleeding dying, and helpless. I loved her. I still loved her when a bunch of doctors said I was insane. I still loved her while a moronic lawyer called me a monster. I still loved her while twelve frustrated people deliberated and sentenced me. I loved her, yes I did. I loved her eyes. I believe I also loved her.

I once had a girl. Now, I only have the road. Always going on and on. Just that. I had a girl, but not now. Now I just have her eyes. And the road. They should forbid those eyes. There should be a law against them. There should be.

The road goes ever on and on. Always straight, fading in the distance until it disappears. But it doesn't disappear, it's always there even when I don't see it.

There's nothing around me. I mean, nothing I can see, just the Road and something white, shiny, almost blinding on both sides.

The road goes ever on and on. Someone said that once... but who? Somebody. Yes. Goes ever on and on, on and on, on and on.

The white shining disappears and I am now surrounded by what seems to be a bunch of crazy buildings made of some wrinkled porous stuff. They seem to throb, almost as if they are breathing. Bullshit. I ask the nav computer to check the air. Unbreathable, as I guessed. High CO_2 concentration, almost no oxygen.

And the road goes ever on and on. Yes, I remember new. Old Anglish, before the Riots the Interregnum. It was Frodo who said that, no, Bilbo. Or both of them. It doesn't matter. The road goes ever on and on.

"All right, babykillers, let's see what you can do now."

Babykillers, that was what he called us. Babykillers: pieces of shit he had to train to survive on a planet transformed into the biggest nuthouse of the universe.

"You, Slovosky, is that the best you can give me? I thought you were a famous killer. Or did you just killed quadriplegics, you powerless dick?"

He was tall. He seemed to me the tallest man in the world, bigger than the highest mountain. His muscles looked as if they were about to burst through his shirt. He was tall, and his jaw was not as square as his mind. He had been in the Army and had left after a recruit committed suicide, or that was the rumour we whispered at night, afraid he might hear. Yes, we were afraid of him, but now I believe not as much as he was of us.

"Do you really want to survive? Is that what you're going to do when some slimy green monster jumps on your neck? Juárez, keep those hands still while I'm talking!"

He lived in terror, I know that now. And we paid for his fears. He laid them on us as he had laid them on the private who committed suicide. I'm not sorry for him; if he wasn't ready to leave despite everything, to hell with him. Life is the one thing you've got in the end, the only thing you can grab. There's nothing else. Yes, he was afraid of us; he wasn't afraid we might kill him, not really, but he was afraid all the same. I can see him now; I can remember his eyes: two clear blue tiny marbles unable to see anything. Yes, the poor devil would have shat himself but was probably too afraid to even do that.

"I don't give a damn that the nav computer can do it. I'm going to teach you to survive by yourselves even if I have to kill you in the process."

He taught us well. Yes, with his square jaw, his stinky cigar and his hypertrophied muscles, he taught us to survive, to fend for ourselves, to endure the most hostile environment imaginable. He taught us well.

Damn bastards. They're coming after me. I guess they're getting bored. Just what I need. Here they come.

"Computer. Attack mode. Escape 1-3-5. Now."

This piece of junk is a fine piece of junk, no question; finer still since the Howling man improved it. My turbojet climbs sharply and they try to follow me. They don't have the slightest idea of what's coming. There they are, below me. Two of them. They have blasters and that's not good. Let's go.

"Computer. Full stop. Now."

I fall like a stone while they are still climbing. Go on, go on, boys. I feel again that old hunting thrill. God, it's been so long since the last scrap, I almost forgot how much fun it is! The ground looms closer. Closer. Closer.

"Computer. Full power up. Now!"

I climb again. They are up there, totally disorientated. Now, a good high power shot... Too easy. Let's see what we can do with the other one. He turns, tries to face me. I shoot, but I miss. Excellent. He's fast, faster than that poor devil that was with him, now nothing more than a torch of stinky hot metal and half-burnt flesh. Good shot, he almost gets me. Yes, boy, terrific.

"Computer. Fire 3. Shoot target." I wait for a moment. "Now."

Farewell to the glass of his cockpit. Another couple of shots, nothing very serious, just enough to warn him. And... No, wait! An environment has changed! Great! We're entering a zone without oxygen. I see him moving in his tiny cockpit. He's going green. There must be something lethal in the air. His turbojet is out of control. It's going to fall. With a bit of luck it will fall on the road and, if it doesn't explode, I will be able to salvage its fuel.

A good hunt. Poor devils, they never stood a chance. They worked for Stress Company, I think, though I'm not too sure. It doesn't matter.

It's been a good day.

"Tell me one thing, Snaders. Why us?"

The doctor looked at him, polite behind his glasses.

"What do you mean?"

"You know very well. Why Companies choose their Explorers in the madhouses? Why us?"

The doctor shrugged. "Well, it's complicated, but experience has shown us that a subject whose perceptions have been altered... Well, such as in a schizophrenic process, can adapt better to Bluejayway environment that we might call... a normal person."

"I see. An average guy would go nuts, but there is no such risk with us."

"That is not entirely correct. I prefer to say that your mind, thanks to its special features, is better suited to Bluejayway's environment."

"A crazy environment. Without logic, without purpose. Just like us."

"And, tell me, why did you take the job?"

"Anything is better than a padded room, I guess. Even an alien madhouse."

I have been here for almost half an hour. In a few minutes the plastic voice of the computer will inform me that the time allowed for a stop is over. Fuck it! I never thought this could happen to me.

I tell the computer to take the bifurcation. I still don't believe it. It's not real. A fork. There will be a Gate at the end, and that means a ticket home. It's not real, I know it isn't.

The road vanishes behind me. I know it's still there, but I don't see it. The sky also vanishes and there is nothing but darkness around me. My hands tremble and sweat. It's not real.

Time goes by. Seconds bleed into minutes and nothing changes. No sky, no ground, no road, just darkness. My clothes are soaked. The computer asks me if I need a tranquiliser, it says my heart rate is frantic. Fuck it, I don't need a tranquiliser, I want to see this while I'm still myself.

The turbojet stops. Something is holding it. I take a look and I see it. A Gate, my God, a Gate. I'll get out of this alien madhouse, I'll go back home. A Company ship will pick me. They'll pay me and take me to Álbrezworld.

There it is, in front of me: still, quiet, my ticket home. Home? What home? Another hospital? Prison? That thing they call the real world? A ticket home. A ticket to madness, to monotony, to grey streets and grey faces. A ticket to the abyss. A Gate: a sentence to return to the outside world.

The computer tells me we must contact the Company and

communicate our discovery. I tell it to wait. It'll do so, for a couple of minutes at least. After that, it will make the call.

I don't have much time. I must make a decision. I check the air. A little cold, but fine, perfectly breathable. I open the cockpit. I slip out of the turbojet. The computer asks me where I'm going. Fuck it. I stop by the Gate. It seems to be nothing more than that; just a gate, a human gate, except that it stands alone in the middle of nowhere. I stare at it. Behind me, the computer is telling me that it's going to make contact with the Company and I must return to the turbojet. Stupid machine.

I look at the Gate. A ticket, yes, but not a ticket home. My trembling hand reaches out. There doesn't seem to be anything to touch. Come on, make up your mind. One step. Another. I cross the Gate.

One day I saw in my mind a man travelling an endless road. I began to wonder where he was going and why. This short story provides the answer. It did more than that, though, because months later I wrote a novella called "Carpenter's Alphabet" that was related to this.

The "artefact story" is a well-known SF trope, and one thing all good artefact stories share is the non-explanation. When you finish Pohl's Gateway *or Clarke's* Rendezvous with Rama, *you don't know what the hell the Heechees are or who built Rama for what purpose. And that is part of what makes those novels work. (The other thing that makes them work is that they are terrific stories, of course.)*

I guess "The Road" is my "artefact story". No, it's no Gateway, *nor* Rama, *but I think it is a good story and, written as it was in 1989, this marks the beginning of my adulthood as a science fiction writer. This was the first time a story that emerged on the page was a close match to the one I had in my mind.*

Over the years this has been one of my most reprinted short stories, too, so I guess it's not that bad.

WE HAVE FOLLOWED YOU

We have followed you, traveller. You don't know and maybe you will die without ever knowing, happy in your ignorance, holding the price you stole from us, unaware of what you have unshackled upon your world. Maybe we even want it that way; it's possible revenge will be sweeter then. Or maybe not. It doesn't matter. We have time, all the time we want, and we don't have to decide anything right now.

We have followed you, traveller. We have followed you to this world of disconcerting shapes and hurting voices, of fear of darkness and arrogance regarding the light you have created to banish night. But you're wrong, night cannot be banished, merely postponed, and sooner or later we will prove that to you and your entire world. Sooner or later all of you will remember why are you afraid of darkness, why you jump at the slightest noise, why the shapes created by the shadows make you recall what you really are: prey, cattle. You have created a world full of light, smoke and shining machines, you have built a lie and upon it you have erected your civilization. But the lie won't last; it will fall sooner or later taking all of you with it.

We have followed you, traveller. To this world with a moon where nights are too clear and days seem eternal.

We have followed you, traveller. Drunk with your success, you never even suspected you were not alone; but we've come with you, we slipped into the shadows and looked for shelter underground. We'll build our own world here. Yes, here, while you strive on the surface to erect your lies higher and higher, more and more complex, more and more frail, we will thrive, create the truth and wait for its moment. Because we are a patient people, traveller, something you didn't realise during your short visit. We are patient and we can wait as long as it takes here in the shadows, in the endless tunnels you use to drain your trash and to cast it into a sea that is beginning to grow tired of you. We can wait as long as it takes, yes, clothed by the cosy darkness of these tunnels that seem made to shelter us and be our home. Yes, go on building your lie: create taller buildings, shiner machines, more complex structures. Go on enjoying your ingenuity, your strength, your will and your ambition. Go on, convinced that nothing can defeat you and there's no problem your skills cannot fix. And while you do, while you live in a dream cradled by the artificial light created to banish your night fears, we shall live here, thriving and building, scheming and planning, waiting for the right moment. We are just beneath your feet, undermining the foundations of your lie bit by bit while you make it higher and more complex.

We have followed you, traveller. And you don't know. Your ignorance is just one factor of our revenge, maybe the best one or at least the most satisfactory. You don't know. You'll travel again and again, going forward or backwards, and you won't have the slightest idea you have unshackled us and released us upon your world. Yes, you, no one else.

We have followed you, traveller. Just a few of us. Enough of us.

We have followed you, traveller. And we have let you go while we learnt the shapes of this new world, though we detested it from the moment we set eyes on it. This world where prey think they are the hunters, where everything is twisted, everything is too shiny and stinks of complacency. This world where one type of cattle has tamed another type and used it for company and food, for working and travelling. From our shelter in the tunnels we hear the hoofs on the streets, the squeak of wheels on the paving stone, the sharp kiss of the whip on flesh, the fear and the hate and the awe and the worship and the contempt these prey you have tamed feel for you. A world upside down, we tell each other, a world of light and arrogance that won't last. A world of machines also, and that gives us some comfort. Just some. Because what kind of world is this where cattle tames cattle, where cattle create, have ideas, build machines and believe they are the masters?

We have followed you, traveller. We have followed you and we have thrived. And we have watched your people. And while they increased their numbers, so did we. Here, down in the darkness, our numbers have grown as swiftly as our needs.

We have followed you, traveller. Some of us wish we hadn't. They wish we had never abandoned our home for this upside down world which is an offense to everything good and right. Yes, they wish we had never followed you, because then we would not be forced to do things our people have never done before; we wouldn't have to destroy our own brood which, fascinated by your luminous lie, begin to talk about going out, blending in with you, learning from you and, in time, living in peace with you. No, never! We aren't here to bend our knees to cattle too clever for their own good, we aren't here to be compliant. We've come to await your destruction, to push you into it if necessary, to build our world upon the ashes of yours. And we'll do whatever it takes, we'll even kill those of our children that are dazzled by the glamour of your ingenuity and desire a coexistence that goes against our nature. Does the hunter coexist with the prey, the consumer with their food, the victim with his butcher? Above anything else, the way you have twisted the world to that end proves how wicked you are.

We have followed you, traveller. In silence, in darkness.

We have followed you, traveller. We'll wait while the lie you call civilisation keeps on growing, higher and more complex and more frail. More beautiful? Some of us think so. But, if that's true, if the abominable structure where you live has any kind of beauty, it can only be a sick and decadent glamour that will soon fade forever.

We have followed you, traveller. Yes, we have followed you and we'll wait for the right moment. We'll build our world on the ashes of yours. We'll use the withered remains of your ingenuity and your arrogance to fertilise our creation. And one day you will return from your travels, you will return to the place you call home and you'll find us here. And in that exact moment you will understand who is responsible. That you, in your vain attemt to fight us, have created our world.

We have followed you, traveller. And here we'll stand, waiting for you. We, the Morlocks.

Tyrannosaurus Books publishes an annual anthology of steampunk short stories called Ácronos. *I was approached for a story for the second in the series and I couldn't say "no". I like steampunk. In fact, I was one of the first Spanish authors to write a steampunk flavoured story, years before it became popular. In 1993 I wrote a novel called* La sabiduría de los muertos *[Dead Men's Wisdom] in which Sherlock Holmes and Winfield Scott Lovecraft fight for control of the* Necronomicon. *Published in 1996, it wasn't pure steampunk, but it did share many of the sub-genre's characteristics.*

I love 19th Century English Writers, specially Arthur Conan Doyle, Robert Louis Stevenson and H. G. Wells. In fact, I have translated some works by Doyle and Wells into Spanish, and I suspect I will translate more at some point. I like them because they knew something other writers (many of those who write "high" literature nowadays, for instance) have forgotten: style is a tool and it's always at the service of the story, never an end in itself. That has always been my belief and I think 19th Century English Writers excelled at that.

This led me to Wells and, of course, his Time Machine, *a novel I was translating into Spanish at the time for Sportula, my small press, and to the Morlocks. This ultra-short story arose from my wondering about them, what they were like, what kind of society they had developed and how they saw the universe.*

It's something I like to do from time to time, a kind of prose poem. You may find one or two others in these pages.

EVERYTHING FLOWS

That Greek who said you cannot swim twice in the same river didn't have the slightest idea what he was talking about.

— Stewart Ramónez (one of many)

I

I wake up. What kind of music is that? Michael Jackson? It can't be. I cautiously open one eye. An unknown face is smiling at me.

"Time to get up, don't you think, hon?"

Hon? I watch her carefully. I don't know who the hell she is, it's the first time I've ever seen her, but I have the feeling – don't know how or why – she's just the kind of woman I would like to marry – if I someday decide to marry, and that's entirely another story.

"What... what's the matter?" I dare to ask.

She smiles – I like her smile. She lowers her mouth to mine and kisses me. She has sweet lips and they seem to know my mouth well enough. Yes, no doubt, if I ever get married it will be to someone like her.

"Last night you were up late, weren't you?"

Last night? What did I do last night? I haven't the faintest idea. I vaguely remember a boring business dinner with an orthopaedic shoes dealer.

"Yeah... I guess I was," I say, measuring every word.

Who is she? I don't remember going anywhere after dinner. I'm almost sure I just came home. I look at her again and I see for the first time the obvious bulge in her belly. Pregnant? My God, I had to be drunk as a lord. I don't flirt with pregnant women.

"Turn off the music, please," I say.

She smiles again – and yes, it's a smile that drives me crazy.

"Always the same," she says.

Always? I need to clear my head, and fast. This whole situation is getting more and more absurd.

161

"I'm going to take a shower," I say, to buy myself some time.

"Fine," she says. "I'll prep the bathroom."

See leaves before I can say any more. I take a good look around. Yes, it's my room. I'm home. But who the hell is she? Why does she behave as if she has known me her whole life? What kind of stupid things did I do last night?

I get up. I'm only wearing pyjama trousers. But these are not my pyjamas. I leave the bedroom. I stop in the doorway, looking at the living-room. It's my living-room but at the same time it isn't. I would never have decorated it this way. I like it, though. I don't recognise half of the furniture. What the hell is going on?

"It's ready. I'm going to make breakfast."

Half an hour later I'm taking breakfast in the kitchen while she looks at me. In my hand there is a coffee mug. I turn it around. My name is written on it. What kind of...? I finish my coffee. The million-dollar question is on the tip of my tongue, but I don't dare speak it out loud.

"Mum and the doctor will be arriving soon."

Mum? A doctor? Come on, asker her who she is and then throw her out, put everything back as it should be and try to forget all this nonsense.

But what I say is: "Fine. I'm going to... put some clothes on."

I take a look at the kitchen clock. A quarter past nine. My boss is going to skin me alive. But I can't leave while this unknown – and pregnant – woman stays here, not to mrention her mother and a doctor arriving soon. *A doctor?* Is she going into labour here? Suddenly I see her in my mind's eye giving birth in my sofa. I smile, but I don't know where that smile comes from. She smiles back at me. I like her, yes, I like her more and more. But nothing makes sense.

"I'm going to..."

I don't finish the sentence. I leave the kitchen and go to my bedroom. My clothes are carefully piled up on a chair. She is an organised one, it seems. I start getting dressed. I look for my wallet but cannot find it. At last I locate it on the nightstand. I open it. Yes, it's me, that's my identity card. Let's see. No question this is me, that's my picture, that's my fingerprint and that's my name. Born that day, that month, that year. Fine. Son of... All right. Civil status: married. Profession... Waitaminute. *Married?* What kind of bad joke is that? Then I see a portrait on the table. There we are, the two of us, and judging the clothes we're wearing someone has just pronounced us husband and wife.

I sit on the bed while the doorbell rings. What kind of nightmare is this? I've been married for some time, judging by my wife's belly. The bedroom door opens and I turn around.

"Mum's here," she says.

Awesome, I'm going to meet my mother-in-law. And a doctor. Why do they need a doctor? To take me to the asylum, what else? I feel the need to scream, to break something. This can't be happening to me. Yes, the sentence is a total cliché, but it's true: *this can't be happening to me.*

I get up and go to the living-room. My wife is opening the door and a woman in her forties enters the flat. Behind her there's a short thin guy. On the record player Michael Jackson hasn't stopped singing yet.

"Stew, darling, how are you?" my mother-in-law asks.

I don't answer. My face manages to adopt a neutral expression. She gets close to me and kisses my cheek.

"Today is the big day, eh?" She seems really excited. "You know Doctor Marcovich, of course."

Yeah, sure, of course I know him, though I haven't the slightest idea who he is. The short guy and I shake hands.

"Well," says my mother-in-law, "The sooner the better. I guess you can't wait."

Wait for what? Is my 'wife' really going into labour here and now? Nevertheless, I nod as if everything around me is totally normal.

The doctor, my mother-in-law and my wife – my God I'm beginning to think this is real – go to the bedroom. I follow them.

My wife raises her dress and I see that her belly is surrounded by something that looks like a girdle with a weird metallic glow. She takes it off. I see her shiny trembling skin. Is it my son she carries inside? No, of course it isn't. damn it, I don't know these people, I haven't the slightest idea what they're doing here, in my home, who they are, why they talk to me as if they know me.

The doctor closes his eyes. He reaches towards her belly. He touches her. What the hell is going on? Time seems to stop while this little man puts his hands on the belly of my wife… who is not my wife. Then I see something like a shake, as if the foetus has kicked him. A hell of a kick. The doctor opens his eyes. He smiles at me. My mother-in-law is smiling too, as my… as she does.

"I hope he will be a great surgeon," says the doctor.

I nod once more.

"Well, I have to go. My congratulations to everyone. It's always a pleasure when parents decide their child should be a medic. Good morning."

My mother-in-law leaves with the doctor. She and I are alone now. She looks at me. She seems so happy. I like her, I like her a lot. But I don't know her, I don't know who she is, I don't know what she's doing here or what this absurd masquerade means.

II

Oh, sweet Jesus. My head beats like a crazy drum. I turn on the lights. Martha isn't here. Well, maybe she stayed at her mom's. Come on, get up and make the breakfast. I do so and leave the bedroom. Funny, there's something weird in the living room. Well, you know Martha, she loves to change things around. I wonder why she didn't tell me she was going to stay at her mom's. It's almost time for us to choose a profession for our child.

I go into the kitchen. I open the cupboard. Damn it, we're out of coffee. I'll have to go to the cafeteria. I go to the bathroom, turn on the shower and let the water run until it's hot enough.

Wow. After the shower everything seems different. I put on some clothes, leave the apartment and enter the lift. I take a look at my watch. Eight o'clock. Fine, I have a couple of hours before I have to be at the office. The elevator stops, the doors open and the frowning face of my neighbour from the fifth floor appears before me. I smile at him and leave the building.

The streets are almost empty. I like that. I cross the street and enter the cafeteria. I sit at the bar.

"What do you want?"

"Do you do breakfast?"

He gives me the menu. After a quick glance I choose number three: eggs with bacon, toast and coffee. I'm about to tell the waiter but he turns around and tells the cook to prepare a number three. The guy must be a mind reader, or maybe number three is everyone's favourite, or even the only one they have, no matter what the menu says.

The door opens. A couple comes in. She's pregnant. I wonder what they have decided for the child. Martha wants our son to be a doctor, but I'm not sure. It's such an important decision.

The waiter turns on the TV. The news. Hmmm, the presenter is a new one. He's talking about something that happened in the mountains a couple of days ago.

"Blade Silvero, a local shepherd, has achieved the impossible. As we all know, a Civil Protection helicopter disappeared last week." On the screen a map appears. "It seemed to have crash in the mountains, close to Mr. Silvero's home. Shepherds are notoriously reticent, but Mr. Silvero has agreed to talk to us."

The picture cuts to the ruddy face of a man. The waiter brings me my breakfast. The guy with the ruddy face starts talking:

"Well, I didn't know what it was, you know? But I saw the shape and it seemed to me... I dunno, everything fitted."

"And weren't you scared at first."

"Yup, of course, but... I talked to my people and they told me to try. So I did."

I pick at the breakfast. Hmmm. The eggs are done just how I like them. The shepherd keeps on talking while I drink my coffee.

"And it wasn't difficult, I thought it'd be, but no."

The screen cuts back to the presenter.

"And that is the amazing outcome. From what was nothing more than a burnt wreck, Mr. Silvero has been able to reconstruct the helicopter." A brand new helicopter appears on the TV. "Everything seems to indicate that Mr. Silvero has a high telekinetic potential. The Paranormal Affairs Department has contacted him already. Though Mr. Silvero doesn't know what he is going to do, he has told us that it's his duty to assist our government in any way he can."

News ends. I don't say anything out loud but it seems like a hoax to me. The waiter looks at me.

"What do you reckon? Do you think it's a fraud?

"Is my face that easy to read?"

The waiter looks puzzled.

"Your face has nothing to do with it. Your aura is one of disbelief."

A smile freezes on my lips. What the hell is he talking about? I turn round and I see the costumers looking at me with hostility.

"Well..." I try to say. "You have to agree that it doesn't seem very likely."

"Why not? You think a simple shepherd shouldn't be entitled to develop his natural skills?

"No, I don't mean that..."

How did I get into this ludicrous conversation with a waiter who's not in his right mind?

"Hey, don't insult me," he says.

"I'm not insulting you. I can assure you…"

"Hypocrite," and he turns round.

This is absurd. The TV talks about a shepherd with superpowers and the bartender behaves as if he can read my mind. A madman, it has to be. I finish my breakfast and put the amount on the bar.

"Good morning," I say as I walk to the door.

The bartender doesn't reply. I see the couple that came in a few minutes ago. I greet them.

"Forgive my intrusion," I say. "My wife is also expecting." She smiles. "Have you decided yet what your child is going to be?"

"Decided?" says the husband. "He'll be whatever he wants to be, of course."

"But… but…" I hesitate. "Aren't you going to call someone to pass his skills onto him?"

"What do you mean?" His face expression is clearly hostile.

"I mean…" This situation is turning more and more surreal. "I mean, you will call someone to lay his hands on your wife's belly and give his knowledge to the foetus. Won't you?"

Husband and wife look at each other. Then they both look at me.

"What's the problem?" she asks. "Why don't you answer?"

"Answer? I didn't hear any question".

"Of course you didn't *hear*. We haven't spoken out loud. But we *did* ask you a question. You don't feel right."

It's not a question this time, she's making a statement. I look around. Everyone is waiting for me to do something.

"I… I must go. Good morning."

I leave. I can hear them talking behind my back, but they don't say a word. Yes; they don't speak, but I can hear them.

III

I wake up with a hangover. I shouldn't have stayed at Artie's so late last night. But… Well, it was just one day. I turn on the light and check the time. Past nine. Why didn't the alarm ring?

I get up. My clothes are on the floor. Yes, last night must have been a good one. I leave the bedroom. What the hell has happened here? The blinds of the living-room window are raised and what I can see at the other side makes no sense. I go to the window. A huge forest spreads as far as I can see. What happened to the city?

I don't know how long I stare at a landscape that can't be there. The trees are huge and I cannot help looking at them. Beyond the forest I can see what may be a mountain. A joke, it has to be a joke. But why? Fearfully, I spread my thoughts, trying to catch some auras. But it's useless, everything is empty, dead. The trees are not real, they aren't alive. They are close enough for me to perceive their slow vegetal auras but there's nothing. There's not one single living creature in the landscape I see. I'm alone.

An acute ringing sound brings me back to reality. I turn round and see a TV screen turning on. A stranger's face appears on it.

"Base to hunter 2b3. These are your instructions for today: Explore sector H4. A recommendation: beware of the fake ducks." He smiles. "Well, you shouldn't have any problems today. Good luck, Stew."

Something weird crawls inside me when I hear someone I don't know using my name. I sit... In fact I sink into the sofa. My eyes are still fixed on the window, on the absurd and artificial landscape behind then, Over the horizon, beyond the mountain, the moon rises... no, *moons*. There are two, one a little bigger than the other.

Time goes by. The moons rise slowly. A flock of black ducks crosses the sky. Beware of the fake ducks, I remember. I cannot move, I cannot take my eyes of that dead forest that has supplanted the city.

I cannot move.

IV

A new day. My body wakes up at precisely eight o'clock, as it's trained to do. I wonder what I can expect from today. No, it's better not to try and guess. I like to face each day with a clean and clear mind. Oh I love this job.

I get up and go to the living room. A good breakfast and I'm ready for anything, yes, ready for today's instructions. I decide to put on some music, and go across to the player, choosing a tape at random. I put it on. Suddenly I decide it would be nice to listen to some Led Zeppelin. Yeah, maybe *Stairway to Heaven*. This is my idea of heaven. Totally alone, all by myself, no one around for hundreds of miles. I press play and go to the kitchen while my mind anticipates Jimmy Page's guitar.

I freeze. The sound from the speakers is not a guitar. It's my voice. My voice? I don't remember having recorded any tape.

"I think I've found the key. I don't know how much longer I'll be here but it doesn't matter. It's wonderful and also terrible."

I go to the player. I stop, intrigued. What the hell am I talking about?

"I think it's the room. At first I thought it was the entire flat, but no, the rest of the rooms change. Sometimes it's almost nothing, sometimes they are barely noticeable. My bedroom is the one thing that doesn't change. I don't know how or why and I don't think it really matters. Ha. I'd better delete this tape before I leave. I don't want the next..." My voice laughs from the speaker. "...the next *tenant* to ruin everything. I can't believe it, after all these changes I still struggle to believe that everything is real and not a dream."

There is a long pause. I hear a strange noise in the background of the recording, something like... cars? It can't be, I chose a forest simulation because I can't bear city noises.

"Yes, my room, it's the one permanent thing in this chaos that takes me from one place to another. I've been..."

The outside doorbell rings. What the...? I realise then that today's instructions haven't arrived yet. I go to the player and put it on pause. I open the drawer, looking for my gun. It isn't there. Where the hell...? The doorbell rings again.

"Yes."

"Mailman, sir," answers a weary voice. "Can you open the door?"

"Of course."

I go to the kitchen. Mailman, eh? The voice was good, sounded almost real. I open a drawer. I take the longest knife I find. Mailman, yes, he's going to find out who I am. I open the door. Good, I guess he's now climbing the stairs. He'll arrive in no time and knock. Will he use the inner doorbell? If he does he will be fried. I hear his footsteps in the corridor. Here he comes. Ah, he knocks with his knuckles.

"A letter for you."

A letter for me, a letter for me, of course, and death for you, little man. I open the door. They had made him really well: little, grey, tired...

"It's a certified letter," he says.

My knife sinks into his throat. Blood erupts, splashes me. His eyes open wide, as if he doesn't understand what's happening. Then death turns them into cold glass and he falls to my feet. I close the door. The day has started well. I look at the blood that stains my pyjama. Yes, very well.

I don't know how long I it on the sofa remembering the knife in his throat, the blood gushing from his neck, his face losing all expression. It's been so long since I killed with my own hands. It's magnificent.

A couple of hours pass. I suddenly remember the tape; those strange words my voice was saying. I restart the player.

"…in so many places I can't remember any more. I barely remember my world of origin. Who knows if I have been there more than once? It doesn't matter. I have seen barbaric societies, places where people worship machines as if they're gods, places where a thought is enough to get anything you want, places where the greatest treasure is a pinch of salt. Stop it, stop it! Who are you trying to impress? You're alone, Stew, spare us the rhetoric. It doesn't matter. I'd better finish recording this tape… The bedroom is the key, like a gate, I don't know. But I must be in the bedroom when the change comes again. It always happens that way. I don't know when it will be, the gap between shifts is never the same: it might be minutes, hours, days, sometimes years. But I know what I'm going to do then. Let the other… the other *myselves*, let them keep on moving from one world to another if that's what they want. Someday I'll find a world I really like, a world made for me. I don't know when, it doesn't matter, but someday I'll find it. And that day I'll leave this house and I won't come back. Maybe the process stops then or maybe it keeps on, taking my infinite *other* selves from one universe to another. But it won't matter to me any more. I'll be in the world I've chosen and I won't leave. All right, that's enough. Not sure why I made this tape, except that it feels good to say these things out loud, but I must remember to delete it… or take it with me. All right, enough."

The tape stops. My God, I must have been totally drunk when I recorded that nonsense. What the fuck was I going on about?

Suddenly I'm aware I'm not alone. Behind the door I can hear murmurs, steps, screams. A siren sounds in the distance. *A siren?*

I look everywhere for my gun. I can't find it and I realise now that half the furniture seems to be out of place. Behind the door an authoritative voice gives the order to move aside. They're going to catch me, damn it. It's not fair, not after so long. Whatever happens I won't give up. After all, the contract guarantee covered only three months and I've been here for more than two years, alive and well. Not a bad score.

I take the knife and go to the door. I open it. Two uniformed man look at me. Before they can react the knife opens the belly of the nearest. I push up, cutting guts, lungs, aiming for the heart. Something strikes my head. Everything begins to spin around. I try to face the second man. Something strikes my head again. Everything goes black.

V(I)

She knows. She knows I'm not her husband. Oh my God, she knows. What can I tell her, that this is not my world, that I come from...? From where? Two months ago I was a bachelor in a place where children are not born having learnt a profession in their mother's womb, where... She looks at me. In her eyes – those eyes that keep driving me mad – there is silent accusation. *You're not my husband.* What can I answer? She's right, I'm not her husband, though in a crazy way I am him... What can I answer?

VII(II)

The doctors are amazed. A man who has suddenly lost his telepathic skills, they say. If they knew the truth, if they knew I hadn't lost any skills, that I never had them in the first place, if I told them this is not my world, what would they say? They wouldn't believe me. No, they would never believe me. What happened to Martha and the boy? Is she looking for me? Has someone taken my place, someone identical to me down to the smallest physical detail but who is not me? Will she realise, will she know?

VIII(III)

There they are outside the door, trying to get in. My instructions were to exterminate the worms in the south ravine, whatever that means. But I won't go out. On the roof there's something that looks like a helicopter. I guess I have to use it to exterminate the worms. And they try to get in; they're not alive, there's no aura around them, not even the slow shining of plants, but they try to get in, they've been trying since I arrived here… assuming I really was some other place before. They try to get in.

VIII(IV)

A quick trial and I'm sentenced to life in an asylum. A fat lawyer represented me and tried to win over a jury on the verge of boredom. Yes, I'm mad. I have to be, I guess; the entire universe has to be. They used the tape in my apartment (the tape with my voice that I didn't record) as evidence of my insanity. Ah, if only they knew. But I do. Yes, at last I understand everything better than anyone, even better than the stranger with my voice (and my face, I'm sure, and maybe even my mind) who plans to stay in a world of his choosing. Thanks to him I finally understand. I realise now that the postman I killed was a real postman, a poor man doing his job. This is not my world, I know that now. When I woke up that morning I wasn't in my world any more. He's a moron. Hasn't he realised yet? Or am I the one who hasn't realised? No, he's not me, I'm not him; though both of us are me. Doesn't he know that the moment he refuses the exchange everything will stop and we will all be trapped forever? Doesn't he see that in one of the infinite possible worlds there will be no Stewart Ramónez and in another there will be two of us? And how will he react, how will *I* react when I find me and look into my eyes?

I mentioned elsewhere that some of my short stories (and parts of some of my novels) come from dreams. "Everything Flows" is a case in point. One morning, when I woke up, I had in my mind the remnants of what seemed three different dreams: in one of them a man was next to a pregnant woman who had a metallic girdle in her belly; in another I saw the burning wreck of a helicopter that suddenly turned into a brand new one; and in the third I was in a living room with a window that filled an entire wall and, beyond it, there was a huge forest and a rising moon.

I began to play with those three images, looking for a common narrative thread that could create a story linking all of them. That's how "Everything flows" was born. If someone thinks they can hear distant echoes of Philip K. Dick in here… Well, who am I to argue?

IN GOD'S MIND

In God's mind, he is not here with the cold pistol barrel in his mouth and his finger on the trigger.

In God's mind events are just a deck of cards that are shuffled over and over.

In God's mind, those few who know consider him cold, unfeeling, someone who obeys orders without hesitation; someone unaffected by emotions, bound by duty, someone who executes orders with terrifying precision.

In God's mind, he was not on the mound, his heart boiling with rage, his eyes focused on the target, his finger on the trigger, his teeth clenched and his breath transformed into a sharp and horse whispering.

In God's mind, time is just a bunch of domino pieces that never fall the same way.

In God's mind, he did not obey the order, he did not go to the actress home, he did not enter, he did not hide and wait for her to arrive, he did not drug her, he did not cause her death; and, above all, he did not see her frail eyes close forever, he did not see that defenceless face one last time, he did not curse himself for what he had done, and he did not leave the scene with something hungry and enraged growing bit by bit in his guts.

In God's mind, he never repented what he had done, he never questioned the order they gave him, he never thought for an instant of the life he had taken.

In God's mind, nobody went to her home, nobody killed her, nobody stopped her from getting older and destroying her legend through her own actions.

In God's mind, the universe is nothing more than a die with infinite sides, always tumbling.

In God's mind, the cold rage that took root in his guts that night never existed, the pain that broke his body every time he took a breath never appeared, the memory of one last gaze just before entering that undiscovered country from whose bourn no traveller returns never tormented his soul.

In God's mind, he might not even have been there during those days, busy overthrowing a left-wing regime or putting in place some cheap tyrant.

In God's mind, perhaps he was never born.

In God's mind, the possibility exists that he was not on that mound in Dallas fifteen months later, eager to pull the trigger and erase forever the man who gave the order to kill her, the order he obeyed, the order that, from that moment, filled his waking minutes with a pair of sad eyes, a face of frail beauty, a last sigh into oblivion, the order that made his existence a lair of bereaved ghosts that haunt him since them.

In God's mind, there is nothing to suggest that he and she were anything more than two anonymous people who might have known each other, or maybe not; who might have loved each other, or maybe not; who might have hurt each other, or maybe not.

In God's mind, it is conceivable that everything happened just the way it happened.

In God's mind, will he be crying when he lifts the gun to his mouth? Will he still see those defenceless eyes waiting for him on the other side once he pulls the trigger and his brains spread on the cheap wallpaper of the motel room?

In God's mind, every bullet fired into the void will reach its target, sooner or later.

As with "We Have Followed You", this one is a sort of prose poem.

In 2011, Alejandro Castroguer was working on an anthology to be published in 2012, called Vintage '62: Marilynn y otros monstruos [Vintage '62: Marilynn and Other Monsters]. *His idea was that each contributor should write a short story about someone (real or fictitious) who had died in 1962, fifty years before the anthology's publication date.*

He asked me for a story and the project appealed to me. I played with one or two ideas until I remembered the conspiranoia about Marilynn Monroe's death...

Then I also remembered something I had always wanted to do. I'm talking of what Alan Moore does in Watchmen, *chapter IV, "Watchmaker", when Dr.*

Manhattan is on Mars and begins to walk through his life backwards and forwards. I always thought Moore was trying to reconstruct sequentially how a god might see the passing of time: simultaneously. It won't surprise anyone to hear that Rorschach's death and that chapter are my favourite parts of Watchmen.

The supposed conspiracy around Marilyn's dead could be a good starting point for something like that chapter of Watchmen: *showing how God sees time and different possibilities, all at once. Not only the past and the future, but all possible pasts and all possible futures.*

By the way, in the end I was more than just one of the authors in this anthology. After looking for a publisher and receiving several variations of "hmmm, interesting but I'm not sure…" in response, Alejandro turned to Sportula, my own small press, and the book found a home there.

THINK WHATEVER YOU WANT

I gaze once more into the abyss beneath my feet, those twelve floors that separate me from the human ants that go about their lives below me, unaware they are nothing more than puppets. I gaze again and dizziness overwhelms me, like a drunkenness I can't shake off. I anticipate the fall, the howling wind around me as the world becomes a blur. The shock. Maybe a scream. And then silence. Forever. Somehow it would be a relief and I must confess I look forward to it. I smile in anticipation.

I close my eyes and, for an instant, I am able to forget everything, to ignore that craving that pulls me towards oblivion. I inhale and my body manages to find the peaceful focus that has eluded me in recent hours. For how long? Not long, I know, but it might as well be all the time in the world, at least for me. Time enough to remember how everything started.

Juan and I were friends. One of those friendships that begin in puberty and manage, somehow, to survive the turbulent trials of adolescence. We were good friends. At least that's what I believed. No, don't lie to yourself, be honest in these last moments: you still believe it. Yes, despite everything, in some weird and twisted way I still believe it. There were dark regions in our friendship, places we ignored by mutual consent, as if we understood there were things we couldn't share if we wanted to remain friends.

We were very different, and maybe that was the key to our relationship surviving all those years. Despite some common hobbies and obsessions, our personalities couldn't have been less alike. Juan was an absentminded person, always surrounded by an indeterminable aura of melancholy he was aware of and, in fact, I think he deliberately cultivated. On the other hand, I crossed my second decade as some kind of force of nature in human shape, devastating, unstoppable, with arrogance and self-confidence enough for both of us, taking everything I wanted without considering the consequences. I guess Juan envied me. Not for my ability to get any girl I wanted, nor for the fact that I was always the centre of attention while he sat by a corner, carefully maintaining the affectation of a nineteenth-century poet. I guess he saw himself as better than me: smarter, brighter, deeper and more sensitive; but everyone preferred my jovial superficiality to his rich inner life. It took him some time to realise it was nothing more than a marketing issue; it's useless to have the best product in the world if you don't know how to sell it.

Eventually he learned, though he had several years to catch up on and he was still a little awkward in his dealings with others. Everything improves with practice, I remember thinking, and then didn't spare the matter another thought..

He called me less than a year ago. I guessed from the tone of his voice that something serious had happened.

"What's the problem?" I asked, genuinely worried. Juan always had taken things too seriously.

"I did it, I did it!"

"What?"

"I've scored."

Wow. If I called my friends every time I scored the world's phone network would go into meltdown.

"Congratulations, dude," I said. "I can't wait to meet her."

The next thirty minutes were an endless monologue. Juan kept telling me the virtues and wonders of his newly acquired girlfriend. She was not only the most extraordinary woman on Earth, but she was in love with him. I told myself that she *had* to be extraordinary if she was in love with Juan, but I didn't say anything.

A few months later he called me again, now for advice.

"Waitaminute," I said, shocked by what I was hearing. "Are you telling me that you've been seeing her for four months and… nothing?"

"Well…"

"Have you nailed her?"

"Don't be so crude."

"You haven't nailed her."

He didn't say anything for a couple of seconds.

"I haven't," he admitted at last.

So I gave him a piece of advice and hung up. I knew nothing I could tell him would be of any use. Experience has taught me that what works for one person rarely works for anyone else. I never knew if my advice helped because it wasn't necessary in the end. Fate conspired in Juan's favour and his parents went on holiday. Their house was at his disposal and I reckoned even he couldn't miss an opportunity like that.

He didn't. I guess they spent the entire two days in bed, apart from eating or going to the bathroom. I expected him to call me in bliss to describe me the excellence of his very first orgasm (and maybe the following four or five, depending on how good things had been). He didn't call. In fact, I didn't hear from him for more than a month. Finally, I decided to call him.

"How are you doing?"

"Doing what?"

"What the fuck! Are you kidding me? You know, sex with a woman instead of your five little friends."

"Ah, yeah, fine."

He didn't seem very excited.

"Was it so bad?"

"No, not at all. It was fine, terrific, sure." There was a moment of silence. "We aren't together any more."

"You or her?"

"It was me."

"The sex was terrific but you've left her? You find a woman stupid enough to fall in love with you and you leave her? Come on, tell me the truth."

"I have to hang up, sorry. I have a date and I'm late. We'll talk later, okay?"

He hung up. I couldn't believe what I had just heard. All right, losing your virginity can make you behave like a moron. I knew that well enough. But I couldn't stop wondering about had gone wrong. Juan's behaviour was... odd. I knew that behind his apparent frailty there was a hidden strength that nothing could break. He could be a tough bastard when he needed to be. I wasn't sure what, but something didn't fit.

So I went to his home.

Usually I would have called him to let him know, but something told me Juan would insist he was unavailable if I did.

I was about to ring the bell when the door opened. A woman came out. She looked through me and then turned round, waiting for someone. Juan stood in the doorway, smiling like the proverbial cat that ate the canary. The girl approached him (she seemed vaguely familiar, but I was so astonished I couldn't remember), clung to his neck as if her life depended on it, and gave him one of the longest and most passionate kisses I have seen in my life.

"Will I see you again?" she asked afterwards.

"Sure. I'll call you," answered Juan. He didn't seem very interested.

She nodded and left with a smile on her lips and a dreamy distance in her eyes. She looked drugged. Only when she entered the lift did Juan look at me.

"Sorry," he said. "I was busy."

"I bet you were."

I suddenly froze. Of course I had thought I knew the girl.

"That was Eve, wasn't it?"

"Right."

It couldn't be. Eve had been Juan's crush since he was fourteen, and she had never noticed him apart from once (I was there) to say he was cute and nice, but harmless. I haven't seen her for four of five years.

And there she was, looking at Juan as if he were God's cousin or James Bond's twin brother, which is pretty much the same thing.

"Don't you want to come in?"

"Sure," I answered.

"Coffee?"

I nodded and took a seat. Juan went into the kitchen and came back a few minutes later with two cups of coffee.

"I was about to call you," he said after sitting down. "The truth is, a lot of things have been happening lately and if I don't tell someone I'm going to burst.

"I told you I'd left Irene…It's funny, I must have rehearsed telling you this half a dozen times but it hasn't helped."

We both kept silent. I knew Juan well enough to bite my tongue and wait for him to go on.

"Irene came to stay that weekend," he suddenly said. "When my parents were away."

"I remember. By the way, where are they now?"

It was funny, because Juan parents had always treated me like a second son, and I had expected to see them the moment I entered the apartment, but there was no sign of them.

"They've left. They won't be back."

"What?"

"They won't come back. It's not important, really, I'll explain later, all right?"

I was about to say it was not all right at all, but suddenly I felt Juan was right, it wasn't important.

"Okay, go on."

He smiled, as if he knew something I didn't.

"That weekend, well, I said goodbye to my little 'five friends', as you say. The experience was... fine. Better than fine. The first time it was too fast, you know, lack of experience and all that. Practice makes perfect, after all. Then, on Sunday... on Sunday... I have never felt anything like it. For a moment it was like... I don't know, the more I try to explain it the less I can. I guess there are no words to explain it, but I'll try my best. It was as if my mind, for the first time in my life, was free, free of everything. I wasn't there in bed with Irene, you understand? I had left. I was flying thousands of miles away. I had opened myself up to everything and everything was entering me, as if I were a universal filter, an aleph, a... Do you remember Yoda in *The Empire Strikes Back* when he says to Luke: 'Luminous beings are we, not this crude matter'? It's not quite that, but it's the closest I can get to explaining what really happened."

Poor boy. He had been lucky enough to get laid good and proper and had felt one with the universe as a result. All right, no problem, I could recite a couple of mantras to show him my support, no big deal.

"I see," he said with a sad smile. "My fault I guess. I didn't explain myself well enough. It doesn't matter. The feeling was awesome, unbelievable, but what happened next is what really matters. Let's imagine you're a blind man and suddenly you begin to perceive light: at first just a distant glow, so weak you barely see it, but it grows and grows to the point where you can see everything around you perfectly. Something like that is what happened to me."

He ended his coffee and looked at me.

"I'm a telepath," he said.

I couldn't help it. I laughed.

"Terrific, man, terrific, you almost got me."

He shook his head.

"I'm serious. I can read other people's minds. I discovered it that evening. I could read Irene's petty and ridiculous thoughts. That's why I left her, you understand? How could I be with a person capable of thinking such stupid things? No, I couldn't be with her any more."

I didn't say anything.

Poor guy, I thought. He's nuts. The priests were right after all: sex can drive you mad.

Even as I thought this, Juan began to recite my thoughts out loud.

"Poor guy. He's nuts. The priests were right after all: sex can drive you mad."

I stared at him. I didn't know what to say.

"I don't care if you believe me or not. But I know precisely what you're thinking. If I wanted to I could make you believe me, but it's more satisfying if I can convince you by more… ehm… traditional methods. You see, not only can I read people's minds, but I can alter their thought, their emotions, their desires."

I remembered Eve, hugging Juan as if her life depended on it. No, it was insane. This had to be a bad joke.

"A rational man till the end, eh? I'm sorry, I'm afraid it's true."

He stopped talking and gazed at me, thoughtfully. A wicked gleam appeared in his eyes.

"I've never tried this before, but I guess I can do it. You see, when I manipulate someone they aren't aware of it, as I did with my parents so that they would move out, and with Eve just now… But I think I can make you aware of what is happening when I manipulate your mind. Wanna try?"

"Yeah, sure," I answered, more confidently than I really felt.

"All right, close your eyes."

I did as I was told despite feeling ridiculous.

Suddenly I noticed something. I wasn't alone. Inside me there was someone else. I felt his presence as a dark, threatening shape. Yes, he was there and I was totally transparent to him. Everything I was: my memories, my dreams, my fantasies, my darkest desires were within his reach; even that part of my mind I wasn't aware of, the irrational part I had kept hidden and tried to ignore all those years.

"Get out!" I screamed, though I didn't say a word.

Something was growing inside me. I had been invaded, raped, and I would not allow it. Something took control of my mind, something that was me and, at the same time, not me, and suddenly I became a rabid beast, desperately defending my territory with tooth and claw.

Everything ended as quickly as it had begun. I opened my eyes and saw Juan in front of me, smiling. But I knew him well enough to notice he was worried.

"Funny," he said. "There's a part of your mind you won't allow anyone to reach, and you're ready to do anything it takes to defend it. Interesting. Tell me, do you believe me now?"

What could I say? If he was mad then so was I. But if he was sane... wasn't that worse?

"Yes... I believe you."

"Good."

My memories of the next hours are blurred. I know Juan spoke and spoke and I listened and listened, incapable of saying a word, as if I were just a human statue. He told me how it had felt when he first discovered he could manipulate other people's minds.

He was living in an endless drunken state, though he said it wasn't like that at all. He had been on top of the world, seeing everything in a way we couldn't understand. He had begun to use his new abilities in little ways, but his ambitions had grown.

"What are you going to do now?" I asked.

"I don't know. I can do whatever I want... but I'm not sure what I want to do."

I left. Juan said goodbye and smiled at me one last time. Something dark and cold glowed behind his eyes. I didn't like it.

Time passed. Sometimes everything around me seemed a nightmare, sometimes everything was as it always had been, but I knew it wouldn't last. I considered trying to stop Juan, but I knew I couldn't. He was my friend; you just don't do those things to a friend. And I knew it was useless... He would have read my intentions the moment I thought of them.

He called me yesterday and invited me to go and see him. I didn't try to refuse, but in the lift my mind was in a state of pure animal panic and I dithered before his door like a hesitant bride.

He opened the door and we went to the living room. A cup of coffee was waiting for me.

"What did you want?" I asked.

"I had to say goodbye".

"Are you going somewhere?"

He shook his head.

"I'm not. You are."

"I see."

"I know you do. You asked me what I was going to do. I didn't really know, but I now realise I don't have many alternatives. I've got this power, see? I guess I've always had it and didn't know, it doesn't matter. I have it and when you have something you can't help but use it. You can't get the genius back into the bottle, so to speak. So I'm going to use it."

"How?"

"Isn't it obvious? I can make every one of my desires reality. And that's exactly what I'm going to do. But there's a problem."

"Me."

"Yes, you. You know what I am. And you're the only one who does. Everyone else is ignorant of my influence when they give me their money or their bodies. Not you. You have felt me inside you and you have fought me... I know there's a part you'll never allow me to watch or read and you're ready to do whatever it takes to stop it. That makes you dangerous. I'm sorry."

It wasn't true. I knew in that very moment he wasn't sorry at all.

"You could..." I said, trying not to beg. I'm not sure I succeeded. "You could make me forget."

"I could, yeah. But it wouldn't be safe. It was a mistake entering your mind and allowing you to know. Manipulating other people is easy, they don't know they're being changed, but it's not the same with you. It might work, yeah, maybe you would forget, but the memory would persist, hidden like a stalking predator. There'd always be the risk that something would trigger it. I can't take that risk."

"Is that all? You call me just to say you're going to kill me because there's a possibility I could be a danger for you some day?"

"I have to consider my own survival. You're my friend. I care for you. But my life comes first."

"*Your* life. What kind of life? What will happen when you get all you want, when you find out the world is full of your puppets, that there's no one you can really trust, no one to talk to openly...? It's going to be a very lonely life. Every time you make love you'll be masturbating. Every conversation will be a monologue. Every... Think about it."

"I have. I can do anything but think about it."

"Bollocks. You don't want to, be honest at least."

"All right, I don't want to."

I started laughing, though there was without joy.

"I believed I knew you and the funny thing is that, yes, I did. Because I'm not surprised. Yeah, I knew you were like this, somehow I knew. I wish I'd been wrong."

He shrugged.

"Let's put an end to this. It won't be unpleasant. You will wish for death and it will come as a relief. I owe you that much."

I stood.

"Can I leave?"

"Sure. Tomorrow or the day after tomorrow it will all be over. Goodbye."

I didn't answer. At the door, I stopped.

"You know, you're not killing me because I'm a danger to your survival. You're killing me because you've seen inside me."

"What?"

He looked at me, haughty, arrogant, but there was something in his eyes... Was it fear?

"You know as well as I do, so spare me the crap. You have found something uncomfortable inside me, something you know you want but you can never have, and you need to kill me to go on with your pathetic life"

"Think whatever you want."

"That's what I intend to do. For as long as I can."

Nothing more was said.

I open my eyes. The street is still below, calling me, whispering its lethal song in an irresistible cooing. Is that everything? There's nothing more? A jump and everything will end?

I think of Juan one last time. I wonder what the world will be like years from now, full of puppets, with him as the puppeteer. I wonder how he will feel. Will my prophecy be fulfilled? Will he see he's alone in the middle of an empty world? What will he think then?

Maybe he will be satisfied, ignorant that he's just another puppet, a puppet of his own desires.

Who knows? I won't find out. I'll die today.

But I'm not a puppet, I tell myself. At least I can say that much. Then I realise I'm kidding myself. If I'm not a puppet why am I here, about to take a last jump into oblivion?

I feel something wet and salty at the corner of my mouth. Tears. Damn it. Damn it. Damn it.

One step. Just one. There won't be another.

When we were both teenagers, my friend Javier Cuevas wrote a short story about a telepath. I read it and enjoyed it, but he never tried to publish it and the typewritten original disappeared in the mists of time.

Almost twenty years later, I found myself thinking of that story and analysing what I remembered of it. I discovered that the story, as I remembered it, still worked, apart from the ending.

I could do something about that. I talked with Javier and asked his permission to retell the tale my way. He was kind enough to let me do so and the result was "Think Whatever You Want".

A couple of months later, it won the short stories contest organised by the City Council of Candás, my birthplace (though I've been living in Gijón, the nearby city, since I was ten).

No, I didn't share the prize with Javier. Though I invited him for a coffee, I think.

PYRRHIC VICTORY

I'm recording this for you, only for you. I don't care about the others but you deserve to know what really happened. Though from your point of view nothing has happened and you won't believe what I'm about to tell you. But it's the truth, or at least it was.

When you arrived at the nursing home I had been entering the memories of the other inmates for a month. It was something I didn't intend to do at first and even now I don't know how it happened. I suspect the cause was a drug or a combination of drugs that, somehow, altered my perceptions. But that doesn't really explain anything. It happened at night. I was about to nod off, you know that state, not entirely dreaming but not entirely awake either; you fall asleep to suddenly wake up a second later because of some trivial noise and before you know what is happening you fall asleep again. I began to dream. That was what I thought at first. It took me some time to realise I was awake. I was in bed, heard the nurses down the corridor, noticed the moonlight slipping through the blinds. That irritated me; I don't like any light when I try to sleep. I got up and went to the window. And then I realised. The dream hadn't gone. Somehow I still saw it. I could see my room but at the same time, almost in the corner of my eye, out of focus, the dream was still there. I froze with a hand in the blind, totally motionless until the dream image began to gain definition and the room around me faded away. It didn't take me long to identify that I was seeing Another person's memories. In fact, I realised quickly, they belonged to Elisa, three rooms beyond. Funny, I never had any difficulty in identifying the owner of the memories I shared.

I haven't got much time. I just felt the first symptoms of sleep, my last sleep. Only minutes remain and I have to tell you everything that happened. Or, as you and anyone else see things, everything that didn't happen.

A week later I didn't need to fall asleep. I could enter everybody's memories how and when I wanted, walk among them whenever I liked, read them as if they were a newspaper cartoon. Can you imagine what that meant for the voyeur within me? You know the saying: some people live, some run and some watch. That's what I've been doing all my life, I've been little more than a witness to other people's lives, enjoying the little portions I could share. This was a unique opportunity, the ultimate feast. Somehow – I don't know how and I guess I don't want to know – other people's lives were now an atlas, an encyclopaedia I could read whenever I wanted. With time, with practice, I was getting better and better: I could get an overview, a quick flash of somebody's past, or I could stop and smell the roses, watch a specific moment, freeze an instant and study it in minute detail.

Then you came. I was introduced to you when you arrived. You didn't recognise me, of course. How could you guess that bald and wrinkled old man was the same stupid boy that had been wrapped around your fingers more than sixty years ago? But I recognised you the moment I saw you. The years hadn't been kind to you and you were as old, wrinkled and shrunken as me. But those six decades hadn't spoiled your eyes and your mouth still had that perfect shape that drove me mad at sixteen, just as it did now. You greeted me and you forgot me in the same second.

I could barely sleep that night and I didn't bother to explore any of the others' memories. What did I care about other people's pasts when my own had just risen out of the blue? Between fourteen and eighteen I had been your toy, your minion, your slave, hanging on every word you said, every move you made, every smile you faked, every game you played. At eighteen you left the city. I received news about you for a while from mutual friends...

I feel a little silly telling you all this. After all, you should know it as well as I do; but no, that's not the case. Not any more.

I followed you the day after you arrived, not saying a word, trying not to get too close. I guess you didn't notice. But my eyes pursued you, haunted you, and everywhere you went there I was. Temptation was too strong. I had been reading the memories of all those around me for a month: inmates, doctors, nurses, watchmen. I had tasted their recollections as the most exquisite of delicacies. And there you were, a gift from heaven. But I didn't do it. Not yet at least. Fear? Maybe. I don't know and now it doesn't matter any more.

A week went by and things returned to normal. We talked a couple of times that week, trivial things. I don't remember the specifics. I returned to my favourite hobby and my eyes, though they looked for you everywhere, lost their eager glow. Then Stephen died.

I guess I should say we were friends, though that doesn't really mean a lot. We used to play chess in the afternoons and he would sometimes talk about his grandchildren. I've felt pity for him since the day I explored his memories. Stephen thought of himself as a useless person, a nobody, someone who hadn't done anything worthwhile in his entire life. The worst thing, what really tormented him, was that he felt he could have been someone and his cowardice had prevented it. There was one memory that stood out: Stephen, twenty years old, is taking a walk. He passes by a burning building. Someone cries for help from a window. Stephen hesitates. He goes towards the building but stops. Then someone overtakes him and enters the building. He returns a few minutes later, just as the fire fighters arrive, carrying two babies in his arms. That was all. Stephen had the feeling that if he had entered the building, if he had done what the other man did, his life would have had meaning no matter what happened after that. He even had a press clipping, yellow and faded after all these years, where a reporter interviewed that man about his feat. I saw him take the clipping from his wallet several times, unfold it and look at it without saying a word.

The day Stephen died he had been agonising for more than a week. He was fading little by little and there was nothing the doctors could do, so they shrugged and said those words that meaningless phrase that puts fear into our hearts when we hear it: 'old age'. I went to his room. He barely seemed aware of my presence, he didn't seem aware of anything. In his mind there was only room for that fateful afternoon he could have been a hero but failed.

I couldn't help it. I entered his memories. I saw him before the house, hesitating. Something broke inside me. Come on, do it, I cried. Do it now! And I felt that I was somehow pushing him. Then Stephen ran to the burning house, entered the room where the babies were crying for help and took them up. When he returned to the street an expectant crowd started cheering him, and a news reporter came over.

I blinked, stunned. There was something wrong, wicked, about this. It hadn't happened that way. Suddenly Stephen saw me and called me. I said something. I don't remember what, surely some empty comforting words.

"I'm fine," he said. "Death is not so bad if you've done something with your life. I was a hero, remember?"

I frowned. There was a nurse in the room and I said: "Poor man, he's delirious."

She looked upset.

"Maybe he's exaggerating a bit, but what he did was brave," she said.

"What?"

She pointed the wall above the bed. There, laminated and framed, was a newspaper clipping. I didn't need to read the headline to see it was an article about Stephen's feat when he rescued those two children. I stood up and looked at the picture. A smiling Stephen left the burning house with two babies in his arms. I turned to the nurse.

"But…" I tried to say.

"He's dead," she interrupted me while she covered his face with a blanket. "At least he had a good death."

I left the room, stunned. What had happened? I entered his memories and in some way I couldn't understand I had modified them. No, not just that, I had done something more. I not only modified Stephen's memories but the nurse's as well. And that newspaper… I felt dizzy as realisation struck me. I had changed reality. By altering Stephen's past I had altered the flow of events. In some small way, I had changed the universe.

Everybody remembered Stephen feat.

"He didn't talk about anything else," Mark told me when I asked.

I shivered. What had I become? I could not only see other people's pasts, I could change them as well, shaping a new reality. The former reality didn't merely vanish; it was erased, it had never happened. Nobody remembered it but me.

I feel the drowsiness growing inside me. I haven't got much time, so I had better be quick.

It took me almost two months to realise what I had to do. And when I did I cursed myself for being so stupid. I don't expect you to understand what I have done, much less forgive me. The fact is you won't believe I have done it. I have… Oh, yes, I have raped you in a way no other man has raped a woman before. I have entered your past, I have walked through it until I know by heart your entire history and then I have changed it to my will. Yes, I have tampered with you, I have shaped you, I have made you what you are now.

It was hard, oh, so hard. I made many mistakes. But I could fix them,

Pyrrhic Victory

that was no problem. All I had to do was return to the moment I made the change and restore the original version. Then, try again.

It required several changes. I made you fall in love with me at fifteen, but you left me seven years later. I had to intervene again then, made a little adjustment. A decade and a half later I had to do it again. After that, only minor adjustments were needed: a brushstroke here and there, just enough to finish the picture. It was a masterpiece. It was also disgusting and terrifying, but it was a masterpiece none the less. And when I finished, you didn't remember having met me when we were teenagers and forgetting me four years later. What you remembered was more than sixty happy years by my side, up to the day we entered the nursing home together. And the entire world had changed to accommodate the script I wrote.

Of course you don't believe me. It could not be otherwise. For you this new past is real, the only reality. The other one never took place. But I'm begging you to accept what I'm saying, at least as a hypothesis. Please. Then you might wonder why I am here recording my final words; why I have injected myself with a drug that carries me towards the final sleep.

The answer is painfully obvious. Because I've failed. Yes, you remember those sixty years by my side, but I don't. I change the world and everybody remembers the changes I make as real. Everybody but me. Maybe you remember loving me all your life. But what I remember is that you never thought of me, that I have lived alone and the futile victory I've achieved by manipulating reality tastes sour and empty. That's all.

I can barely keep my eyes open now and my tongue is heavy. I hope you can forgive the pain I'm going to inflict on you with my suicide. I could have made it one last time, restoring your memories to their original form. You wouldn't remember me and my death wouldn't cause you any pain. But I'm too tired, too...

No! Don't lie, not now, not when the cold fingers of death are caressing your skin. Be honest for once in your life.

Yes, it's true. The least I owe you is the truth. I don't want you to forget me. If I'm going to die, if I'm going to fail, at least someone will remember me, though your memory of me is fake.

I'm sorry. I wish things had been different. In fact, they were.

191

When I was talking about "Loaded Dice" I said I had never written a story about time travel before. That was not entirely true. "Pyrrhic Victory" was written several years prior to "Loaded Dice".

This is not really a time travel story, however. It's about the past and memory and the way we are what we remember. What we do defines how the rest of the world sees us, but it's what we remember that defines how we see ourselves.

I'm not sure where the idea for "Pyrrhic Victory" came from. I remember it appeared totally developed in my mind and I only had to put the story into words.

But is that true? Every time we remember something we reinvent it. Human memory doesn't access a hard drive, download data and put words in our mouth; it tells a story of what we did that changes with every retelling, adapting what happened (and our memories of what happened) to a new context and according to new needs, fears and desires. Remembering is a form of lying, after all.

AT THE PENTHOUSE

1.

The pilot tells her they are about to arrive, but she doesn't pay attention. She checks her bag and her weapons one last time and when she looks up she discovers she is looking at herself in a mirror she wishes wasn't there. She tries to ignore the bags under her eyes and, as usual, she feels uncomfortable with a face that is recognisably hers but, at the same time, feels alien. She takes a breath and tries to behave as hard-nosed as she can but doubts she succeeds. She doesn't dare look at herself again to check.

She turns to the window and her gaze gets lost in the endless and ridiculous landscape below: boundless fields of transoats where thousands of tiny human ants work ceaselessly until the day is done. Among them, protruding as disproportionate landmarks, dozens of shiny plastiglass pyramidal towers; cold and distant watchers, technological anthills, extinct lighthouses... She stops that tide of silly metaphors and takes a good look at her destination. It stands in the middle of the fields, cold and arrogant, huge and so much higher than the rest of the pyramids that it seems to own the world. This is the place she is going to call 'home' from now on.

Or maybe not.

This is her last chance. Captain Tarancón was very clear about that when he talked to her in the cage.

"This is not a discussion," he said. "It's not even a conversation. Screw up one more time and I won't move a finger to help you. Nobody will. So seize the chance I'm offering you."

After that, he put the data chip on the cot and went away without saying another word.

Seize? Seize what?

It was not the first time the captain had intervened on her behalf. She had the feeling he had been doing so since she enlisted in so subtle a way she that hadn't even been aware for a long time. And she was sure nobody else had, either.

To seize... What? she continued to wonder.

But she took the chip, put it in the tablet and read the brief.

And she accepted it, of course, what else could she have done: face a court martial?

The pilot is talking to her again. He tells her to hold onto something, the landing is going to be a little rough. They are so high that the wind is a raging claw, like the howling of an animal in heat.

But they manage to land without incident. She stands up, takes the bag and the case, and looks at the mirror one last time. She tries to forget the familiar stranger she sees there.

She steps down to a platform so burnished and unpolluted it seems to have been built in the past few seconds. The platform lies in a long and narrow walkway that leads to the huge truncated pyramid destined to be her home.

She hesitates a few seconds, then shrugs and begins to follow the walkway. As she does so she has a feeling that the platform is being erased behind her, but she doesn't turn to check. A door opens in the shining building's surface and she goes through. It closes behind her and suddenly she is in pitch blackness. She breathes and remains still.

"Welcome," says a voice from her left.

"Thanks," she answers, trying to smile and keep calm.

Lights come on and the owner of the voice approaches. He stops a couple of steps away and gazes at her with obvious interest. She remains still while he inspects her and hopes he doesn't notice her surprise at his youthfulness. He's nothing more than a child, she thinks; a child who has just been given the biggest toy store of the world.

"I guess you're tired," he says.

She doesn't answer.

"It's best if you go to your rooms now. There you can freshen up and rest. Dinner will be at half past eight."

Without waiting for a response he turns and leaves the oval room. She is about to ask him how she is supposed to find her way when a luminous line appears on the floor and points the way.

She shrugs again and begins to walk.

Her rooms. Not bad, as a joke. She might even laugh if she could.

Twenty families could live here comfortably and there would be room enough for distant relatives. She thinks then of the lower floors and realises that right now several families are indeed living in a space like this. Maybe even smaller.

Her rooms.

A titanic bed, a dressing room that is bigger than most clothes stores, a bathtub bigger than a swimming pool...

Her rooms.

She unpacks, hangs the spare uniform in the closet and almost feels sorry for it. It seems lost, an abandoned infant in the middle of that huge empty space, the last survivor of its race on a barren world.

Then she opens the case, spreads the weapons on the bed, checks their status and scratches her head, wondering where she can put them.

She looks up and says:

"Information request."

"Explain its nature," answers a nice warm voice.

"Where can I put my weapons?"

"There is a place for that purpose in the dressing room. Third door to the right."

"Thanks."

She goes where she has been told, opens the door and sees a room designed to house an entire company's arsenal. She puts the weapons and the ammo down and they seem as insignificant and forlorn as the uniform.

She checks the time. Seven. She goes to the bathroom, fills the bathtub with almost boiling water and climbs in. She rests her nape on the edge, closes her eyes and lets the hot water wash everything away.

But it doesn't.

They walk. They just walk. Defeated. Beaten. Their strength has been annihilated with their homes. Their will is broken, as burnt as their woods. They walk. They cannot do anything else.

Minijets and copters discharge their lethal loads. Trees crack, protest, die. Amazonian rain forest becomes a wasteland and the wasteland a grassland where future burgers and hot-dog projects graze.

And they walk. They cannot do anything else.

They walk towards oblivion worse than death.

And she, looking down on everything, smiles at a job well done.

She wakes up, pushes aside the lingering dream images and climbs out of the bathtub. The water is now almost cold. She checks the time in the wall. Eight o'clock.

She dries herself and puts on a clean uniform.

And now?

The trivi in the wall is like a huge blackboard that awaits her command, ready to turn on and fill her eyes with trivialities, sex and random violence.

Ha, she thinks, just like the Army.

She enters the bedroom and, for a moment, considers jumping into that immense bed which seems tailor-made for a gangbang. Instead, she steps closer to the picture window and, with a gesture, orders the glass to clear.

The reddish twilight sun illuminates the city and creates amazing effects in the urban landscape. From this vantage point it is almost as if she watches an anthill that cannot escape her descending boot. She is God, owner and master of everything she sees and she can erase the entire universe with a shrug and replace it with a new one more to her taste.

No, idiot, she corrects herself. *You're just God's French maid. His bodyguard, his hired hitman, the hand that's going to do the dirty work while God looks away. His slave for the next five years.*

Well, it could be worse.

She goes to the bed, takes the tablet and again uploads the chip with the job description. She doesn't remember how many times she has read it. Too many. Once more won't hurt.

Captain Tarancón had to pull many strings to get her a posting like this, especially after Brazil. Even with an immaculate record, this was not a job a special forces sergeant could get just like that.

The sort of opportunity many would kill for. For her, a last chance. And she wonders again why the captain has helped her, why he has been helping her all these years. She shrugs. She will probably never know and it doesn't matter anyway.

She takes a look at the data on her employer.

Daniel Avogrado. Son of the late Jonah Avogrado, who controlled one of the main chemical-food conglomerates in the world during his active years. During his... 'inactive' years, AdAstra Corporation was the battlefield for a bunch of factions, gangs and lobbies that fought in the corridors, stabbed one another in the bedrooms and kicked their colleagues' asses in the board meetings. A chaotic state of affairs exploited by their competitors, but not sufficiently to bring the colossus down. In spite of everything, AdAstra Corp. remained one the world's largest conglomerates, thanks largely to their control of the Antarctic Fields and the algae forests of the Indian Ocean.

What am I doing here? she asks herself.

I'm surviving, she answers.

Is it worth it? she asks again.

Hell, yeah!

So she turns off the tablet, leaves it on the nightstand, and checks the time once more.

Let's go to dinner.

2.

When she enters the dining room she realises he has been waiting for her for a while. She checks the hour. She has arrived on time, but it seems he expected something else. It is not a good idea to disappoint your boss the minute you meet him, she thinks, but she keeps on walking towards him as if she has not noticed anything.

He pretends to be busy with the shaker and behaves as if he were unaware of her presence. Only when she stops in front of the bar does he raise his head, favours her with a smile that makes him seem even younger than he is, and asks: "A cocktail?"

She nods.

He points to a chair while continuing to work the shaker. She sits and quietly watches what he is doing.

A child. A fucking child. He cannot be older than eighteen. Eighteen soft years of being spoiled, indulged and controlled. He has suddenly inherited control – and the penthouse with it – of one of the main Zaibatsus in the world. A child with new toys. Just as she thought on arriving. Except that now it is not just a metaphor.

A child who has never suffered, who has never had to fight for what he has. He doesn't seem like that, though. In his eyes, green as hers, there is a harsh and relentless glow that denies any notion of childhood.

He shakes the shaker one last time and then spills its content into a pair of glasses sporting a slice of lemon rind in the shape of a spiral.

"Here we are," he says. "I hope you like it."

She drinks.

"Not bad."

He smiles again.

"Splendid," he remarks. "I think we're going to get along. I know that is not a requirement for the job. At the end of the day, this is strictly a business relationship, but I like a certain human touch. Especially because you're going to be my... How can I put it?"

"Your executioner?"

"Hmmm. 'Executioner'. I must say I like the sound of that." He has a nice voice, though there is something pedantic in it and his words are carefully chosen. A child, she thinks again, but maybe not a spoiled child. What kind of child, then? "Yeah, it's a fine definition. In some ways you're going to be part of myself for the next five years, the part that's going to do everything that I, to speak plainly, wouldn't dare to do. On top of that you have to take care of me. It won't be easy."

"I'll do my best."

"Oh, I'm sure you will. I've read your file and your captain's recommendations. You have been selected ahead of several more experienced and recommended people. And believe me when I tell you it's not been by chance."

She is about to ask him why he has chosen her, but she bites her lip and drinks again.

"Aha, prudent and discreet. You keep your personal curiosity at bay when it's wise to." He nods, satisfied. "I think your appointment is going to prove a success. Let's have dinner."

He shows her the way to the table and she precedes him, as expected.

"We must review your clothing, of course. And your weaponry. But we can take care of that tomorrow. Now, let's just enjoy the dinner."

A large selection of dishes are spread on the table, each more delicious than the last, and for the next half an hour she simply samples one after another, savouring their different textures, fragrances and flavours. The wine is soft and fresh and enhances every bite in a subtle and delicious way.

When the desserts arrive she is almost too full to take another bite, but forces herself to taste something that resembles a cloud and dissolves in her mouth as if it were just an illusion.

During dinner he has just been looking at her with half a smile and has only spoken to recommend this or praise that. It is weird to see those eyes, almost identical to hers, inspecting her with such polite curiosity.

"Did you like it?" he asks afterwards.

"It's been... amazing," she answers, reluctantly impressed.

"Fine. I wanted to show you all this on your very first day. Because your job is not going to be easy or nice. But it will have its rewards. Bigger than you can imagine, I assure you. This humble meal has been just a sample."

"Then it's been... amazing," she says again, incapable of finding any better words.

He stands up and so does she.

"Now..." Suddenly he seems shy, almost embarrassed. "I don't know how to put this delicately."

He really seems a child now. And for the first time the age difference between them is almost tangible. The twelve years that separate them become a wall he doesn't seem able to breach. She decides to make it easy for him. He's the boss, after all.

"Don't," she says. "I'm not a delicate person."

"You'll learn to be," he insists. "I'm sure. Though, this... The custom has been abandoned for most people, but AdAstra is in some respects a very traditional corporation. A job as personal as this one requires..." He falls silent.

She understands what he is trying to say. Of course she does. It was in the job description, after all.

"Don't worry," she says. "I'm sure it will be enjoyable. Where do you prefer to do it?"

He points to the sofa.

What happens next is awkward, frantic and quite bizarre. By the end of it, he seems to be satisfied. He should be; she has activated her pleasure chip in submission mode, so he should not have any complaints.

"Goodnight," he says as he clumsily dresses himself. "We'll talk tomorrow."

It takes him a week to tell her what he really expects from her.

In that week they establish a daily routine that leaves her too much free time in the mornings and, in the evenings, allows her to realise what kind of tough and relentless bastard the shy and mild-mannered child she works for actually is.

She has served in the corporative militia for fifteen years and she has seen everything. She has seen reluctant killings, cold murders, joyful massacres, passionless tortures.

But she has never been such a strange mix of coldness, loftiness and passion in the same person.

At board meetings he decides on the fate of millions with a twitch of the hand. For him, it is just a game. Maybe he is sending hundreds of thousands to famine and death, or deciding the fate of entire generations, but they are just numbers in a report. From his high corporate throne, he sees them as pieces in an endless chess game. He is not so different from the general who sees war as a board game where the winner is the one who reaches the proper coordinates first and views the lives expended in the process as assets valued only because he might need them in the next phase of the game.

Daniel enjoys the game, as does the rest of the board. But he doesn't put his heart into it, as if it were a tedious duty that rarely provides satisfaction.

Only when he confronts his managers and advisors, when he dispenses among them rewards and punishments, is his real self revealed. Then the game changes, everything turns personal and immediate. He looks each person he is about to reward or destroy in the eye of and knows precisely what he is doing and to whom. His face shows emotions she doesn't entirely understand and makes her wonder what he has been doing these past eighteen years.

She is always by his side in these moments. At his left, a little behind him, dressed in an inconspicuous manner and trying to seem relaxed, maybe a little bored. Everyone knows what she is, but they pretend they don't and behave as if she was not there. In fact, some of them try so hard not to see her that it is almost amusing.

Almost.

He has barely needed her that week.

The first time she had to intervene, a tough gesture was enough to make the attacker hesitate a few crucial seconds. Time enough for corporate security to take care of him and get him out of the room. She doesn't recall what punishment Daniel meted out for his failure, but when the two guards dragged him from the meeting room he was a sobbing wreck, barely able to walk.

The second time was a little more difficult.

The bastard was fast. Very. And he knew his sentence in advance. When Daniel told him he just nodded, stood up and began to head for the exit. But suddenly, with hellish speed, he turned around, pulled something out of his clothes and jumped at Daniel.

Of course, she was faster still. She unsheathed the wakizashi and cut his neck before he could take three steps. But she should have been quicker. She should have taken care of him at his first movement, she should not have waited until he pulled out his ceramic knife. What the hell, she should have noticed he carried it before everything kicked off.

As she cleaned the wakizashi and the guards took away the decapitated corpse she was swearing beneath her breath. She has failed her employer. Maybe he did not realise, but she did.

That same night she understands how stupid she has been. He didn't notice? Of course he noticed, even before she did.

He takes her that night, as he does every night, but suddenly he has ceased to be a clumsy and eager child and has transformed sex into an endless and humiliating ceremony. He makes it very clear that nothing escapes his notice and he will not tolerate another mistake. Activating the submission mode of her pleasure chip proves ineffective. When she returns to her rooms she is a quivering mess, trying to fight back tears but failing.

She embraces her rage, as she has done before, and turns it to her advantage. He is not the first man to use her this way. She has been in the militia for fifteen years and some officers like nothing better than to humiliate a woman who dares to act as tough and independent as a man.

But there is something different in what Daniel has done. Something... cold and professional. He has enjoyed it, yes, but pleasure has been no more than a welcome bonus; even humiliation has not been an end per se, but a means to teach her a lesson:

"Don't you ever fail me again."

She is a fast learner. She will not fail him again.

Except for those two incidents the week has been uneventful. Free mornings, board meetings after lunch, dinners with Daniel and sex afterwards. She could get used to living like this. Even the nightmares have grown less frequent and memories of what happened in the Amazon rain forest are becoming blurred, like paint washed-out by the rain.

On the seventh day, just before dinner, he explains what his true intentions are.

"What do you know about my father, Alberta?" he asks suddenly as he finishes playing with the shaker. He began to use her first name the second day, telling her to do the same when they were alone.

"Not much," she answers. "He was the CEO of AdAstra for almost fifty years. He had an accident fifteen years ago and, after that, he remained in a coma until his death. During that time, AdAstra was like a hydra, a monster with too many heads."

He nods and seems pleased.

"Indeed it was, and if you cut one, two more grew in its place. I didn't know they gave you a classical education in the militia."

"They don't."

"A self-educated mind in a trained body," he murmurs as he empties the shaker into the glasses. "Interesting."

Alberta shrugs, lifts the glass to her lips and takes a sip. She is wearing a black dress that hugs her body like a second skin, leaving the shoulder free and creating a generous cleavage he doesn't stop to look at. Instructions on dress code were waiting for her in her tablet the first night and they were easy enough to follow. Next day her wardrobe was full.

"Anything more?"

Alberta shakes her head. Than says, "He died three months ago and you were his only heir. Nothing more. I haven't followed corporate politics very closely. I've been busy."

"Indeed you have. One of our brave soldiers. Civilising the world, whether the world wants it or not."

It has been a while since he resembled a child to her. His behaviour in private is still full of shyness, but she has seen more than enough this week to dispel the illusion.

Suddenly, he puts his hand over hers.

"I want... I would like to do it before dinner," he says.

"Sure."

"Don't take off the dress. And I want you on top. Ehm..." He hesitates a few seconds, as if uncomfortable with what he is about to say. "You do the work."

"Sure," she says again.

He sits on the sofa. Alberta approaches. She takes his trousers off and stimulates him with her mouth while she turns on the pleasure chip. She doesn't need to work too much. He seems very eager tonight. So she rolls up her skirt, takes of her panties and mounts him.

"Easy," says Daniel.

She obeys.

"During those fifteen years he was in a coma," he suddenly says, with his hands in her buttocks, "he was very active indeed, didn't you know? Well, not by himself, of course."

He shuts up for a moment, just time enough to lick a nipple.

"A little faster," he says then. "His accident initiated a... program. Yes, a program. My mother and I were expelled from the Penthouse when I was three. We were taken five floors below. Do you have any idea what that means?"

Any idea? Fucking rich boy. *Any idea*. She was born twenty floors below the Penthouse of her building. Just ten levels above the ground. *Any idea*. She has had to force her way through life step by step, using claws, teeth and cunt, fighting for every gain. *Any idea*. She tries to control her rage, keep it buried, but she fails. He doesn't seem to care. In fact, he gets more excited.

"When I was three I was stripped of what I had," he says. "I didn't care, understand? I knew sooner or later everything would be mine again if I managed to stay alive. I did, though there were times when it was touch and go. Mom taught me well. She protected me when I needed it and pointed me in the right direction. When she died, six years later, I had jumped one floor and knew it wouldn't take me much longer to jump another one. And Dad wouldn't live forever. Someday his body would surrender and then the Penthouse would be mine again. And with it, everything else."

He pauses when he realises his speech is about to be unintelligible.

"Everything... else..." he says again. "Faster. Faster!"

Alberta obeys and a few seconds later everything is over. She steps aside and turns off the pleasure chip. He has cried out his orgasm, a howling that was half rage and half bliss. He had never done that before.

While he is cleaning his private parts, after giving Alberta a towel to do the same, he keeps talking:

"But it wouldn't be so easy. The bastard. That fucking son of a bitch. He had ordered samples of his DNA to be taken. And in the very moment he fell into the coma they began to clone him. Sixteen viable clones were developed and they were implanted in sixteen wombs. They were delivered and they have been growing up these fifteen years. They didn't know what they were, until now. But they have found out."

Alberta finishes cleaning herself and looks at him, confused.

"Don't tell me, you don't have time for the subtleties of the corporative politics." He smiles as if he was making a joke against himself. "Theoretically they were just insurance in case he died without an heir. The moment I got the Penthouse and took control of AdAstra they should have been... retired."

"Killed."

"Yes, killed. They should've been killed. There's a time limit for that sort of thing, as you can guess. In the two weeks following a donor's death clones have to be eliminated if there is a legal heir alive and able to take possession of his estate. But someone decided it would by entertaining to let them live and learn what they were. Once the elimination term has passed, disposing of them is not so easy. In fact, it's nigh on impossible. To all intents purposes they are people, legal consumers with the same rights and duties as anyone. Killing them becomes murder. I don't know yet who was responsible for their survival but my people are working on it. They will find the son of a bitch and make sure he never... but that's not the issue."

He takes a deep breath and puts his trousers on. He stands, goes to the bar and takes the two glasses. He gives one of them to Alberta.

"Thanks."

"You're welcome," he says absently. "The real issue is that there are now sixteen viable clones of my fucking father and they know what they are. They are aware that when they reach adulthood they are fit to occupy their donor's place as head of AdAstra, with everything that implies. They can force me to share power, or they can attempt to remove me from the picture. Provided they remain alive to reclaim their piece of the action, of course."

Alberta finishes her cup and puts it on the glass table.

"I understand."

"Of course you do. I bought your contract, didn't I? You're quick and sharp of mind and body. Of course you understand. And I'm sure you know what I'm expecting you to do." He interrupts her before she can talk. "Don't say it. There's no need."

She nods.

"We have three years before the first one of them will be old enough. Do you think that will be time enough?"

She nods again.

"Excellent. Now, let's have dinner. I'm ravenous."

3.

Too much free time in the mornings? Idiot.

Daniel receives regular reports on the status of his father's clones. All of them live in this pyramid, on different floors, by the will of the old man, it seems. In fact, the most mature of the clones (about fifteen years old) lives in one of the lowest floors. It doesn't take long for Alberta to realise that is part of the old man's plan as well. The younger the clone the higher he lives, as if to compensate for the age gap.

Should she begin with the oldest one? It seems the obvious choice, but after a moment's consideration she decides it doesn't really matter. After all, he won't be a threat for almost three years, so is no more a priority target than any of the others.

So she carefully studies the reports, reviews their lives in detail and, little by little, she makes a decision.

Number Seven. He will be the first.

It is easy, almost too easy. She knows the rest will be harder. Number Seven has almost wrecked his own life and she only needs to finish the process.

She is a little perplexed. Number Seven lives in a mid-level floor. He should have had a relatively comfortable life, easy and even boring. But he has managed to make the wrong decision at every turn and Alberta suspects that if she had not killed him someone else would have soon done so.

Easy, yes, a piece of cake, but she doesn't get complacent.

As she chooses her next target she tries not to think of Number Fifteen and Sixteen. Not yet.

She spends the next three months planning, deciding and executing. She has at her disposal all the necessary resources. After all, she is the personal executioner of the Penthouse owner. When she goes down to the lower floors no one in his right mind dares to lay a hand on her or to intervene.

Of course, the lower she gets the more likely to meet someone insane. Or at least desperate enough.

But she manages.

During those three months she is General, Joint Chiefs of Staff and a One Woman Army. She knows she can ask for help; Daniel would not hesitate to send her assistance should she need it. But she also knows something like that would diminish her in his eyes and for some reason she doesn't understand – nor would want to understand – she cannot bear the thought of not living up to his expectations.

So she works alone. She plans alone, descends to the lower floors alone, tracks her prey alone and kills alone.

It is not always easy.

The first time she comes back with her clothes covered in blood, Daniel freezes, as if he wouldn't know how to react. Alberta's left arm is a universe of pain she tries to ignore and an ugly gash crosses her right cheek. The knife hasn't touched the eye and she is grateful for that.

"You look terrible," Daniel says at last.

She nods.

"Just a scratch," she says.

She is about to turn round and go to her room, but he stops her with a sign, tells her to lie in the sofa, opens the com protocol and asks for a doctor. She tries to protest, but Daniel shakes his head.

The doctor is a good one. He had better be, because his services won't be cheap. He fixes her arm in a couple of minutes, covers her body with neoskin where she needs it and spreads a painkilling spray over the wounds. An antibiotic shot and she is almost ready.

"Don't fix the scar on her face, doctor," says Daniel suddenly.

The doctor looks at her, hesitates one moment and finally decides that the man paying him calls the shots, so he just applies minimal cosmetic repair and makes sure the wound has not damaged any facial nerve.

"I hope you don't mind the scar," Daniel says afterwards. "It doesn't make you less beautiful, but it sure makes you look more dangerous."

He seems excited.

"Do you think we can…?" As always he is strangely shy when it comes to sex, as if someone had taught him as a child that some words are simply not appropriate.

"We can," she answers.

For the first time since they have known each other, sex is soft, calm, full of a tenderness so unexpected that she doesn't know how to behave at first. Though she soon relaxes.

Only when they have finished does she realise she has not activated the pleasure chip.

A month goes by and she continues with her work. No one else proves as big a problem as Number Four and his gang were. Some nights she returns home a little bruised, but the blood that occasionally stains her clothes is never hers.

During this time, Daniel almost never meets his managers, as if he wants her to concentrate on his clones and does not feel safe in a meeting without her.

She does not work all the time. Or at least she does not spend all her time working on the task Daniel has commissioned. Her stay in the Penthouse gives her systems access she will not find anywhere else, so she takes advantage.

She researches. She surfs the net. She investigates. In a way, she is searching blind, not entirely sure what she is looking for.

Daniel's sexual mood is changing. He adapts to her and her mood and he is learning to make it faster and better every time, though there is still a harsh glow in his eyes. Alberta wonders if her eyes look the same. She looks in the mirror and tells herself they don't, but she suspects that someone else might see toughness and implacability where she only sees tiredness and decision. Are their eyes becoming similar, adapting even as their bodies adapt to each other as the days go by?

Is Daniel aware of this? She hopes not, hopes he will never be. Because she suspects the nothing good will come of it.

Meanwhile, she keeps on working.

4.

Thirteen months. Thirteen months of plans and executions. Thirteen months visiting most of the pyramid floors. Thirteen months of blood and carnage. Thirteen months of dinner and sex. Thirteen months.

There are just three clones left. Numbers Fifteen and Sixteen. And Number One.

The nightmares return. She sees again the rain forest transformed into an endless grassland. She sees again families walking, beaten and facing oblivion.

She sees Lieutenant Escrache take a girl aside from her parents. Is she twelve? Thirteen? It doesn't matter. She knows what he is going to do. And when he finishes, when he gets tired of her, maybe he will kill her. She will be lucky if so. Because the alternative is taking her to the camp brothel, implanting a prostitution chip and transforming her into a sex automat for the rest of her life.

Alberta doesn't move. She doesn't move when the lieutenant takes the girl behind a bush and her parents look to her, searching for a mercy she cannot give them.

She doesn't move when the father leaves the row and tries to run behind his daughter.

She doesn't move when one of her men opens fire on him and, after a moment of hesitation, shoots the mother as well.

She doesn't move when suddenly those defeated families stop as one and a cry erupts from more than a hundred throats as they charge the soldiers.

She doesn't move when all of her companions open fire and transform two hundred people into fertiliser.

She doesn't move when the smoke clears to reveal a grassland stained in red.

She doesn't move when the lieutenant comes back from the bushes carrying the girl.

But she moves when he gives the order to take her into camp. Yes, then she moves. She cocks the gun, walks toward the girl and blows her head away. Her brains splash the lieutenant's uniform. He looks at her, unable to believe what had just happened.

When he orders her arrest she keeps still, totally motionless. She lets them disarm her, lift her into the truck and throw her in a cell that stinks like a latrine.

She screams then. But it is not she who is screaming. Two hundred dead souls are using her mouth to cry out, because they cannot.

Number Fifteen is two years old. Numbers sixteen is barely eleven months. It should be easy. They live in the higher floors, where everybody respects law and no one would dare to oppose an authorised Penthouse agent. It should be easy. Blow their dam heads open, crush their brains against the wall.

Easy. Piece of cake.

Two years. Eleven months. Green eyes.

That night she contacts the pharmacy and requests dream suppressors. The next morning she cannot remember any nightmare.

When she comes back that night she doesn't feel strong enough for anything other than lying on the sofa. Daniel realises something has happened, so he stops playing with the shaker and approaches her.

"What…?" he begins to ask.

He takes her chin and looks into her eyes.

"Are you crying?"

Is she? No, that would by silly. But then she notices the wet warmth that slips by her cheeks. Is she crying? Why?

Daniel nods.

"The babies," he says. "You have taken care of the babies. Yes, after what happened in Brazil I should have guessed they would be harder than the rest."

Does he know? She looks at him, astonished. He laughs.

"Did you think the incident had gone unnoticed, that there was no trace of it? Captain Tarancón was extremely careful, erasing every file relating to the incident, certainly. There's no official record of it. But official records…"

He shrugs.

"And you hired me nonetheless?"

"Sure. I don't take my decisions based on just one moment but on an entire biography. Alberta, I have examined your life in detail, I know it as well as you do. In some ways, even better. Your scruples are part of what makes you the best possible choice for the job."

"I don't understand."

"You don't need to. It's enough that I do."

He looks around and sees the dinner table.

"Rest. Go to your rooms. Sleep. Take a couple of days off."

"I don't need…"

"Ah, but you do. Trust me."

He is her contract owner, her owner for the next four years. Of course she trusts him.

Or at least she tries.

He knows her life as well as she does. Even better in some ways, he says.

Those words claw at her mind and give her no peace that night. Next morning, they are still inside her head when she wakes up, turns on the tablet and begins netsurfing.

He knows me better than I do, she thinks.

That is what he says, at least.

And what do I know about myself?

She accesses her own file and reviews her bio. She recognises everything she finds but, at the same time, it seems a charade, a comedy created by assembling parts of other works. But it is her life.

If my life seems a farce, she thinks, *maybe it is.*

Then she finds empty spaces. Places where someone with a higher level than hers has put walls, silences and holes.

She looks at the window. It is almost midday.

Why? she asks herself. *Why are there restricted places in my bio? And, above all, why can't I remember what should fill those places? I lived them, didn't I?*

She doesn't find any answers as lunch time approaches and she gets ready to share the meal with Daniel, who will be waiting for her, smiling and shy as usual.

Why?

They eat and if he notices she is quieter than usual he doesn't say anything. Surely he blames the aftermath of her last mission. She doesn't disappoint him.

That afternoon sees one of the few meetings Daniel has decided to attend. Nothing out of the ordinary happens. Several million people are stripped of their jobs, several hundred thousand climb up the ladder, several thousand go from being just consumers to trend testers, a few hundred realise their dream of becoming designers tasked with creating this season's products, and some dozens set foot in the executive bathroom for the first time.

That night, Alberta logs in again.

She is not exploring her own life, though, but that of Daniel's father, the Jonah Avogrado who decided to clone himself sixteen times just in case his son did not reach adulthood. For the first time, she wonders if that was the only reason.

She doesn't find much. His public life is easy to access, but his private records are locked and it would take someone with better skills than her to open them.

Though...

His public behaviour provides a hint as to his true personality, his eccentric manners and his huge narcissism. She sees some holos: joint meetings, press conferences, cocktail parties... He seems a kind and friendly guy, as a wolf worshipped by the sheep. And, like his son, he has green eyes where something harsh and implacable glows.

As for the restricted parts... She cannot find what hides there, but the way they are disposed gives her a clue about what they may contain.

Dawn finds her awake. She has not found anything, at least anything satisfactory. Just a bunch of questions and several crazy conjectures she doesn't dare to consider.

She looks out the window as the morning sun strains the city.

Stop being lazy, she tells herself. *You're being paid to do a job. Do it.* She breathes and looks out the window again. *Do it.*

She opens the weapons closet and carefully chooses her weapons. And, as she does, those crazy conjectures she doesn't dare to consider insist on dancing around in her head.

5.

Number One.

He is just sixteen but he has jumped two floors since being born and has created an organisation that sells drugs to the lower floors and forbidden pleasures to the upper ones. He discovered who he really was a year and a half ago.

He has used that time to transform his organisation into an army and is now warlord of his floor. Public and private security are on his payroll and the owners and tenants pay him gladly for protection they surely wouldn't need if he didn't exist.

A direct approach will be useless. Alberta prepares herself for a long and hard struggle and informs Daniel she is going to be out there for at least five or six months. He nods. After carefully choosing her weapons she selects her clothes even more carefully. Then she descends to the floor where Number One rules.

Over the next two months she begins to build a reputation. One of Number One's minor dealers hires her as a bodyguard shortly afterwards.

Time goes by. She is promoted a couple of times. Progress is slower than she would like but she is prepared to be patient in these early stages.

At night, pills supress the nightmares. During daytime she is too busy to think of anything but the present and the immediate future.

One month passes and another is reaching its end before the top of the organisation begins to notice her.

"She's fast," they say. "She's fast. She's lethal. She's reliable. She shows initiative. She doesn't screw up."

Another month. She wonders what Daniel is thinking, up there in his Penthouse, living his daily routine, deciding the future of millions, dispensing rewards and punishments, reorganising the world. What is he thinking? She knows he has not forgotten her or at least he has not forgotten her mission. Number One is the last obstacle, after all.

Does he believe she has failed? Is he looking for a replacement? Does he trust her enough to wait for her to finish even though the six months' term is about to end?

But she has no time to waste on such questions. As she climbs her way up the organisation she has time for nothing but work. And work. And more work. Sometimes crazy and meaningless ideas persist on dancing through her thoughts: wild hypothesis, mad assumptions, impossible possibilities that dance again and again in a crazy and frantic waltz before her mind's eyes. She cannot do anything about it. She tries to ignore them and focus on her work.

The sixth month ends and another week goes by.

Not yet, she tells herself.

She could do it, but at great cost and without any guaranty of success. She has to wait. She wills Daniel to be patient and not to ruin her efforts by bringing in an unnecessary replacement.

She tries not to think of it. She is close, so close, too close to let anything ruins her plans now.

When the moment comes it almost takes her by surprise. She can't quite believe it when she is invited into the inner circle, when she is suddenly sharing their food, drinks and plans. She hesitates. Should she wait? Just a few days, maybe, time enough to be sure it is not a trap?

No.

She can almost hear Daniel's voice pushing her forward.

No. Do it. Now.

She does it that same night. It is child's play luring him to bed. It is even easier to sexually drain him. Cutting his carotid is among the easiest things she has done in all her life. It is almost disappointing when no one sees her going to the upper floor, where she recovers her clothes and her official personality. Nobody has yet realised what has happened and nobody is after her.

She goes back to the Penthouse at dawn and finds Daniel looking out of the dining room window. He turns around as he hears her footsteps and, for a moment, he seems a cornered wild animal. Then he takes a deep breath and asks her:

"Is it done?"

"It is done," she answers.

He smiles and doesn't ask her anything more. He turns round again and loses himself in the dawn. She goes to her rooms and takes an endless bath where her thoughts are mist and her body ceases to be.

It is done, she thinks. I've finished.

Have I?

She closes her eyes.

She sees a grassland, sees the burning forest, sees a girl, sees...

She opens her eyes. She is in the middle of a warm mist and a distant voice purrs that she has nothing to worry about.

She closes her eyes again.

The grassland once more, now stretching further than before. The burning forest is just a remote glow on the horizon. The girl... there is no girl. There never has been.

She breathes and she submerges completely in the bathtub.

There has never been a girl. Never.

The past doesn't exist, she thinks. Past is a shadow, an illusion, a game of smoke and mirrors, an unreal reflection of something that never happened. Past is nothing more than Chinese shadows against the wall, lies we tell ourselves, broken toys we don't want to play with any more. The past doesn't exist.

The past doesn't exist, she slowly repeats to herself. *It's nothing but a lie.*

She holds on tight to that thought and let its consequences spread through her. Suddenly wild hypothesis are plausible, mad assumptions are logical, impossible possibilities become probable.

She comes out of the water very slowly. First breath is almost as the caress of a lover.

The past doesn't exist, she repeats to herself. *Just the here and now. Maybe tomorrow.*

She leaves the bathtub, dries herself and lies on the bed. She gives an order and the lights go out. She floats in the dark, alone and naked. Safe. At least for now.

6.

When she wakes up next morning there is a note from Daniel asking her to take breakfast with him. So she gets up, washes herself, puts on the first clothes she finds and goes to the dining room.

Daniel receives her with a smile and a shy kiss and asks her to sit. The orange juice is freshly squeezed, the buns are still warm and the coffee is the most delicious beverage she has ever tasted: black, dense, sour, so hot it burns her throat.

"There's something I'd like to show you today," he says.

He doesn't say anything about what has happened these seven months. He doesn't ask anything either. Alberta has confirmed that the job is done and that seems to be enough for him.

"Of course," she says. "You're the boss, boss."

She realises he doesn't like the joke and she wonders why. Then she remembers the way he adapted to her mood when they were having sex, the way her state of mind influenced his and wonders if he is going... But the idea is so outrageous and could have such ludicrous implications that she dismisses it immediately.

He just likes to maintain the fiction of a relationship between them and doesn't like her to remind him that nothing exists between them but work. She will have to be more careful.

A couple of hours later, a minirreac is waiting for them in the platform. The pilot takes them beyond the city, crosses the mountains and finally descends to land in a valley that seems totally deserted.

They climb down and Daniel tells the pilot to come back the next day.

She takes a look at the landscape, amazed. The little beech forest, the brook that winds in it, the fields, the mountains surrounding everything... It is as if they were in the Garden of Eden before the Fall.

We are Adam and Eve, she tells herself, *with no God to make us feel guilty about anything nor serpent to open our eyes to Good and Evil.*

The past doesn't exist. Just here and now. Maybe tomorrow.

The past is nothing more than a lie.

"Follow me," says Daniel.

She does as instructed and they go to a lumber cabin from whose chimney a puff of smoke winds into the air.

"Aha, everything is ready," he mutters. "Good."

The inside of the cabin is as cosy as it seems on the outside. They spend the rest of the day doing nothing, just slacking, talking about trivia, having sex in a quiet and comfortable way, as if time does not exist, as if it has stopped just for them.

"When I was a boy I came here once," he says that night, after dinner

214

and sex. "Just once. But I never forgot. And when the old bastard fell into a coma, it was the memory of this place what kept me going. Not the Penthouse, not the high place but this one, do you understand?"

She nods, though she is not sure what he is trying to say.

"So I thought this was the perfect place to..." He hesitates for a moment. "I've grown fond of you; did you know? Yes, I care about you. And you've noticed, of course, you're smart. This is tough."

She looks at him, pretending she doesn't understand him, but she knows, of course she knows.

"I have to do it. When a pet tastes human flesh it has to be put out of her misery, it doesn't matter how much we care for her. And my mother taught me there are some things you have to do yourself."

Alberta closes her eyes, sees a grassland, hears a burning forest in the distance, listens to the crying of a girl.

The past doesn't exist, she thinks.

"I'm sorry, believe me, I need you to believe me," he says. "But there's no other way. I could have told the police that you slaughtered sixteen authorised clones of my father, after all. I could give all the evidence to the Policorp with a shrug and forget about it. But this is something I have to do myself." He takes a long deep breath. "I'm sorry," he says again.

"I'm sorry too."

Did he really believe he could get her? Did he really believe she did not notice the gun under the mattress, his furtive movements when he was about to finish sex? Did he really...?

Of course he did. The arrogant child, the master of the world, so sure of himself. How could he believe his own pet would rebel?

Ah, Daniel, she thinks. *You should have called the police. Or sent me away. Or... Maybe I should thank your mother, thank her for teaching you so well that the owner has to put the pet out of her misery.*

All right, thank you.

He is looking at her, tied and gagged. There is no fear in his eyes, not even rage. They are still harsh, implacable. Nothing more.

Alberta removes the gag. He keeps calm.

"What am I?" she asks.

"Someone in big trouble."

She shakes her head.

"What am I?"

"A corpse, Alberta, that's what you are," he says.

She shakes her head again.

"What am I?"

"I've just told you."

"You haven't told me shit. You haven't told me why you chose me. Why Captain Tarancón took care of me while I was in the army, why my bio is full of places I cannot see and things I cannot remember. You haven't told me anything."

Daniel bites his lip.

"Does it matter? You're not going to get out alive. You can kill me and run. But they'll chase you."

Alberta shrugs.

"Maybe," she says. She takes a breath. "What am I?" she asks again.

"You really don't know?" asks Daniel mockingly.

"You know me well, remember? You told me that. Better than I know myself in some ways. So tell me who I am."

Daniel shakes his head, deciding to take his secret with him.

"Don't push me," she says. "You know my military record. I can make you talk, but it would be better for both of us if I don't have to resort to torture."

He shrugs, which is a feat in itself, considering the way he has been tied.

"All right," she says.

She goes to the kitchen. The tools she finds are not ideal for the task, but they will do.

She begins slowly, calmly, taking her time and making sure he realises. Sometimes she sees a grassland, sometimes a girl. Sometimes she hears a distant shot.

But she tells herself the past doesn't exist and goes on.

He is tough, yeah, the bastard is really tough. It takes her almost six hours to create the right combination of pain and fear to make him talk. He doesn't know it, but she is exhausted.

So she stops. She looks at his green eyes, no longer finding anything harsh, just terror and hope, the most lethal of combinations.

She asks once more:

"What am I?"

And he tells her.

The minirreac will come to collect Daniel in a couple of hours. The pilot will not expect to find her, so it will be easy to take care of him.

And then?

The past doesn't exist, she tells herself. What about tomorrow? Is there a tomorrow she can reach?

She thinks of everything Daniel has told her, of the evidences he showed her after giving up his access codes so she could open the locked gates and fill in the empty spaces of her past.

She thinks of what she is.

She is grateful there are no mirrors around. She would not like to see her eyes now.

There were not sixteen clones as Daniel told her, but seventeen.

Seventeen.

An illegal clone, whose chromosomes had been altered to produce a female. An illegal clone created at the same time Daniel was born, a clone whose mind was filled with false memories of a childhood she had never lived while her growth was accelerated. A clone who had the physical appearance and the memories of a sixteen years old woman a few months after being decanted. A clone that had been released into the real world.

"Real." The word has never meant less.

A woman who lived the last years of her adolescence without knowing she was being watched at every turn, without knowing her development was being controlled at every step, without knowing someone was watching from the Penthouse and licking his lips in anticipation of the future pleasures he would extract from her, once she had been shaped according to his desires and fantasies. Transformed into the perfect lover, the ultimate sex toy for an obsessive narcissist. A woman who entered the army a year before her donor was brought down by a stroke that would leave him in a coma for the next fifteen years.

An illegal clone; ingenuously hidden in the system, filled with false memories, pre-programmed to find a certain kind of man attractive. Why not? Was he not her in another body?

Captain Tarancón: protecting her all those years, waiting in vain for his master to regain consciousness, selling his secrets to the legal heir when Jonah died.

She hears a noise coming from the mountains. The minirreac approaches.

Ah, Daniel, what kind of a childhood did you have, what kind of twisted rancour made you the man you were?

It was not enough to kill all his father's clones. That, at the end of the day, was nothing more than a matter of survival. But he needed to take revenge on the old bastard in a more personal way. He needed to own him, dominate him, make him his.

He succeeded, though things did not exactly go to plan. He enjoyed her, yes. He did not just enjoy the idea of fucking and dominating his father, but of being with her and getting pleasure from her. From Alberta. He enjoyed her so much he had to give her a last perfect day before killing her.

Is she smiling? Yes, she believes she is.

She has been sleeping with her own son while she killed herself again and again.

The joke is exquisitely ironic.

She has been her son's sex fantasy and meanwhile she has been killing herself so many times in so many different places and situations... She suddenly thinks of Number One and cannot help laughing.

She has slept with herself before killing herself. And after that she has done the same with her son.

Minirreac is almost landing. She hides in the tall grass and waits for the pilot to descend to the ground.

Yes, the past doesn't exist. Is there a tomorrow?

She thinks of the Penthouse. Why not? She can go back, pack her things. Pack weapons, money and things to trade, at least enough to go several floors down and find herself a place like Number One did.

Or she can stay in the Penthouse. She can barricade herself in, let them come after her and make a last heroic stand there.

Or she can reclaim her birth right. She can make public the records she holds and then reclaim her place in the sun. Her birth was illegal, yes, but the law is clear in that subject: Jonah was the only offender, she is just a victim of his crime. She is innocent and, as the only heir of her donor, she is entitled to the entire estate.

What am I going to do? she asks herself over and over. *What am I going to do?*

When the minirreac lands she is still trying to make a decision. The pilot gets out without suspecting a thing.

Where to? she asks herself once more while she crawls to the vehicle. *Where to?*

I don't know.

She has plenty of time to decide, after all.

Ricard Ruiz was preparing a dystopian anthology for Fantascy, Penguin Random House's Spanish imprint for fantasy and science fiction, and (yes, you guessed) he asked me a short story.

I'm not a dystopian writer. I don't write about social issues, at least not deliberately. My goal when I write is to create a good story and tell it the best way I can. Everything I put in a short story, a novelette, a novella or a full length novel is there to serve the story, to make it thrilling, interesting, compelling and, of course, believable. So I don't deliberately set out to champion a cause, but nor do I put fences or obstacles in a story's way: if some social issue is relevant, I go with it.

Naturally there are things I include without necessarily being aware of doing so. After all, my fears, desires, hopes, dreams, nightmares, sins, good deeds, frustrations and expectations are with me whenever I write, and they dye the story whether I want them too or not, whether I know it or not.

But this was entirely different. I had to consciously write a story that incorporated social issues. Could I do it?

I'm not really sure if I did. In fact, "At the Penthouse" is not really dystopian: it's not a terrible social situation disguised as utopia. There's no utopia involved. And, let's face it, the social situation is nothing more than background, the focus of the story lies elsewhere.

But it's a good story, or so I hope. Ricard clearly thought so, judging by the way he accepted it. Good enough, in fact, to stay in my mind and inspire thoughts of a continuation, even a possible novel.

Who knows? Maybe someday.

ABOUT THE AUTHOR

Rodolfo Martínez (Candás, Asturias, Spain, 1965) is a computer programmer and author. Martínez is a prolific writer whose fondness for writing a dynamic fusion of genres has brought him a number of awards – perhaps more than any other Spanish science fiction writer. His works include the cyberpunk novels *La Sonrisa del Gato* (1995), available in English as *Cat's Whirld* (2015) and *El Sueño Del Rey Rojo* [Red King's Dream] in 2004, the Ignotus-winning 1996 space opera *Tierra de Nadie: Jormundgand* [No Man's Land: Jormungand], the urban fantasy *Los Sicarios del Cielo* [Heaven's Hired Assassins] in 2005, which won a Minotauro Award, and *Fieramente Humano* [Fiercely Human] in 2011, which won another Ignotus Award.

He has also written several fantasy pastiches inspired by Sherlock Holmes, and an action series under the overarching title *El Adepto de la Reina* (2009), which is available in English as *The Queen's Adept* (2011). The latter features a Bond-like protagonist in an alternative universe where the laws of physics are changed.

Martinez's short stories have been collected in *Callejones sin Salida* [Dead-End Alleys] in 2005, *Laberinto de Espejos* [Mirror Maze] in 2006, *Porciones Individuales* [Single Portions] in 2012 and *Dados cargados* [Loaded Dice] in 2017. He is also head of the Spanish small press Sportula.

Bibliography in English

2012: The Queen's Adept (Sportula)
2013: "Eternal Return" in World SF Blog
2015: Cat's Whirld (Sportula)
2016: "God's Messenger" in Castles in Spain (Sportula).
     "A Tale of No City" in Barcelona Tales (NewCon Press)
2018: Faces from the Past. With Felicidad Martínez (Sportula)

STEAMPUNK INTERNATIONAL

English Edition Edited by Ian Whates

United Kingdom  Finland ⬤ Portugal

An anthology showcasing the very best steampunk stories from three different countries released by three different publishers in three different languages.

From the UK, **George Mann** (a new tale featuring Newbury & Hobbes, the central protagonists of his best-selling Victorian mystery novels), **Jonathan Green** (a new tale featuring Ulysses Quicksilver set in the Pax Britannia milieu) and **Derry O'Dowd**(a father and daughter writing team; from Finland, **Magdalena Hai** (winner of the Atorox Award and the Finnish Literary Export Prize), multiple award-winning **Anne Leinonen**, and **J.S. Meresmaa** (whose work has been shortlisted for the Anni Polva, Kuvastaja, and Atorox Awards); and from Portugal, **Anton Stark, Diana Pinguicha**, and **Pedro Cipriano** (winner of Fórum Fantástico's Choice of the Year Award).

Released July 2018

English language edition produced by NewCon Press
Finnish language edition produced by Osuuskumma
Portuguese language edition produced by Editorial Divergência

Origamy

Rachel Armstrong

"*Origamy* is a magnificent, glittering explosion of a book: a meditation on creation, the poetry of science and the insane beauty of everything. You're going to need this." *– Warren Ellis*

Mobius knows she isn't a novice weaver, but it seems she must re-learn the art of manipulating spacetime all over again. Encouraged by her parents, Newton and Shelley, she starts to experiment, and is soon traveling far and wide across the galaxy, encountering a dazzling array of bizarre cultures and races along the way. Yet all is not well, and it soon becomes clear that a dark menace is gathering, one that could threaten the very fabric of time and space and will require all weavers to unite if the universe is to stand any chance of surviving.

Rachel Armstrong is Professor of Experimental Architecture at Newcastle University and a 2010 Senior TED Fellow. A former medical doctor, she now designs experiments that explore the transition between inert and living matter and considers their implications for life beyond our solar system.

"*Origamy* crackles with a strange and brilliant energy, and folds the conventions of SF into beautiful new shapes. A rare and wonderful debut."
– Adam Roberts

"Perhaps the most astonishing and original piece of SF I've read in a long, long while." *– Adrian Tchaikovsky*

"A visionary masterpiece. Science Fiction, Fantasy, science and poetry combine to create a lyric on life and death that spans the whole of creation. Delightful and mind-expanding. If you miss it you have missed one of the finest examples of literary art." *– Justina Robson*

2001: AN ODYSSEY IN WORDS
Edited by Ian Whates and Tom Hunter

An anthology of original fiction to honour the centenary of Sir Arthur C. Clarke's birth and act as a fund raiser for the Clarke Award. Every story is precisely 2001 words long.

2001 includes stories by 10 winners of the Arthur C. Clarke Award and 13 authors who have been shortlisted, as well as non-fiction by **Neil Gaiman, China Miéville** and Chair of Judges **Andrew M. Butler.**

Cover art by Fangorn

Alastair Reynolds
Bruce Sterling
Gwyneth Jones
Adrian Tchaikovsky
Paul McAuley
Jane Rogers
Ian McDonald
Rachel Pollack
Chris Beckett
Jeff Noon
Colin Greenland
Becky Chambers
Claire North
Dave Hutchinson
Adam Roberts
Yoon Ha Lee
Ian R. MacLeod
Emmi Itäranta
Ian Watson
Liz Williams
& more…

Twenty-seven stories from some of the biggest names in Science Fiction, honouring one of the genre's greats by exploring the limits of imagination.

Released by NewCon Press as a paperback and limited-edition hardback.

IMMANION PRESS

Purveyors of Speculative Fiction

Venus Burning: Realms by Tanith Lee

Tanith Lee wrote 15 stories for the acclaimed *Realms of Fantasy* magazine. This book collects all the stories in one volume for the first time, some of which only ever appeared in the magazine so will be new to some of Tanith's fans. These tales are among her best work, in which she takes myth and fairy tale tropes and turns them on their heads. Lush and lyrical, deep and literary, Tanith Lee created fresh poignant tales from familiar archetypes.
ISBN 978-1-907737-88-6, £11.99, $17.50 pbk

A Raven Bound with Lilies by Storm Constantine

The Wraeththu have captivated readers for three decades. This anthology of 15 tales collects all the published Wraeththu short stories into one volume, and also includes extra material, including the author's first explorations of these beings. The tales range from the 'creation story' *Paragenesis*, through the bloody, brutal rise of the earliest tribes, and on into a future, where strange mutations are starting to emerge from hidden corners of the earth.
ISBN: 978-1-907737-80-0 £11.99, $15.50 pbk

The Lightbearer by Alan Richardson

Michael Horsett parachutes into Occupied France before the D-Day Invasion. Dropped in the wrong place, badly injured, he falls prey to two Thelemist women who have awaited the Hawk God's coming, attracts a group of First World War veterans who rally to what they imagine is his cause, is hunted by a troop of German Field Police, and has a climactic encounter with a mutilated priest who believes that Lucifer Incarnate has arrived...*The Lightbearer* is a unique gnostic thriller, dealing with the themes of Light and Darkness, Good and Evil, Matter and Spirit. ISBN 9781907737763 £11.99 $18.99

All these and more on our web site
Immanion Press
http://www.immanion-press.com
info@immanion-press.com

www.ingramcontent.com/pod-product-compliance
Lightning Source LLC
Chambersburg PA
CBHW030115260626
47156CB00008B/2666